AN UNKINDNESS OF SHADOWS

"Offers a nuanced and sympathetic portrait of British gay life from the late 1940s to the days of Thatcher."   —PUBLISHERS WEEKLY

"In Justin Margrave, John Linwood Grant has created the finest travelling companion that you could hope for when venturing into the dark world of art and the arcane."

—PRIYA SHARMA, author of the Shirley Jackson Award-winning books
Ormeshadow and *All the Fantastic Beasts*

"*An Unkindness of Shadows* is a thoroughly absorbing and impressive outing that rings with the voice of a true original, and proves a terrific exhibit for an author that all lovers of the macabre should be reading. There is pathos here, and wit and tragedy. There are secrets, horrors and ghosts. In the swift time this reader reached the grace note of the last tale, one could only imagine that others will also be left hoping that Justin Margrave returns."

—GINGER NUTS OF HORROR

WHERE ALL IS NIGHT, AND STARLESS

"A cornucopia of dark delights, this collection is highly imaginative, extremely well written, and a delight to read. Weird fiction at its finest!"

—TIM WAGGONER, author of *Your Turn to Suffer*

"In Grant's fiction, not a single soul gets away unscathed."

—POLLY SCHATTEL, author of *The Occultists*

THE ASSASSIN'S COIN

"With elegant, effortless prose, John Linwood Grant has created a compulsively readable work of eerie suspense."

—AMANDA DEWEES, author of *A Haunting Reprise*

A PERSISTENCE OF GERANIUMS

"Grant skillfully evokes the sensibility of Edwardian Britain in a series of supernatural tales distinguished both by their elegance and by their wit."

—JOHN LANGAN, author of *The Fisherman*

AIN'T NO WITCH

"Melding magic, hoodoo, and a no-nonsense, sassy protagonist, Ain't No Witch delivers a silky smooth reading experience you can savour."

—A.F. STEWART, author of *Fairy Tales and Nightmares*

An UNKINDNESS of SHADOWS

The STRANGE ENCOUNTERS of JUSTIN MARGRAVE

JOHN LINWOOD GRANT

Also by

JOHN LINWOOD GRANT

The Assassin's Coin

A Persistence of Geraniums

A Study in Grey

Where All is Night, and Starless

Ain't No Witch

JOHN LINWOOD GRANT

The
STRANGE
ENCOUNTERS
of
JUSTIN
MARGRAVE

An UNKINDNESS
of SHADOWS

LETHE PRESS

Published in 2024 by Lethe Press
www.lethepressbooks.com • lethepress@aol.com

Cover design and layout by JeremyJohnParker.com

ISBN: 978-159021-772-6

CREDITS

Still She Stares: One to *Six*, *The Madness of Queen George*, *Les Effrayantes*, *At The Courtly Place*, *Elk Boys*, and *Auntie Vi* are all new to this collection.

The Beasts of Kemberdale first published in 'Lonely Hollows', Pavilion, 2023

These Pale and Fragile Shells first published in 'Strange Tales: Tartarus Press at 30', Tartarus 2020

The Smoke Market first published in 'Spirits and Ghouls', Flame Tree, 2023

The Children of Angles and Corners first published as *The Woden Jug* in 'Terror Tales of the West Country', Telos, 2022

Where the Thin Men Die first published in the author's collection 'Where All is Night, and Starless', Journalstone, 2021

CONTENTS

STILL SHE STARES

ONE

Camden, 2015

TRUE NIGHT NEVER FALLS in London.

The evening sky is bronzed by a million street-lamps, stiff gibbets hung with burning orange and caustic yellow. At least there is an order, a pattern, to these. The rest is mindless glare—neon signs shriek nonsense, pleading for attention; security lights flare and die, flare and die, never sleeping, in shadowed yards. A sad moon haunts the horizon, and the distant stars—outshone by winking beacons on office block and high-rise—are close to admitting defeat, humanity's amps and volts more potent than the fusion of their boiling hearts.

Or so it seems to Marcus, staring at this monstrous city from the pavement outside his gallery. He misses darkness; he misses the night sky of Trinidad, though even there the battle of light is being lost, the Land of the Hummingbird succumbing to the glare of investment and tourism...

"Lorcas wants to talk to you."

Stefan's hand is gentle on his shoulder, smoothing the over-expensive suit Marcus has borrowed for the evening.

"Is he going on about putting money up for our expansion again?"

"Of course."

He cradles his thoughts on the evening so far. Can you have half a success? Attendance has been reasonable, and their event has at least been noticed—a few art critics, a clutch of artsy journalists, and rather too many corporate buyers, interested in snapping up 'ethnic' works for the endless corridors and boardrooms of business. And Peter Lorcas, a tedious man with the temperament of an ageing terrier, an investor with more bombast than bite. Marcus's gallery *The Hummingbird* is small, but stands on prime property, a deal arranged by his sharp Trinidadian grandmother—she sent much of her money along with the Windrush generation, but not herself. Wise woman.

But expansion? An excess of ambition has ruined many a small business.

"Tell him I'm still not interested. I can't cope with him tonight."

Stefan tugs at a lock of his wild blonde hair and scowls, but ambles off in acquiescence.

Ten, twelve yards down the street, a woman in designer denims is being sick in a doorway; her designer friends stand well back to protect their clothes and their pretence at dignity. One of them is giggling.

Marcus abandons the nights to its own problems, and turns to go back inside, to 'mingle', as everyone says he should. He straightens his tie, reflected in the smoked glass of the gallery's frontage, and...

Tap. Tap. Tap. The sound of an iron ferrule on paving stones.

A second shadow has arrived, a presence at his back.

"I wouldn't have anything to do with Peter Lorcas either," says the shadow. "But more importantly, I wouldn't sell the Perot you have on display."

Marcus swivels on one heel.

"Sorry, what?"

The man with the cane must be seventy or eighty years old, and the word 'large' comes to mind. It isn't that he is especially overweight, or exceptionally tall, but there is a feel to him. Bold against a crisp linen suit, a burgundy silk cravat bursts untidily from the neck of his shirt, making his face seem almost marble-white, as is the flowing hair which brushes his collar. Critic? Collector?

Marcus hesitates, puts out his hand. "Welcome to *The Hummingbird*. I'm Marcus Evenche, the owner."

"I know." The man dispenses a polite nod. "Margrave."

A warm, dry palm; a strong handshake. Closer to, you can see a younger man still lives inside him, beneath liver-spots and a hint of jowl—amused brown eyes and lips untouched by the blue of old age, though he clearly needs that stick.

"Well, do please come inside and look around, sir. I'm afraid I've accepted an offer on the Perot, but—"

"When we're inside, dear boy."

Marcus and Margrave—a slim, dark frigate escorting an aged, out-dated ship of the line. God, what a ridiculous image. And why did he say 'sir' to the old man?

"Good Lord!" A waspish critic from an arts magazine loses her grip on a glass of Sancerre, managed to catch it before it shatters on the stone floor. Ignoring the wine splashed down her purple tights, she clatters forward on ludicrous stilettos.

"Good Lord," she says again. "Justin!"

Murmurs, heads in sudden motion.

The large man straightens his cravat, looks around. "Incarnate and in circulation, Jenny, despite the tales of Archie and his surviving cronies."

People begin to gravitate to the newcomer, small satellites of curiosity. Stefan, always the smoother operator, has disappeared, but reappears a moment or two later with another bottle of wine. Red wine, not the cheaper white laid out for the punters.

"That's Justin Margrave, you moron!" he says in Marcus's ear. "Man was a legend in the seventies and eighties. Friends with Hepworth, Moore; made some careers, ended others. They say he could cancel an entire auction at Christie's or Sotherby's with one word. And he's as gay as Dorothy on acid."

"How do you know all that?" They are not heard by others; the gallery reverberates to an awkward buzz of false flattery and genuine interest, all aimed at the new arrival.

"I read, sweetheart."

Stefan holds out a glass of wine; Margrave hesitates, his eyes on the younger man.

"Salentino, Mr Margrave. A 1983 Salice Salento," said Stefan.

Marcus bites his lip. He'd been saving that for their anniversary. It was bloody expensive.

"How apt—a fine old wine for a foolish old queen." Someone titters; Margrave takes the glass, and drinks. "To *The Hummingbird*."

Marcus gulps the tepid Sancerre, and puts on a smile. Phones flash for candid shots, or are prodded by hasty thumbs, despatching gossip across London Town. This is some sort of accidental coup, it seemed. Stefan certainly knows what to do with unexpected publicity—he is circulating, saying the right things, making introductions. The reviewer from *The Times*, who only 'popped in' on his way to another late event, pumps Marcus's hand.

"Most interesting evening, most interesting," says the journalist, and Marcus doubts that he is referring to the paintings on the walls. But it will surely mean a few inches for his gallery in either the reviews or the gossip pages, so what the hell.

Despite the unexpected excitement, one by one the guests do depart, though a few like Lorcas have to be eased towards the street. By two in the morning, only the three men remain—Marcus, Stefan, and Margrave. They can't bring themselves to call him Justin.

"Would you care to look around a while longer, Mr Margrave?" Marcus slides one bolt home on the front doors, just to discourage casual intrusions. The old man is staring at one side wall, where a range of works by Trinidadian and Guyanese artists hang—*The Hummingbird*'s speciality.

"My apologies, but no. I heard you have Perot's canvas 'Who Doh Hear', and knew I had to come."

Why would that piece be of such interest?

"Yes—it was shipped over last month, from an estate sale outside Georgetown. 'Who doh hear, does feel'. One of those sayings they have all over the Caribbean. Those who don't listen, suffer the consequences. That sort of thing."

"Oh, I know what it means, dear boy."

Marcus feels defensive. "Graylet Stein want it for their foyer in the City, as it happens. They've made a very good offer."

"Appropriate for a law firm, I suppose. But you really mustn't go through with the deal."

Stefan shifts uncomfortable from one foot to the other.

"Why not, sir? Something dodgy about its provenance?"

"Oh, it's genuine. But it's an... unhealthy picture."

His cane in use again, Margrave taps his way to the opposite wall, where he stares at the central canvas, a work some two feet deep by three and a half wide. Pride of place.

The reds, golds and greens of Guyana dominate this picture, especially the greens, which come in bewildering shades, a jungle of emerald leaves and pine-blue shadows framing the figure of a reclining woman. The couch on which she lies is barely defined; her slim dark body, wrapped in folds of pale cotton, is crystal-sharp, almost photographic. She gazes 'off-stage', to the left, and her hands rest across her lap, her bare feet on the end of the couch.

"I met Perot once," Margrave strokes the ebony or black onyx head of his cane with large fingers. "He came here, to London, back in the days of the original Caribbean Art Movement."

"The late sixties. The birth of real interest in West Indies art— Winston Branch and the rest." Stefan smiles at Marcus. Showing off.

"A time of excitement in our small circles," agrees Margrave. "All the colourful wonders of the West Indies, eye-openers to we grey children of forties and fifties Britain, who remembered rationing. I knew most of the people involved back then, of course—Winston, Jessica

Huntley, Kamau Brathwaite, so many more. But Aristide Perot... there was a lesson in resentment."

"Resentment against...?" Marcus isn't entirely sure that he wanted to know. Is this old man going to start spouting some disappointing colonialist text? He feels suddenly very Black.

"People. Everyone. Perot was a boor. A misogynist, a homophobe, a coward."

"Oh, I see. That's why you think I should withdraw the picture? Because of his character?"

"Gods, no." He laughs, a throaty sound, and takes another mouthful of wine. "If you followed that rule, you would strip half the galleries and museums in the country of their most prized exhibits. A fair portion of artists are complete arses. Utter bastards, sometimes."

Stefan takes a nervous glance at the bottle of Salice Salento, which is almost empty; Margrave's face grows sombre, exaggerating the pouched skin under his eyes, the furrows across his broad forehead. His gaze seems to tunnel into the painting.

"She was called Celine Granger, a decent girl."

The two men step closer. They have seen their acquisition—in passing—for two or three weeks, and believe they know it.

"One of Perot's best, I'm told," says Marcus.

The old man leans more heavily on his cane. "Possibly. What do you think of the hands?"

Marcus takes out his reading glasses. "A little awkward, perhaps... and, huh, I'd not really noticed before. The fingers are slightly bent, as if she'd been holding something."

"They once held life."

"I don't get your meaning."

Margrave's glance is a disappointed one, as if the two younger men were slow students in the simplest of classes.

"Dear boy, this is the portrait of a corpse."

"Bloody hell," says Marcus. Ridiculous, yet the more he looks, the closer he examines the brushwork...

Those eyes. The pupils are mere black pinpoints, piercing the ivory of the whites. Do they stare not at anything in the artist's studio, but into another world? If there is such a place. His Baptist grandmother would have said so. And the sensual lips—when they drew the picture from its crate, he thought he saw a hinted smile, but now... those curves speak more of rictus. How could he have missed it?

Margrave caresses the wine glass, runs his fingers along the rim.

"Perot poisoned her for suspected infidelity—a lie spread by others, as it happens. After the last rattle of being left that slender throat, he posed the body, and spent the rest of that day painting it. You can tell by the light, the way the shadows shift in places. By the next dawn, Celine had disappeared, her fate unknown."

Stefan shivers. "That's dreadful. But Mr Margrave, you're saying her fate isn't exactly unknown, that she was murdered. But 'Who Doh Hear' was painted a quarter of a century ago, and half a world away. I don't remember reading that Perot was ever charged with a murder, or even accused of one. How can you be certain about any of this?"

"Nothing is certain." He strokes his cravat ring, a simple silver ankh, with one forefinger. "And so why should you listen to poor Margrave, so out of touch with your 'scene'? Names, dates, places—they all become confused for the elderly, don't they? After all, Aristide Perot himself is long gone, lost ten years ago off the Port-of-Spain. He will never tell."

"Supposed to be a boating accident, wasn't it?" asks Stefan. "They never found the yacht."

"An accident. Yes, that seems likely."

There is something odd in his intonation. The couple look to the painting, then to the old man's expressionless face.

"Did you know that there were still Grangers in Georgetown a decade ago?" adds Margrave. "The telephone is a marvellous device."

Stefan's grey eyes widen. "You told her family... about what you think happened. You told them about Perot."

"Did I?" Margrave shrugs. "The former owner of this work knew exactly what I do. He never slept soundly after learning the truth. 'Still she stares,' he said to me, before he passed away in March. Of natural causes, the coroner wrote."

Marcus, whose recent nights have been less than restful, thrusts his spectacles back into his breast pocket and steps away from the painting. He has attributed his insomnia to nerves, to the preparations for their open evening. And that must have been all it was.

"It's always possible that he wasn't a very good coroner, of course," Margrave adds.

Marcus is unnerved, irritated, but the old man's tone, the look on Stefan's long face...

"What do you expect me to do, on the basis of a wild story like that? Please don't say that you believe this picture is haunted."

He can't stop looking at those eyes, that prone form. Is that a touch of pallor on the smooth black skin; are those elegant legs too stiff, stretched out by other hands?

"Haunted? Such an over-used word. Have you been reading M R James or Benson, my dear? No, it is just as I said. 'Who Doh Hear' is an unhealthy work." He draws out a slim leather pocketbook, and retrieves a cheque, which he passes to Marcus. "I think this might serve to un-burden you."

The amount on the cheque is less than Graylet Stein offered, but still...

"What will you do with it?"

The old man passes over a card, ignoring the question. "If you would be so terribly kind as to have it sent to my rooms, I believe all will be well."

A silence between them, a tangible lack of voices. Margrave seems done; the other two have no idea what else to say. Stefan pours the last drops of gleaming red wine into Margrave's glass, and mutters something apologetic about going to fetch more of the Sancerre.

Marcus clears his throat, a harsh sound in the almost empty gallery. "Well, you... you made a certain impact, sir, turning out tonight."

Which elicits a soft, mischievous smile.

"It is a sad thing, dear boy," says Margrave, "To outlive one's own myth, and sympathy is a cruel companion. I rarely promenade these days. But *The Hummingbird* does appeal to me. And now I find that you appreciate the wines of Puglia. Always a good sign."

That voice... should Marcus say it? He does.

"I keep thinking that I know you, somehow. Not 'know', I suppose, but that we've met before."

"Do you? How curious."

Nothing more is offered; nothing given away.

When Stefan returns, only Marcus is there, in the process of lifting 'Who Doh Hear' down from its former place of honour.

"He's gone? Bugger," says Stefan, fumbling with a bottle of white and three clean glasses. "I wanted to ask him about 'Bonny' Cheyvis, and what really happened when—"

"Who cares?" Marcus turns the canvas to face the wall.

"You're not interested to hear more of what he's seen, what he's done? Decades in the business. Decades! Hell's Teeth, the man must hold a wealth of the most fantastic stories—and the best gossip about the worst people in the art field."

"More? Not if it means stories like tonight's. I'm not even sure I believe what he said."

"You sold the picture to him."

"I've gone off the thing. Margrave might as well have it as anyone."

He turns the small, expensive card over in his fingers. There is something written on the back in a neat script, almost copperplate in its flourishes. He has to squint to make out the words.

Brixton, April 1981. *Auntie Vi.*

"Let's have a gander." Stefan takes the card from him, peering at it.

Marcus goes to the entrance, pulls back the bolt again, and steps outside. The street is empty, the revellers gone. Stefan slips fond arms around his waist, bringing the soft scent of cloves and sandalwood.

"April 1981? How old were you back then, eight or nine years?"

"I was seven," says Marcus. "A scared little boy in the middle of the Brixton riots."

"But what does the note mean?"

"I think... no, I don't know."

Stefan's sigh is one of frustration. "What don't you know?"

"God, leave it! I can't remember, all right? Kids get confused."

Marcus leans back into Stefan's embrace, a mute apology for snapping at him, and stares out into the sullied night once more. The moon has almost gone, the stars are lost entirely. Far away, a police helicopter stabs the low clouds with its searchlight, offering a pretence of order; the sky is an inky ochre dome, set down over London as a child might contain a bug, to study it before they grind it beneath their shoe.

What he said to Stefan was the truth. He remembers Railton Road running with fire, the clatter of riot shields, and—oddly—the rusted bonnet of a yellow Ford Cortina, crumpled around a lamp-post. But what exactly happened to a little boy called Marcus... nothing.

"We should order more Salice Salento," he says, "Or at least a decent Primitivo. Dark, and earthy."

"A couple of bottles?"

"A case. For the next time Margrave calls."

Marcus doesn't explain his reasoning, doesn't really have any. But he knows that the old man will be back...

* * * * *

A FORTNIGHT. A FORTNIGHT and one day. Stefan is bolting the doors for the evening—crouched, velvet waistcoat hanging loose on his skinny frame—and humming a show tune, one which he knows irritates Marcus. It's his way of teasing, of chipping at his partner's reserve.

Marcus is about to complain, when he hears a familiar sound.

Tap. Tap. Tap.

"Hang on, Stef."

The old man looms before them, paused outside the entrance with a wrapped bottle in his free hand.

"I have something for you, my dears," says Margrave.

They let him in, naturally.

"Is this a convenient time?"

Marcus wants to ask: 'For what?' Instead... "We were about to take a break, let the day go down. Would you like to join us for a glass, sir?"

"How kind. And look, I have brought with me a bottle of that same Sancerre which graced your delightful event."

Marcus takes the white wine from him, remembering how little they paid for that uninspiring white wine. "That's very, uh—"

"Abominable of me." Margrave laughs. "My little joke, boys. A poor year, better cooked than sipped—or alternatively, used to loosen the tongues and wallets of your clients without costing the Earth. Oh, I've served worse, especially when I did not want my guests to linger too long."

Stefan grins. "A pleasure to see you, sir—but is this... business? Don't say that we've acquired something dubious again?"

"Not that I'm aware of. No, I hear that *The Hummingbird* is slowly growing in reputation—this is a mere social call, to see how my two delightful young entrepreneurs are faring in the cut-throat world of galleries and dealers."

Marcus doesn't consider himself young at forty two, but then, Stefan's recent burrowing on the Internet places Margrave as at least eighty years old, probably nearer ninety. He gestures to a discreet door almost hidden by a stand of pamphlets on Caribbean art.

"We have a small courtyard at the back, Mr Margrave—catches the evening sun. We could sit out there?"

In truth, the courtyard behind *The Hummingbird* was dank and fern-clogged when they set up, but the demolition of an ugly seventies office block opened the space up. A few plants in terracotta pots, seating, and a touch of Art Deco screening created a private place for friends, favoured clients, and their ilk.

Quite which of those categories would fit Justin Margrave has yet to be determined.

"How is the Perot, sir?" asks Stefan, almost immediately.

A subject Marcus would have preferred to let go.

The old man smiles, accepting a glass of Puglian wine as dark as dried blood. "Safe, subdued. I've had to deal with such matters before, never fear."

'Such matters'. Marcus winces, knowing what Stefan is after. Stories, tales of Margrave's many years in the business, perhaps his more salacious exploits—not the words which have been written about him, but the words which are missing...

An odd conversation at first, with Stefan probing, unashamed, and Marcus trying always to keep to relatively mundane matters—the virtues of this artist or that, the relevance of certain market trends, or even matters of technique. Anything which does not return them to 'Who Doh Hear'—or a certain Brixton past. Marcus doesn't want to be seven years old again, doesn't want to hear about Auntie Vi.

"...So I returned from Poland relatively unscathed, but minus an expensive camera, and inclined to be a little more careful around river banks, let us say. Especially those with young ladies lurking in the reeds."

What had that been about? Marcus realises that he's emptied his glass, and that he isn't used to the stronger stuff.

"And the Caustons? That business in the North?" Stefan probes, his blonde fringe falling over his eyes in that way which Marcus finds both annoying and irresistible. Is he doing this to charm the old chap? No, he won't be aware of the effect he has. One of the things which Marcus loves about him.

"Ah. That." Margrave glances at Marcus. "Well now, I do like you two boys. And I *could* tell you the truth of such matters. I could tell you rather more of certain other odd occurrences, but I suspect that to do so would make one of us somewhat uncomfortable."

Stefan's hand on his lover's arm, squeezing; that eager look, beseeching—and the warm scent of his sandalwood, overcoming the dull odour of the litter-strewn streets outside.

Marcus breathes in, out, a slow consideration.

"Oh, he can have his stories, Mr Margrave," he says at last.

"If you are sure, dear boy. But what should I select, out of so many years, so many incidents? Hmm..."

As Marcus reaches for the corkscrew, Margrave leans forward, his fingers tight about the black onyx head of the cane.

"I have it. Let me tell you something of my experiences during the nineteen seventies, partly because they are so crystal clear to me these days—and partly because you are too young to have been involved. A strange period for Britain, really, which is easily looked back on as terribly grim—bombings, power-cuts and strikes; racism and murdered children. Those horrors were with us, to be sure, but alongside all that, other curious events unfolded, ones in which I played a very modest part."

And his voice becomes deeper, a soft rumble in the chest of an old bull...

THE MADNESS OF QUEEN GEORGE

King's Cross, 1974

LISTENING TO THE RICOCHET of rain from cracked paving stones, the scrape of broken high heels, and the scuff of sodden boots, I wished very much that I could be elsewhere. Cigarettes sputtered and sagged in the downpour, as did the lives which drew on them, desperate for one last drag. Outside the station's blind arches, beneath the thunderous grind of the great Deltics on their rails of slick iron, I heard the same old hoarse offers and entreaties from mascara-smeared women in fake furs and ripped tights, from red-eyed teenage boys, as pale and unpromising as spoiled milk.

"Hand job for a fiver?"

"Want to go somewhere dry, baby?"

"I just got to get home, mister..."

A single rain-caped police constable stood by a waste-bin, peering into it as if hoping to find an IRA bomb which would blow him far from this dank desolation. He seemed completely blind to the girl crouched next to the concrete bin, her fingers shaking as she tried to fit a needle to a broken plastic syringe. I watched as she dropped it, found it, dropped it—Sisyphus reborn, female and the worse for that, to find herself here...

I rarely came here willingly. There were the trains, which one could hardly avoid when the North called, but otherwise... this was a land of mould-spotted rooms behind stained Victorian facades, and cheap tricks in alleyways, in hotel foyers, behind a thousand lock-ups and hastily-built post-War monstrosities. And it was the land of George Desmoges, the vain, self-serving queen of a realm in darkness.

King's Cross.

If you knew the true nature of the King's Cross district in those days, you knew of Queen George (or Georgie) as he was widely known. His hands, cramped with far too many ostentatious rings, stretched out across the night, dispensing his own mercurial justice to rent boys and drug addicts, to magistrates whose secrets he hoarded, to policemen who battened on fat brown envelopes passed across the bars of grimy public houses.

I was no adherent of his court, thank God, but I had to know about such people in order to do my job as an appraiser and provenance-hound. The art world, you see, has many circles. Some contain the cut and thrust of creative genius and critical savagery; others are even more unwholesome. These latter include the fences, forgers, bent antiquarians and traffickers who feed the fine, brightly-lit galleries.

Desmoges ruled many such folk, and however hard I tried not to, there were times when I crossed paths with his subjects. Some were disgraced artists, grinding out pigments to ape a seventeenth century portrait or knock out a Picasso or two; others were go-betweens familiar with the back entrances to various museums from New York to Beijing. Saddest were the debtors and addicts who would 'move' whatever needed to be moved—not villains as such, simply men and women impoverished into a sort of dull amorality. They needed the work to eat, to drink, to inject...

Natty Wade was one such man, his survival in King's Cross due not to the paltry income from the sex-shop he ran, but his ability to please Queen George.

"It's my cock, Mr Margrave," he said as we shared an over-boiled pot of tea in his backroom. "That, the poppers I get his crowd on the cheap, and—"

"Your friends at Heathrow and at Dover customs, who know when to ignore a suitcase?"

"Well, yeah, and them. But Georgie—she does love an omi who, you know, don't need to stand near the khazi to go for a slash."

That was common knowledge. Desmoges would only receive, never give, and liked the giver to be well-endowed. I did not, however, want to hear more about Natty's penis—or even to think about it. The state of his stained tea-cups was more than enough.

"Thank you for that, Natty. So you're in favour at the moment. Good for you, I suppose, but you still haven't said why we had to meet." I placed a ten pound note on the rickety plywood table, in the fervent hope that it would speed things up.

The tenner disappeared into my informant's grubby trousers.

"It's something in your line, Mr Margrave—she needs a really smart omi to varda what's she's got her mitts on."

Natty had that habit of referring to the more ostentatious gays as 'she', and throwing Polari, cant, into his sentences. Fortunately I understood. I pushed the half-drunk cup of tea away.

"You asked me down here to talk about one of Desmoges' dubious acquisitions? Honestly, Natty, you know me better than that."

Queen George was an art aficionado and collector, another reason it was hard to totally avoid his presence—though I had refused to deal with him in the past.

"Guv, you reckon I'd bother you if I didn't have to?" He looked offended.

Retrieved the hot tea, I gulped it down in one. Nothing like a scalded tongue to provide a moment's distraction. I had known Natty since he was a child, running errands for Billy Hill's gang in the fifties, and he knew of my dreadful curiosity—poor old Justin Margrave, who sought a simple life writing witty reviews and earning plump commissions, yet never quite avoided being drawn into the most peculiar affairs.

"Let me guess. Someone's offered him the chisel set that the centurions used to construct the True Cross."

Natty wasn't the humorous sort. "She needs to see you. Urgent, like. There's dosh in it for you."

I neither wanted nor needed Desmoges' money.

"No thanks."

The muscles of his face twisted, struggled to find the right expression. "I ain't allowed to go back with a 'No', Mr Margrave, She'll..."

I could imagine what an angry, thwarted Georgie might do, and Natty was barely a survivor as it was.

Acts of charity are so often double-edged. I have 'salvaged' waifs and rent boys in my time, helping them out of that world only for them to overdose or have their throats slit a month, a year later; I have aided less experienced colleagues in the art world, only for them to turn into treacherous termagants and know-it-alls. Apart from doling out the odd tenner, I had no intention of involving myself further in Natty's life, and yet—why make it worse for him?

"Tell me where Desmoges hold court these days," I said.

And between gushes of gratitude, he told me.

* * * * *

THERE WERE WORSE ESTABLISHMENTS in King's Cross than *The Courland*. No, really, there were. Propped between other cheap hotels and rooms for rent, it was one of those places which you knew was 'dirty', but where you didn't have to check your shoes for spiritual dog muck with every single step. It had a bar used by the public, the décor Victorian gin-house with a splash of seventies chic, and a more private lounge beyond that.

"Margrave," I said to the doe-eyed young man in mustard-coloured flares, standing by the closed lounge door. If those flares had been any tighter, I might have guessed not only his religion but the health of his prostate as well.

He simpered, and went to find out if I was allowed into the inner sanctum, making sure that the sway of his small buttocks was on full display—but even if I had been attracted, he had no doubt been touched by the hand of the Queen. Spoiled goods.

At seven in the evening, the public bar was busy, a room full of glances but no direct eye contact—minor mobsters, soiled lawyers, the odd police inspector... they were all there, blending in with office workers trying to get drunk before going home.

And so was Reggie Fitzgerald, antiques dealer and occasional critic, sinking a large whiskey.

"Don't ask," he muttered. "Apparently I'm not up to whatever it is Desmoges wants."

"Did you really want to be, Reggie? Dealing with Georgie has never been a pleasant business."

He was human enough to blush. "The bastard knows of a man in Kazakhstan, who has certain... curios he wants to shift. Nothing illegal, Margrave, before you start on at me, but the local officials are bribe-happy and argumentative..."

I was flattered that Reggie thought me divorced from the more tawdry aspects of our field.

"You're better off out of this, believe me..."

Doe Eyes interrupted anything else we might have said, ushering me through the now-open doorway and into the true gin palace, a luxurious, high-ceilinged lounge bar ruined by cheap red flock wallpaper and too much Formica.

Between the empty tables stood an entirely inappropriate Victorian chaise longue on which reclined the equally inappropriate George Desmoges. The acid green of the re-covered chaise and the lavender of Desmoges' tailored suit hurt my eyes.

"Ah, darling Justin!" He greeted me like a long-lost chum, his round face as welcome to me as a full moon to a poacher.

"Georgie." I drew up a chair, well away from the chaise. My real idea of 'well away' would have been another county.

"Drink, sweetie?" He leaned towards a small table holding two glasses of brandy, pushing one in my direction. He stank of pomade, his pale, slicked-back hair reminding me of discarded rice noodles, and it struck me that a good scrubbing would have made him more palatable. Not much more, though...

"I don't care for *The Courland*'s drinks, thank you—they have a dubious aftertaste."

Doe Eyes giggled; Georgie laughed.

"Justin, Justin... such a serious girl. Ah well, this is business, so..."

Reaching down by his side, he held out something about the size of a man's head, wrapped loosely in green silk. I hesitated, then took it from him. It was unexpectedly heavy.

"It's all right, darling," he said. "I haven't been naughty. I bought this off an antiquarian, one of the really old-school types, who was struggling with his cash flow. He didn't want to sell at first, but I was terribly, terribly generous. I do hope I haven't been taken advantage of."

"You want me to appraise it, tell you if it's genuine."

I still hadn't unwrapped the thing.

"Partly, partly. Have a peek, and then we'll talk."

It wasn't soft, it wasn't dripping dubious fluids. I pulled the material aside.

And was relieved. What I held was a fired clay sculpture which depicted a man, a monarch, swathed in the usual regal robes. Full-length, twelve or thirteen inches tall. Not especially well executed, but it triggered a memory...

"Would this be a maquette for a larger piece?" I turned it in my hands, peering at certain features. Many sculptors made maquettes—models—before they undertook a major work. It allowed them to explore posture, viewing points, and the overall integrity of the composition.

"So my antiquarian friend said. One with particular relevance to this part of our dear city."

What would be so relevant to King's Cross? Intrigued despite myself, I examined the model again, peered closely at the base, and found the initials S G scratched lightly into the clay. Considering the condition of the baked clay, the colouration and general feel...

Desmoges had managed to surprise me.

"I suspect," said. "That this could be a maquette for that ghastly old monstrosity, Geary's statue of George IV."

Desmoges clapped his chubby hands together.

"I hoped, I hoped. Is it... valuable?"

That was a difficult one to answer. As George IV sank into blindness and claret-soaked immobility, a local freeholder had championed the need for a monument to celebrate His Majesty, better remembered as the dissolute Prince Regent. Public subscriptions towards this edifice were—unsurprisingly—less than munificent, but it went ahead in 1830, under the architect Stephen Geary.

The result was a small octagonal building where New Road (later to become Euston Road) and Pentonville met, an inconvenient traffic island cursed by Victorian cabbies. It was eventually topped by Geary's statue of the king. The Morning Post called this addition 'a frightful staring effigy... executed in a style of grotesque vulgarity beyond anything I have caught a glimpse of in a waxwork or hairdresser's window.' The effigy was torn down only a few years later, but oddly, the name King's Cross stuck.

Was the maquette valuable?

"As a curiosity for some ardent monarchist with too much money, or a collector of bizarre historical relics," I said. "Not artistically, no. It is an interesting piece, though."

"And why would that be?"

"It's often said that Geary and his crew built the statue from scratch and on the spot—bricks, cement, and a bit of stone cladding. Clearly that isn't true—he made at least one maquette of what he planned after all."

That pleased Desmoges. "You are so clever, Justin darling—I knew you were the man for my little project."

"Project?"

"I want a statue like this—but full-sized, with my features. A statue of Queen George, to commemorate my status, my achievements."

"You're serious?"

Small, slate-grey eyes met mine, tiny pits of spite and hubris which made matters absolutely clear. He was very serious, and any further signs of amusement would not be tolerated.

"I can find you a stonemason or two, if that's what you're asking," I said.

His gaze became less threatening, but he shook his head.

"Why do you think I had you in particular brought to me, Justin sweetie? I want this done by a proper sculptor, an artist, not some peasant who turns out gravestones and cemetery angels. And I'll go to seven, eight grand, before you ask, with a percentage for you, naturally. Find me the person I need, and explain my requirements to them, there's a dear."

Appraising the occasional maquette or other bauble was one thing; being patronised, being used, was another.

"Why on Earth should I help you out?"

The tiny eyes glinted again. "Oh, I know things about you, Justin—so many things. The unlikely company you keep from time to time, the disappearance of that Caravaggio sketch, even the business at Lincoln's Inn last year and why James Henry Petheridge is now on a mental ward, rather than practising at the bar."

"If you had the courage to use chatter like that against me, Georgie, I'm sure you already would have. And therefore..."

Desmoges smirked. "Well, there's always Natty, or those other charitable cases who seem to attract your sympathy. How many people would you like to see hurt, Justin darling, before you give me this teensy bit of assistance, at absolutely no cost to yourself?"

My shoulders slumped. I did not need additional difficulties in my life. There were ways to thwart Georgie, or redirect his attention—he had rivals, and there were gangs across the city who had little love for him, but that would mean dealing with people just as unpleasant as he was—worse, in some cases. The authorities would be of no use. Despite efforts to cleanse the Met, there remained plenty of officers who could not risk upsetting Desmoges.

Would it be easier all round to humour him?

"I dare say I might be able to find someone." I pushed the brandy away, untouched. "There is a condition. Non-negotiable."

"What?"

"They complete this work for you; you pay up, and have nothing more to do with them. If I hear that you've drawn them further into your nasty little web, then..."

He waved one hand airily. "A piffling matter. All I want is my statue."

I wrapped up the maquette again, and tucked it in the crook of my arm.

"Give me a week or so. I'll send word through Natty."

"Lovely. Toodle-oo, Justin sweetie."

Reggie was no longer in the main bar; the early evening shift had replaced him and a number of other idle drinkers, all nicely turned out with Chelsea-boutique clothes and outrageous lies, looking for booze and benzedrine. And Desmoges's benny-boys were ready with their little plastic bags.

Queen Georgie had only one redeeming feature of which I was aware—unlike the slum landlords, crooked hostel owners and blue-film princes of Soho, Desmoges never knowingly encouraged under-age trade. I even knew of cases where a kid had turned out to be only seventeen or eighteen, and had been summarily ejected from Georgie's 'scene'—including his businesses. By order of the Queen.

In contrast, the railings of Piccadilly were strewn with doped-up teenagers, lost almost as soon as they set foot on the streets. Runaways, drug addicted teens, children from 'decent homes' who could no longer take those nights when their drunken father staggered into their bedrooms, zip already halfway down. Easy meat for the vile, the wealthy, the influential—which gave the area its common name, the Meat Rack.

It sickened me because of what it was—paedophilia—and also because it cast a shadow over 'my kind', our reputations. Whilst so many gay men worked hard to keep their lives intact, decent, caring, in Piccadilly the pimps and murderers sold stray and vulnerable boys to their predatory clients, entirely careless of the result. It was a sick demimonde, beloved of the cheaper newspapers, and a stick which was used to beat any passing homosexual.

Enough. I had a task, and the person of whom I was thinking knew about Georgie—she would make up her own mind. I set off through the damp, dirty streets of King's Cross.

My candidate was also a stray, but by choice and with purpose. Bristol-born, she lived in a squat by Regent's Canal, in the shadow of the gasworks. Not the usual abandoned tenement, but a small warehouse, with enough room for three or four fellow adventurers. A collective, of sorts.

And she had both the hand and eye of a sculptor. Working on this one piece for Desmoges wouldn't get her the critical attention she needed, but it could provide the hard cash she needed to turn the warehouse into a proper studio.

"Now then, Mr M."

I nodded to her as she hammered at a piece of corrugated iron in the corner of the workshop area. She knew I hate being called Mr M.

"Miss Walsey." Now we were even. "Can you spare a moment?"

"You got me an exhibition yet?" She threw the hammer aside and strode over.

Joanna Walsey, twenty seven, with a lean face, a lean body, and the sort of nose that might have matched Wellington's. It made her seem patrician, and intense.

"Time will tell. But I do have a job in which you might be interested. George Desmoges requires a statue of himself, believe it or not."

"You gave my name to that horror?"

"Certainly not. But he's laid up to eight thousand on this particular job—and I would stand guarantor, if you chose to take it."

"Why me?"

"Because I know you could do something worthwhile with the money."

She sniffed, and led me to another corner, where she made coffee, courtesy of grey-brown granules from a tin, and a sputtering electric kettle. The taste was such that I actually thought she had used gravy powder at first.

"A single life-sized statue. Three months, a quarter of the money upfront." I took out the maquette, which had hideously distorted my soft leather shoulder-bag, and pulled the silk away. "Modelled on this, but with Georgie's face."

"Fuckin' hell. What is it?"

I explained the maquette's origins, about Geary and the rest. She wasn't terribly interested in the background, but I could see that the amount offered tempted her.

"I bloody hate Desmoges."

"Most of us do, dear girl."

"How come you're involved in this, Mr M? Always thought you were clean."

"Are any of us?" I was tired of this business already, and it had hardly begun. "I could refuse, yes, but what would come next? You know how he works."

"You're afraid of him?"

I was hurt that she could think that. "I have broader shoulders—and more resources—than most. No, I'm afraid of what he does when he's thwarted, and lashes out. Other people I know would suffer, especially the weakest, the most vulnerable."

"Shit. And that's all the nasty bugger wants? A statue."

"I made it clear that's all he'll get—through us, anyway."

She took the commission.

As I wandered back to find a cab, I wondered what I had begun.

* * * * *

THE PRACTICALITIES WERE SIMPLE. I arranged for a suitable block of Portland stone—resilient but workable limestone—to be delivered to Joanna. Desmoges paid up without complaint, handling everything through Harry Goldberg. Harry the Axe. They loved their sobriquets, these ten-a-penny heavies. Harry was a Krays discard, too dull for the fast cut and thrust of the sixties firms, abandoned in the seventies to make his own way in the protection racket, until Georgie picked him up. Arthritis in his hands made it unlikely that he would wield an axe again, if he ever had.

"I don't like poofs," were his first words to me.

You like their money, though, I wanted to say. I didn't. I did notice that it took Harry only one encounter with Joanna, and a chisel thrust under his chin, to make him keep his distance from the squat. My task was to inspect the work every so often, and report back via Harry. I said that I didn't want to meet with Desmoges again until there was some-thing to show him.

My dislike for this entire business only grew, and so many times, moving through the murmur of a gallery opening, or clinking glasses at *The Ivy*, I wondered why in God's name I had agreed to do this. Was it really to protect others, or did I—at some unfathomable level—want to see the final result, the statue?

Of all people, it was Natty who gave me a sliver of comfort.

"It's all she wants, Mr Margrave," he said, "And all she talks about. I was late with me takings last week, but no one cared—nanti hassle—and

I haven't been called to *The Courland* to do, you know, for weeks. Mind you..."

I was expecting a grim addendum, but Natty was more puzzled than anything.

"Harry says she's not at her best. Says she looks like a right bag of suet these days, and she's havin' trouble gettin' around."

Curious—Desmoges had looked well enough when I was first summoned. Was he really ill? Had he already received news from his doctors, some frightening intimation of mortality? George IV had been a complete wreck in his last months, a corpulent corpse-in-waiting. That might explain why the statue was so important.

I looked in on Joanna, who had the basic form carved out by now, and was starting on the riskier, deeper chiselling which would define limbs, and the later smaller features.

"Stick this one a pedestal in Euston Road, Mr M, and they'll be calling the area Queen's Cross in a hundred years."

She had certainly followed the maquette, and with enormous ability. Even at this stage, the line of the robes had vitality, and there was an inherent strength to the posture; the head was only crudely formed as yet, awaiting its time.

"You seem... enthusiastic," I said. "More than at the beginning."

"It's a job."

I didn't believe that deflection. Her urgency—and her diligence—as she hammered, cut, smoothed... this statue mattered to her, for some reason. Money was not enough to birth this sort of effort, not in Joanna Walsey.

Govind, one of her fellow squatters, was of the same opinion. A handsome post-graduate student originally from Gujarat, he sat with me by the canal, smoking a cheroot.

"It is not good for her, heh? She spends so many hours working... and she stares, stares at photographs of the buffoon."

"Of George Desmoges?"

"Yes." He blew a dense cloud of smoke into the still air. "Does she know him? Personally, I mean."

"I don't think so."

Joanna might have been squatting in King's Cross for three years, but she had nothing to do with Queen George's scene. She had never displayed any interest in matters of sex—with men or women—and had an aversion to any form of drug use apart from the odd cigarette. I was one of the first people who spent any time with Joanna after her arrival in London, after she pestered one of the review magazines for coverage of her early pieces. 'Very promising,' I had commented at the end of a brief column, and I had been watching since to see what she would achieve.

"Artists, heh?" Govind was an engineer—he enjoyed the technical aspects of large-scale sculpture and architecture, the mechanics of it all, but grew bored when the conversation turned to aesthetics.

I nodded in companionable agreement, lacking the energy to point out that many artists were rather dull and workmanlike when you got to know them. Behind the eccentric and visionary geniuses, hidden in the shadows, stood an awful lot of competent plumbers...

* * * * *

A S THE WEEKS WENT BY, I found myself following two narratives. The first concerned Joanna's progress and any minor problems she was having; the second was the growing trickle of gossip about Queen Georgie, who was apparently becoming more and more of a recluse. Something was seriously wrong with him.

Curiosity often leads me astray, and so it was that I did the unthinkable—I requested a direct audience with the queen, rather than waiting for some tedious summons through Harry or Natty. And my request was granted.

My first hint was that the lights in *The Courland*'s private rooms had been turned down low, and a number of bulbs were conspicuously missing from their fittings. Doe Eyes was nervous, tugging at his hair, as he showed me in.

"She's off-colour," he said, and tittered, an unpleasant sound.

Desmoges sat at a table in the darkest part of the main lounge, Harry the Axe glowering from another three or four away from his employer. I was beckoned forward.

"Justin, darling. You have news?" Georgie sounded hoarse, asthmatic.

I took the single free chair, a plastic and tubular steel thing that smelled of disinfectant.

"It's going to plan," I said, and outlined the progress so far.

My purpose, however, was to inspect the man's condition. I won't say that I ever liked George Desmoges's appearance, but this time I *really* didn't like what I saw. I was hardly a thin fellow myself, but here, plumpness had turned to a gross, pallid obesity—his eyes were buried deeper, his jowls wobbled, and his skin was... I'm not sure of the right words. Pitted, oily. Generously-applied cosmetics could not hide the pimples and blackheads which clustered in the folds of his face, or the boils which peeped from under his shirt collar.

He looked like he needed to be lanced. All of him.

"I hear you're not feeling so good," I said, when I had finished my report.

Georgie glared.

"A temporary condition, Justin. How nice of you to be concerned, though."

"I wouldn't want Miss Walsey to go unrewarded. She labours night and day on your statue, after all."

The dip of his head seemed to cause him pain.

"Of course, of course. Fear not, all will be well. I am so looking forward to the result—and you are sure that I will be pleased?" His enquiry held an obvious threat, but I could at least give an honest answer.

"She's has done an outstanding job. Fit for the best galleries and museums in London."

"Excellent." He gestured to Harry, who came over, not too close, and threw a chunky brown envelope on the table in front of me. "A little extra for your girl, to ensure that the work is finished soon. I am so... so very eager for my first private viewing, and—"

A deep, choking cough overtook him. Harry, with a sneer pulling up one corner of his mouth, back away; I hesitated. As the fit passed, Desmoges dabbing at his lower lip with a blood-red silk handkerchief. I could not be sure, given the lighting, if I saw darker spots there, crimson on the red, or not. I can be over-imaginative.

"Not too long, Justin sweetie," he said, indicating that the audience was over.

Not too long for the sculpture to be finished—or for him?

Govind rang me from a corner-shop a few days later.

"Jo says to come over."

"With Desmoges?"

"*Na.* Just you, she says."

I took a taxi to the gasworks, and wandered over wasteland to the warehouse. They had cleared one side of the main floor, and the statue stood alone there on a wooden pallet, all trace of tools and chippings cleared away, the head covered with a paint-spattered sheet. Joanna, dressed in her usual stained boiler-suit, was dozing in an old deckchair next to it.

"She's been working nights on the thing, all week," said Govind, shaking the kettle to try and get it working. "Silly cow."

Were Hindus supposed to say that?

Joanna woke with a start, looking up first at her work, then seeing us.

"There you go, Mr M," she said.

I strolled around the statue.

"Why the sheet? Should I not see the whole creation before I risk telling Desmoges it's ready?"

"Trust me." She stood, placing herself in front of the statue. "You can see enough, can't you?"

Her work—or artistry, if you prefer—on the body of the figure was certainly outstanding. A proud, forward posture, with regal robes sweeping down from broad shoulders which hinted of strength and command. In the raised right hand, a simple sceptre of burnished copper; in the left hand, held close to the chest, a matching orb, though without the excessive faff and detail of the real thing. Some part of the gasworks was probably missing a pipe or two.

I chewed at my cheek. "Jo, you haven't topped this with some hideous caricature, have you? A Mickey Mouse head, or a ferret's face. Georgie isn't known for his appreciation of satire, especially when it involves him."

If I had ever seen a slow smile, that was what I received at that moment. Slow, and secretive, as it spread across her face.

"No," she said. "Hand on heart, Justin. I studied the photos you gave me, and a few shots I managed to find of Desmoges when he was young, looked at him from every angle. It's a true likeness—his own mum would know him."

She had never called me Justin before, not in all the time I had known her, and my neck prickled.

"You've made him look as gross and stupid as he really is, then."

"No." Snapped, impatient. "It's rather flattering, as it happens. Seven and a half thousand quid, remember?"

I should have felt reassured, but I didn't.

"He wants to see it here, in situ, before he decides where to have it erected."

"That's fine. Tell him and his lickspittles to pop in, then."

"Your middle-class suburban background is showing, dear girl. No one says lickspittle these days."

There was nothing to be gained from hauling myself to-and-fro again, so I called Natty, and suggested that Desmoges come over that evening. An exclusive viewing—Joanna, myself, and Govind, Desmoges and a couple of his 'lickspittles'. Except that I said 'friends' on the phone. Natty could be terribly literal when he reported to others. Yes, I wanted to peer under that cloth, but I did manage to restrain myself. This would all be over soon enough.

I took Joanna and Govind out for a bite to eat, somewhere pleasant, free of artists, critics or Georgie's people. Mel and Charlie, the other members of the commune, were away at a juggling event in Oxford, choking down lentil pasties and selling bean-bags or something along those lines. Despite a decent meal and a few glasses of something Sicilian, part of me wished I was with them.

At five to eight, a highly-polished red Bentley cruised into view beside Regent's Canal and scraped to a halt on the broken concrete. A low sun shone through the girders of the depleted gas-holders, casting intricate shadow-squares over all; we walked across a crumpled, graph-paper landscape to meet our guests.

Queen Georgie had to be helped from the Bentley, Doe Eyes wiggling along with a hand under his ruler's elbow, steadying him. Despite dark glasses and a new grey camel-hair overcoat, collar turned up high, Desmoges looked worse than he had the week before; sickly, aged, not as a fine wine ages but more akin to a rotting cheese. Harry the Axe was behind them, his usual menacing self.

"Where... where is it?" asked Desmoges.

"Inside," I said. "All ready for you."

Govind and Harry eyed each other as we walked towards the warehouse's open doors; Joanna was alongside Desmoges, murmuring something about the virtues of Portland stone, and how long it would last. Between coughs, he made approving noises.

His hands looked dreadful, rings almost buried in flesh the colour of off-pork, a slight sheen on the skin, and expensive eau de toilette could not hide the over-sweet smell of him. I was not happy. Not that I cared for his welfare, but I wondered what his reaction would be to the statue when he was in such a condition.

"Oh my," he said, almost slavering as he saw the partly-covered sculpture, which stood higher on the pallet, giving it an imposing premise. "Oh, this *does* look promising."

"I followed your commission, Mr Desmoges." Joanna took hold of one corner of the sheet. "I cut away the stone, every millimetre of it, thinking of you."

Desmoges paused, breathing heavily, noisily. "Are we acquainted?"

The slow smile touched her lips, but not the rest of her face.

"You knew my brother. Andrew."

"I don't remember him. Harry, do we know an Andrew Walsey?"

Harry looked more blank than usual, shook his head.

"He came here, to King's Cross, five years ago, before I did." Her voice was steady, casual, and that worried me as well.

Impatience appeared to struggle with mild curiosity.

"So many do, my girl. And has he prospered?"

"He was gay. He was looking for work and lodgings, but work was scarce—he ended up in one of your many establishments." Her delivery was a monotone, as if rehearsed. "When he couldn't make rent, he was told that Mr Desmoges wasn't a patient man. Andrew would just have to some little jobs for you—entertaining a few of your clients for a couple of weeks. After that, not only would the slate would be clean but he would have a couple of hundred in his pocket. Enough to find a decent bedsit, and get himself sorted properly."

Doe Eyes did that inappropriate giggle of his; Desmoges pursed cracked wet lips.

"We do what we can to help and..." He had to stop for a moment, wiping discoloured saliva from the corner of his mouth. He reminded me of a rat I had once found behind the flat, its corpse twitching because of whatever was tunnelling through the corruption inside. Desmoges had worms under his skin, at least metaphorically. "And boys do come to London with such ridiculously high expectations—it's rather sad. Anyway—"

Joanna gave the man a look I could not interpret.

"My brother died of an overdose, stuffed with your pills, your bennies and mandies. His body was found in a hotel room, trousers around the ankles, vomit spattering the bed. He'd probably been raped whilst semi-conscious, the police said. But funnily enough, they didn't want to do much more with the case, given that it was on your patch."

Desmoges shuddered, and gestured to Harry, who started to come closer, but Govind and I were in the way. Neither the Gujarati or I could be called small men. I didn't know what was happening, nor had Joanna ever mentioned a brother before, but she should get to say her piece.

"And then you gave me a job to do as well, didn't you? It took me a while to realise what had been been put into my hands, but I'm a conscientious woman. I thought about what I would do. I thought long, and hard, and I did it well, Mr Desmoges." Dipping into a pocket of her boiler-suit, Joanna tossed a handful of Polaroids across the concrete warehouse floor. "I even rang your mum in Sussex—she was happy to send me some photos of you as a younger man, seeing as you, such an upstanding citizen, were getting your own statue."

Desmoges was—for a moment—speechless.

Joanna pulled the sheet away.

They say that Gian Lorenzo Bernini was the master of Baroque sculpture—the life, power and vitality in his works have rarely been bettered, and I am rarely unmoved by his figures. Bernini's faces, with the loosening of a single braid of hair, the gasp you cannot hear which comes from drawn-back lips, are rich with humanity, and with questions.

Joanna Walsey clearly understood Bernini.

"Bloody hell," said Govind.

The body of the statue displayed talent and a feel for the human form, but the head, the face...

It was beautiful.

Flawless.

A noble brow, teased with modest, artless locks; eyes which, although stone-blank, seemed to glow, and lips which were parted to offer, to promise, to care. Without lust or desire, providing hope, giving without need for thanks or reward. A young man, gifted, open, almost holy. Pure.

You wanted to bow, or to sob; you could not look long, for fear of how it looked back at you.

This was surely the George Desmoges who might have been, the angel who was to lose his struggle with a thousand tawdry demons, who had become the swollen and diseased man who stood there in his camel-hair coat and Chelsea boots a size too small.

"Do you like it, Mr Desmoges?" she asked. "This is what you have shredded, pissed and spat upon. Your mother would be proud of this—it's all the promise and hope you must once have held—and everything which you have twisted and spat upon as you became King's Cross."

Georgie was on his knees, his limbs jerking uncontrollably; Doe Eyes stared, paralysed, at the face above him. The young man was weeping.

"Do. You. Like. It?" she repeated, staccato.

I turned away, trying to exorcise what I had seen in the statue's face. Too great a beauty brings its own terrors.

"I believe you have the rest of the money owed to Miss Walsey," I managed to say to Harry the Axe.

He blinked, confused, and reached into his jacket, handing me the envelope. It looked about the correct thickness. By the statue, Desmoges was pawing at his chest, his dark glasses on the concrete, his overcoat open. Even Harry could see the monstrosity of his master's face, the dirt-encrusted furrows and ruptured veins which mapped out every fault in the man's soul, every sin. Not a word I use lightly, but to see both Georgie and his statue together... it was almost enough to make one turn Catholic.

Joanna showed no emotion. "Andrew used to read to me when I was much younger. Oscar Wilde. I was a little girl, filled with wonder—and sadness. Do you enjoy reading, Mr Desmoges?"

A spasm left Desmoges unable to do anything but moan.

Wilde.

And finally I understood—not the how of what Joanna had done, but possibly the concept behind her work these last few weeks, behind her growing commitment to the project.

Joanna must have seen my expression. "See, Mr M? I knew you'd get it. The statue was for bloody Desmoges—but I knew that if it wasn't me who made the damn piece, it would be someone else. The money was too good. At first it just brought back a few bad memories, but then... the resentment and hatred inside me started to build. And I'd always wondered about the real power of art..."

For every day that she had chipped at that face and created beauty, compassion, that was also a day where Georgie struggled a little more, felt his pulse weaken and his fingers swell, his belly rot...

Not that such a thing was possible.

Was it?

Doe Eyes, whimpering, edged towards the open doors and the Bentley; Harry shuffled over to his boss and, after some hesitation, dragged him to his feet. You could see that he didn't want to touch the other man if he could help it. Exactly what Desmoges was babbling, I don't know, but his lips were turning blue, his tiny eyes bulging...

They left, with a thin trail of sick marking their retreat.

As we heard the car pulling away, I went forward and handed Joanna the cash, my eyes averted from the statue. Part of me, deep inside, feared that under its gaze, purulence and corruption might begin to show itself beneath my own brow.

I am hardly a sinless man.

"You don't approve," she said.

That brought me to my senses.

"Approval, Jo? Who am I to judge? A sick man just collapsed, having pushed his body too far—sex, drugs, and iniquity. Or... a corrupted soul could not bear your reminder of just how warped and ruined it had become."

I made a mental note to send my commission to Natty Wade. Maybe I could persuade him to set up a proper bookshop, one which didn't need the likes of George Desmoges to keep it going.

"Which do you think is the most likely, Mr M?" She seemed genuinely concerned to hear my view, as if what I said mattered.

I sighed. "I find that I don't want to know. Desmoges is finished. If he lives, you have broken him."

"And the statue?"

"It can't be displayed. Ever. So... I don't know, keep it shut away, safe, or break the thing up. I know, I know, a sacrilege in itself. All right, find a secure lock-up, and I'll pay for it to be stored."

"Was it... well done?"

"Well done? Jo, you have true vision, the makings of a long and very successful career in sculpture." I paused. "And you have another gift, which I hope to God has exhausted itself."

I could not smile at her. I patted Govind's arm, and walked away.

Behind and alongside my path, the gas-holders stood like abandoned crowns of iron and rust, cast off by giants who had lost their kingdoms to men.

"The Queen is dead," I told them as I passed. "Do you think that King's Cross will manage without another one?"

They did not answer.

THE BEASTS OF KEMBERDALE

North Yorkshire, 1975

I SHALL CALL THE PLACE KEMBERDALE, in order to spare those who deserve their anonymity. It is real, though—one of those small communities on the edge of the bleak North York Moors. Perhaps once it straddled a Roman road, or a later pack-trail between more important destinations, but now it stands disconnected, isolated. Farming land, with little to commend it to outsiders—none of the ruined buildings or interesting vistas which delight ramblers and amateur photographers. Sheep on the hillsides; wheat and potatoes in the fields.

Archie Crane mentioned it to me, at a dull party in Chelsea. Archie is a touch pestiferous, and will poke his nose into others' affairs.

"Young Petersen has his eye on a collection held by the local lord of the manor. I say 'lord', but he's just a jumped-up farmer, really." Archie refreshed our glasses. "Anyway, they say there are a few oddities up there, and Petersen thinks they're worth a look..."

The conversation swung to gossip about a sculptor we both knew, and I thought nothing of it until I bumped into Erik Petersen later that week at a wine-bar.

"Fancy an adventure, Justin?" Petersen was a tall blond, a fine echo of his Scandinavian forebears. "I need to go north later this week."

"Kemberdale?"

His eyes widened, then narrowed with suspicion. It spoiled his good looks.

"Are we in competition?"

I laughed. "I don't even know what's up there, and no-one's asked me to go hunting, if that's what you mean. I'm carefree—and commission-free—at the moment.

He relaxed. "Oh, well, I know you're fond of Yorkshire, and you do have an eye for curios, so I wonder..."

"What's the quarry?"

He stubbed out his cigarette and leaned closer.

"I have it on good authority that there used to be a number of quaint practices in the area, the sort of thing that people keep trying to revive."

"Dear God, not druids?" An unfortunate encounter the previous year, involving suburban accountants, had quite put me off that area. Little was worse than middle-class Englishmen—or women—donning robes and wandering round spouting pseudo-Celtic nonsense without the faintest idea of what they were doing.

"No, genuine folk history. Chap up there wrote to say that he has some costumes; mumming, sword dances—that sort of game—including a nice set of masks."

It wasn't particularly my field, but I'd submitted my column to *The Sculptor* magazine, knocked off a couple of articles for *The Times*, and completed a large estate valuation, so technically I was free. Perhaps also relevant to any decision I made, the IRA had been pursuing a fairly determined bombing campaign in the capital that autumn, and everyone's nerves were on edge. One might have some sympathy for aspects of a cause, but not when its wilder elements were blowing up your hotel.

Petersen was easy on the eye, decent company, and reputed to be what we jokingly called 'a cousin of Dorothy'. A wavering candle. I had no definite intent in that direction, but one should always be open to opportunity...

All in all, a trip into the countryside might indeed be a good idea.

"I could be free by Thursday," I offered.

We agreed the details there and then.

* * * * *

OUR FIRST MISTAKE was the car we hired in York. I rarely drove; Petersen was used to London and the flatlands. It soon became obvious that we would have been better hiring a Landrover than the large, comfortable Ford Granada we had been offered. This was late November, and although we'd avoided snow as yet, every route to Kemberdale involved narrow lanes lined with drystone walls, sudden lurches into precipitous inclines, and poorly-metalled country roads. Crossing the purple and dark green expanse of the moors proper, Petersen jerked the wheel at every idle sheep in the road and every bird which broke from cover.

"Christ, what was that?" he said as he almost took us into a ditch.

"Pheasant. For goodness sake, Erik—are you expecting spear-wielding natives to burst out of the bracken?"

In time, and after a few accidental detours, we spotted a lichen-covered wooden post with a sign which could just be made out: Kember 5 miles. The rest of the journey was a low-gear crawl down into a valley bottom, and on through a scatter of stone cottages to our destination.

Kember Manor was the only building of note in sight—a farmhouse fortified in the manner more commonly found on the Scottish borders. No doubt the northern dales had seen their share of sheep and cattle rustling.

I wouldn't have called the manor attractive—the thick walls appeared a mix of gritstone and brick, unevenly plastered, with lank ivy hiding a good third of the two storey building, which could have been 16th or even 15th century. A few small, quartered windows were scattered across the frontage as if afterthoughts, looking out over a pitted gravel drive which meandered between barns and chicken-huts.

"Chap we're going to see is a Samuel Beckshaw. His family have lived around here since Adam; he owns most of the houses hereabouts. Has the only telephone in Kemberdale, would you believe?"

"That's one more phone than I might have expected," I said, conscious that the landscape was fading into a charmless dusk. "Are we going to drive back to York in the dark?"

"No, Beckshaw's putting us up for the night—he wanted me to come as soon as possible."

I hadn't been able to get a straight answer as to whether Petersen was buying any of this stuff, or simply viewing it and looking to catalogue it, but I'd been promised a couple of nights in a decent York hotel when we'd finished in Kemberdale.

Petersen slid the Granada to a halt in a patch of mud by the nearest barn, and pronounced himself content.

"Four o'clock. Not bad time, really."

I said nothing. We were supposed to have been here by two in the afternoon.

A cold wind cut across the manor yard, bringing with it the smell of rank vegetation and stagnant water; it smelled as if the entire area could do with a good hosing down, and perhaps a few barrels of carbolic. But the door was answered promptly by a man at odds with these surroundings—a well-dressed man in his late twenties, clean-shaven, red-cheeked and redolent of Old Spice. There was something slightly unappealing about him, though I couldn't say what.

"Mr Petersen—you made it." He looked relieved to see us. "And this would be..."

"Justin Margrave," I said, extending a hand. His grip was firm, too firm.

"Good, good. Do come in."

He showed us into a large, barely furnished room with whitewashed walls.

"Where the cattle would have sheltered during raids," I murmured, and Beckshaw smiled.

"Quite right. With a few modifications." He indicated a pair of ancient leather sofas, and a set of closed pine cabinets which lined the long far wall.

"By your accent, you're not from Yorkshire, Mr Beckshaw?" I ease myself into one of the sofas, expecting mice to shoot out of its seams.

"Born here—in this house—but I was abroad for years. In France. Came back when my father died this summer. Cancer."

"My condolences."

"Yes."

Not 'Thank you', but 'Yes'. His smile had gone, and I changed the subject.

"So, Petersen tells me you have some fascinating pieces. I'm more in the sculpture line, with a touch of ceramics and bric-a-brac, but still, I imagine–"

"Time presses, Mr Margrave." Beckshaw's interruption was accompanied by the jangle of keys, drawn from his jacket pocket. "I know you'll think me rude, but I'm hoping to rid myself of this lot as soon as possible..."

"Of course." I was used to odd customers, and Petersen had an acquisitive gleam in his eye.

"Let me show you what I have. We can have a drink later, and maybe come to terms."

He unlocked the row of cabinets, five in all. The were tall, not that old, but the contents clearly went back many years, and I found myself stepping closer...

The display before me was reminiscent of a theatrical costumiers I had visited, not long after the war, a warren of a place packed with the most gorgeous and most tawdry racks of gowns and robes, fake jewelled necklaces; sceptres, hats and masks. This looked like its rural, folk museum equivalent.

"Feel free to browse, assure yourself that it's all genuine."

We did, and we did.

Thick woollen robes, dyed green and crimson, smelled of another time; furs were moth-eaten in that way which only many decades could achieve. Petersen lifted out a horse skull, gaily coloured but faded, which must have been from a mummer's hobby horse.

"Early Victorian, at least," he said, showing it to me. "Brass fixings for the pole, heavily used."

In the cabinet nearest me were blades typical of the traditional sword dances of the North—rigid steel with simple wooden hilts, the varnish peeling—and padded black ceremonial jackets. The casual heap of jackets was topped by a basket of belled anklets, typical of Morris dances and similar going-on. And there was much more along the same lines.

"Is all this from around here?"

"I don't know—I didn't collect this junk. I tried to get rid of it all last month, but none of the museums I rang had enough space or interest to come through in time."

"In time?"

"You'll understand in a minute. Here..."

Beckshaw stood back from the last cabinet, holding the door wide open.

This one was shelved—four deep shelves, presenting a display of twelve of the most curious masks I had seen since a Venetian collection I valued back in sixty eight. I had been prepared for the sort of thing that you saw at Mayday and other such times—the papier-mâché dragon's head, the wheat-sheaf mask, the plague doctor and the knight's helmet, battered out of tin cans, but these...

Each was a superb representation of an animal's or bird's head, fashioned with incredible skill. I took up one from the top shelf; it was clearly meant to portray a robin redbreast. If worn, it would cover most of a man's head. The small black eyes—volcanic glass?—glittered, the short beak was ready to stab, and the lacquer around it as red as arterial blood.

I squinted over my glasses, and could see a patina to the lacquer, a series of those tiny cracks which come with age. The mask was made of wood.

"This is surely carved, painted oak, yet it's so thin, so beautifully crafted. Quite a find."

Petersen, running his fingers down the mask of a horned bull, agreed.

"Better than I'd expected. Have you any idea how old these are, Mr Beckshaw?"

"As old as the manor?" The man had a look of immense distaste. "They've always been here. My father coveted the masks; I hated them."

"Hard to hate a wooden mask," said Petersen, but there we differed. The stare of the robin was cold, even aggressive... I put it down.

I have no peculiar talents, but it has often been said that I am receptive to the 'feel' of things. Useful in my line of work, because it means I have an eye for forged paintings, and for mutton passed off as lamb. However important—or valuable—these masks were, I did not trust them. An otter's head had lips drawn back, sharp teeth exposed; the bull was a mask of anger, not placid strength.

"Ritual." I murmured. "A local custom, some performance at certain times by the villagers and hill-farmers?"

"The Beasts of Kemberdale," said Beckshaw. "Much of the collection in general was brought together over the last fifty years, but as I said, the masks have been here for generations. They belong to whoever holds the manor. They're brought out each solstice, and worn in procession around the limits of the dale. It's a private thing; no outsiders, no reporters or folklorists allowed. I always refused to take part."

Petersen look blank, poor boy, but dear, clever Margrave could provide.

"They call it 'beating the bounds'" I said. "Still goes on in various places around the country. Costumes sometimes, and willow sticks—a sort of ritual to remind everyone of the boundaries of the parish or community. Ordnance Survey for beginners—for those with an old-fashioned sense of the land."

Beckshaw locked the mask cabinet, and going to a small cupboard, pulling out a bottle of whisky and three glasses. He said nothing until we were seated and supplied, the bottle to hand. It wasn't very good whisky, but the burn of it was welcome.

"So, you hope Erik will take this lot off your hands?"

Beckshaw poured himself a hefty refill. "Those damned 'heads', if not the rest. I remember my father taking them down and stroking them—they always frightened me." His face darkened. "He spent more time with those bloody masks than with his own son. When he died, I wanted to burn them, but when I suggested a good bonfire... well, I started to hear what I took as veiled threats from some of the local people."

"Burn them? That would be a terrible waste." Petersen sat on the edge of the sofa, next to me. "They are... magnificent."

Which is not what you say if you're thinking of purchasing an item. You point out the flaws, the limited market, the plunging pound—anything you can, including the price of butter and your tragic war wound, to soften up the seller.

"What sort of threats?" I asked.

Beckshaw's face was redder than before.

"Oh, I don't know that they were serious, but they annoyed me. The locals are tight-mouthed, short on words. Tight-knit, as well—few enough marry outside Kemberdale. They said things like 'Would be a bad do for thee, maister,' " He shuddered. "It's like living in a bloody Brontë novel."

Another whisky, and Beckshaw began to say more of his late father. He was not only the one who had owned the collection which lay in the cabinets, but the one who had amassed it, gathering remnants of Dales traditions as they fell from practice, and nurturing those which persisted. The masks were his beloved centrepiece.

The manor house settled; cast iron pipes complained at the boiler's demands, and the large room closed in on us. I sipped my drink, feeling an unease I couldn't shift. I had the sensation that even through an inch of pine, the masks were staring at us—and listening to the waspish sound of Beckshaw's continued narration...

"...Yet never a word from him," Beckshaw was muttering. "His own wife—my mother!—for God's sake. Influenza, fatal, because he wouldn't fire up the heating, and wouldn't take her to hospital. They came close to charging him with negligence, but never a complaint from her..."

"So you left at fifteen, and never came back?" Petersen nodded, clearly half-cut. "Well, Beckshaw old chap, I don't think there'll be any problem relieving you of all this."

He took out a notebook, scribbled in it, and showed it to the other man—probably didn't want me to see how little he was offering for the collection, in case I poked my nose in.

"Fine, fine," said Beckshaw, barely glancing at what Petersen had written. "It's all yours. The sooner the better."

"Why the rush?" I asked.

He scowled. "The Winter Solstice is near. Soon they'll trail up here, wanting the bloody masks out again, all the paraphernalia of the procession. Just as they always have."

"It sounds a harmless enough affair." I thought it odd that, if he felt so strongly about the things, he hadn't quietly broken them up. Was he more superstitious than he'd admit to us?

Perhaps he felt his father's spectre peering over his shoulder, not just the disapproval of the Dalesfolk.

"Harmless? Damn the lot of them, and damn my father!"

And then I grasped what was happening. This wasn't the first 'vengeance' sale I'd seen after someone's death. Not just removing unpleasant memories, but deliberately selling off objects beloved of the dear departed—out of pure spite. By his lock, stock and barrel sale of local history, Beckshaw was getting back at a whole community, as well.

I offered one last mild suggestion.

"Why not simply donate the 'Beasts' to the village?" I stood up, my legs stiff from the car. "Call it a bequest from the manor, and then have done with the place."

"Bollocks," said our intoxicated host. "I won't give them the satisfaction of keeping that crap. Kemberdale and its masks can go to hell. I'll teach them that this isn't the Middle Ages."

Petersen merely giggled; I said nothing more.

A few minutes later, the lord of the manor showed us to our rooms on the floor above. Plain rooms, with good beds. Too tired to consider other options, I stretched myself out, trying not to think.

I was sure that something dark was on the horizon...

* * * * *

MY COMPANIONS were quiet at breakfast, which was slabs of gammon, eggs a-plenty and hot tea. I let the food amuse me for a while, and then asked Petersen about his plans. He chewed on the fatty meat and tried to smile. He wasn't used to hard drink.

"I'll ring around this morning. Need a haulier from Whitby or Middlesborough—we can't get that lot in the car."

It was a sort of plan, immediately scuppered by the fact that the phone line was down.

"It happens," said Beckshaw. "November's the devil for storms up here."

There hadn't been a storm in the night. I wondered if the November was also the devil for a truculent villager with wire clippers?

"I'll take a stroll," I said. "I'm sure it will be fixed soon."

Why would it be fixed, though? No one else around here had a telephone. I suspected that Petersen might have to drive to some more modern part of civilisation if he wanted to make arrangements.

I have always been fond of Yorkshire. It is, in general, a vast and fascinating county with a vehement sense of its own worth—'God's Own Country'—and a dour suspicion of the South. And of Lancashire, and the Midlands, and... well, you get the picture. Generous in person, and yet insular. Kemberdale was little different from any other small dale in aspect, but as I walked down from the manor and along the main road, I felt I was being observed.

A lone ploughman worked a field by the roadside, a team of horses turning the wet soil, and I thought of the hobby-horse skull in its cabinet. These people were closer to the earth than most, for better or worse. Beckshaw and Petersen had no sense of it, but I—

A stoat or weasel darted across the lane, their scramble followed by a shriek of rooks in the gaunt trees above. And there were wrens in the hedgerow ahead.

"Who killed Cock Robin?" I asked myself aloud and thought of black, gleaming eyes.

I passed a roofless schoolhouse with 1743 carved into its stone lintel, and next to that, a low cottage with a woman sitting outside, peeling potatoes. She paused in her task, her fingernails broken, her fingers caked with mud. Her hazel eyes met my gaze.

"He mun relent," she said. "We knows as why tha's here. We all knows."

I had nothing to offer. "The masks? Not much I can do, to be honest. Mr Beckshaw's made his choice."

I thought I caught a glimpse of a face at the window of the adjoining cottage. Kemberdale was definitely watching me.

"T'ain't his to make. He mun relent, or..."

She went back to her work, making it clear she had nothing else to say.

I, too, thought Beckshaw should relent, and leave well alone. But I didn't like the sound of 'or...'

Back at the manor, I asked our host if he had a shotgun.

"Rabbits," I added, without offering to explain further.

He seemed surprised, but brought down an absolute beauty, with a box of cartridges. A genuine Purdey up and under, twenty eight inch. I silently assessed it as worth seven, eight thousand pounds. To him, it was some casual relic of his father's time here.

"I don't shoot," he said, which was fairly obvious.

If I was wary of the masks, I coveted this gun. A collector's piece, like a diamond discovered in a coal scuttle. I muttered something about cleaning it, and he lost interest.

The promised rain came, heavy enough to worry Petersen. He looked bleary-eyed.

"Don't fancy taking the Granada through this. I'll drive to Whitby first thing tomorrow, and have a chap follow me back with a van. We'll be out of your hair as soon as we're loaded, Mr Beckshaw. You have my cheque."

"One more day?" said Beckshaw, somewhat morose. "But yes, that's good enough."

Whilst Petersen spend his afternoon cataloguing the collection, I lay in my room and read or pondered. So Rafael Beckshaw, our friend's father, had been a typical hard hill-farmer, clearly uncompromising, even cold to his only child. There were no photographs of him, but pages at the back of the huge family bible ran through the generations, scribbled down by successive patriarchs. The earliest entry was 1612. And there was one picture of his wife, taken in the forties or fifties, by her outfit. She looked sad, harried.

The 'Beasts' had brought her no comfort, whatever they offered the rest of Kemberdale.

After a dinner which consisted of beef, potatoes and a rambling explanation by Petersen of what he might do with the collection—donations to favoured museums and pure profit-making—I retired early. The rain had not stopped. It had made a lake of the yard; it hammered against the roof tiles, and spoke of nothing good.

I kept the Purdey with me, and wondered why I found myself too often in these awkward, unsettled situations...

* * * * *

THE NOISES IN THE NIGHT were not the house timbers, nor the heating pipes. I had been dozing, above the room where the collection was kept, and was sure that I had heard the heavy main door grate open.

I threw on my jacket, and crept to Beckshaw's room, the shotgun with me. I shook him gently.

"Beckshaw, there's someone in the manor."

His eyes flew open.

"What?"

"Downstairs. There's someone downstairs. What do you want to do?"

It wasn't my house, and I doubted that anyone around here meant me any particular harm.

"I want to chase the buggers off," he said, sliding out of bed and dressing.

I roused Petersen, who had been drinking again and was slow to respond. When he was up, we gathered on the landing.

"They won't want to tackle three men, whoever they are," said Beckshaw.

I sighed at 'whoever they are'. Who would the intruders be but Kemberdale, come either to take the masks—or make a crude and direct point about their disposition?

We went barefoot down the blackened stairs, wincing at every small creak, until we stood before the room which held the collection. Any chance I might have had to urge caution was ruined by Beckshaw throwing back the internal door and striding in.

Oil lanterns stood by the door to the yard, setting long shadows across the room, but my attention was drawn rather to the six figures by an open cabinet. One of them was the ploughman I had seen earlier, I thought; the other five were already masked—the robin, the otter, and the bull; the raven and the boar. I shivered at the sight.

The ploughman stood back, holding a powerful representation of a wolf's head, whilst other masks lay on the floor.

"They are ours, by right," said Cock Robin—a man's voice, muffled but strangely high and melodic. "If we must take them, we shall not be kind—"

Beckshaw lurched forward, but the Bull intervened, slamming into the man and felling him. Petersen gasped, and with the usual stupidity of youth, tried to grapple with the Bull, the largest figure there. That gained him a driving fist to the belly, and the attention of Cock Robin— the beak thrust, and Petersen shrieked, blood running from his cheek.

I am not a man of action. I am slightly overweight, in my middle years, and inclined to favour comfortable seating. I was, however, concerned about how far this would go. I made my own move, mostly to protect Petersen, grabbing at Cock Robin's mask and pulling it from his head...

There are moments in our lives, moments when our souls take precedence over our clever minds or earnest hearts. Such moments are rare, but this was not my first, and so I stood, rather than ran screaming.

Beneath the mask of glittering black eyes and cruel beak, was... a stark and unexpected sight. From the man's collar rose a feathered head with eyes of dark ice and a wicked beak, open to show a bird's darting tongue. The feathers moved gently, alive, with his breathing; he was, undeniably, the mask that he had worn.

I fell back, grasping the Purdey. I knew that I was sober, that this was real—and more, I could smell them now, the warm, musty scent of damp animals, close around me.

One by one the others took off their masks. The Bull, a blunt, over-large head with thick lips and wide nostrils, bovine anger glinting in his eyes—not a man, no, not a man. The Otter, river-sleek and ready, his companions each as their masks made them.

Five beasts stood before us, the Beasts of Kemberdale, and the ploughman, still holding the wolf mask.

"If I were t'wear this," he said, "I'd be as them. It's the way, tha sees? Our way to be Kemberdale, an' keep it as it always were. The Beasts, and the Boundaries, all ours."

Cock Robin came closer to me, and trilled, called, with a song that spoke of bare hawthorn and tangled hedges; fierce combat, and conquest. Of the short, sometimes violent life of small birds. The Otter barked, and gave me swirling, icy waters—the soft sweetness of a trout caught in mid-leap... and a threat.

This was possession, a possession which went beyond surface appearance, and a terrifying one at that; it reminded me of dear Arthur Keen, now long gone, who had spent time among the Sámi people of Northern Finland, and tried rather too many mushrooms. To wear the skin of the seal was to become the seal...

Petersen moaned, holding the side of his face. Blood ran between his fingers. Beckshaw was blank and bruised, crouched against the cabinets; it was up to me, and I was a dealer as well as a critic. I was used to negotiations. I pointed the shotgun at the hare mask on the floor, not that far from Beckshaw.

"If I fire, the Hare will be shattered, one of your Beasts no more. Lost, gone from Kemberdale."

Cock Robin shrieked; the Bull grunted, but they held back. That hesitation told me all I needed. I doubted that anyone living had the art to make such potent things again—if they had, this intrusion would not have been needed.

"Two cartridges—two masks. I might even manage to reload, but I don't want to do this, believe me."

"Tha's not frit, not like t'others." A harsh croak from the Raven. "Tha knows how it mun be."

Frightened? Well, I might be later, but for now...

"So we understand each other," I said. "We can make a deal—"

"No!" Beckshaw tried to rise; the Raven turned its huge black beak to him and cawed an obvious threat.

"Steady," I warned them all. I eased myself to one side and helped Beckshaw up, with the Purdey steady.

"Beckshaw, your father is rotting away quietly wherever he was buried. There's no vengeance to be gained, no 'win' for anyone here if the masks are destroyed. You can sell this place and have a life—back in France, maybe. I don't know."

His anger struggled with fear, and with my slow, steady words.

"Be a more generous spirit than Rafael Beckshaw. Let these people be, let Kemberdale keep its ways."

As his shoulders slumped, the Boar, motionless until now, bent and picked up the hare mask. Whoever was beneath the tusks and bristled snout was female, powerfully built—or was that also a property of what she had donned? She held the Hare out to him—as if to demonstrate that he still had one last chance to join them, to be part of this...

"No." He turned away, shuddered. "Just take the damned things. Get them out of here!"

Cock Robin trilled, and I watched as they gathered up the rest of the masks from the cabinet, cradling them with care; as they formed a solemn, silent procession out into the night. Would these people be themselves again, by dawn? Which was real, the image or the creature beneath? I had no idea.

The whisky bottle was empty, but all was saved by discovery of a rather nice cognac behind it in the cupboard. Beckshaw was silent; I propped Petersen on one of the sofas, and cleaned his wound, which was long but shallow.

"Could be worse, Erik. He might have had your eye out. Cock Robin is a fighting bird, you know."

"What... what happened?" He had retreated into himself.

"We were visited. The poor light and jostle of local villagers confused you, and you gashed your face on a door." I surprised myself by chuckling—a nervous reaction, I suppose. "That's what I'll say, down the wine-bars."

The brandy helped my companions drift off to sleep again where they sat, and allowed me to sit quietly by the empty cabinet which had held the masks. I had a good friend in Hull—a land agent—who would be able to help Beckshaw shift the Kember Manor estate quickly, if certain aspects of the story were trimmed. Petersen could turn a profit on the rest of the paraphernalia in the other cabinets, and would be able to show off his scar for a few weeks. It gave his fine Viking face even more character.

And I? I had lost nothing by the trip, and if Beckshaw wasn't too mad with me, he might be persuaded to part with the Purdey.

Ah, you will say, but more importantly, I had learned the truth of the Beasts of Kemberdale. To which I might agree, except that what I witnessed had no rational explanation. It is fortunate that, unlike Archie Crane, Justin Margrave knows how to keep his mouth shut.

Outside, in the deep dark of Kemberdale, unsullied by street-lamps or other acts of man, the triumphant song of a robin pierced the night...

LES EFFRAYANTES

London, 1976

MY FRIEND DID NOT LOOK AT ALL WELL.

Admittedly, I had not seen him for a very long time, but the change was alarming. Lying on his nursing home bed, Peter Carew was a skeletal figure, with little more substance than the striped dressing gown he wore. A drip line fed into the raised veins of his right hand, leaving him to hold his cup of tea awkwardly in his left. His thick thatch of pale yellow hair, once so appealing, was thin and grey now, straggled across a blotched scalp, whilst his face had the sunken contours of an archaeological find, not the man I had known.

He had been a handsome chap in the nineteen forties, when we had both been in central London—I as a teenager, a volunteer with the Auxiliary Fire Brigade, and Peter as a young man who... well, he never said. Something official. Something that you didn't tell anyone, for fear of German agents listening in. 'Careless talk costs lives', as they said at the time.

"I won't last, Margrave. So no point in giving me any of that hopeful, you never know, gas."

"How long?"

"Two, three months. I can't take another bad bout of pneumonia——the docs say my lungs are shot, and the rest of me is giving up anyway. I have the immune system of a milk pudding. Remember those, at Grace's Caff?"

"Skimmed, powdered milk, and lumps of flour. Enough to put anyone in hospital." I tried to laugh, and did a poor job of that. "Look, I didn't know you were even back in Britain, Peter."

The matron at St Leonard's, Bermondsey, had called me completely out of the blue that same morning, to say that they had a new arrival, transferred from a hospital ward in Kent. It would be very much appreciated, she said, if I could come to visit a Mr Carew. He was asking for me, in his better moments. I was already aware that St Leonard's was a hospice, and so I sought out a cab within the hour.

Carew and I were never intimate—although it was clear to me that he was homosexual, and I think he knew it of me. It was simply that as a junior in the Auxiliary, I was sent on all the fetch-and-carry jobs, and somehow we ended up bumping into each other on the street every week or so. Sometimes it was crossing one of the nearby parks or city squares, sometimes at Grace's, which, whilst dreadful in any culinary sense, was cheap and cheerful. We talked about the war in general, politics, and wine—Peter's father was a wine merchant. That was my introduction to the concept of a world beyond 'red or white', and a fascination which never left me.

I was sorry to see him in this condition.

"I had one or two things to see to, Margrave, before... you know."

"Is there anything with which I can help?"

"Do you recall that night in Pimlico? January the seventeenth?"

I did, unfortunately.

"And you remember what I gave you—that little disc? Did you keep it, as I asked?"

"It's somewhere in the flat, I imagine. Not exactly sure where, but I certainly never got rid of it. Does it matter to you?"

He looked at me as if I was mad.

"Matter? Does it matter?" he said, harsh-voiced, only to sigh and sink back onto his pillows. As his dressing gown fell open for a moment, I saw a number of ugly dark brown lumps, above his breastbone and at one side of his neck. He covered himself up again.

"I'm sorry," he went on, in a softer voice. "I haven't told you yet, have I? My brain's in a fog these days. And the painkillers..."

"I can go and fetch the disc, if you'd like."

"Not yet. Margrave, could you do something else for me first? Without badgering me, until I'm ready?"

It was hard to argue with a dying man. "Naturally. What is it you want, Peter?"

"I need you to find a woman called Edith Raines. I... I worked with her, during the war. I'm fairly sure she's alive, but I'm not certain where she is these days. There's a small tin box under the bed with what details I have, old addresses and so on."

"You want her to come and visit you?"

That alarmed him. "No, she mustn't do that. But... she has the other one. The other disc. Unless... no, she'll have it. She has to. Look, I need both, and then I'll explain."

Although he wasn't to know, I'd had stranger requests, and undertaken far stranger missions. I reassured him that I would do what I could, and left him to doze.

On the way out, I managed to catch hold of a doctor, stressing the whole 'dear old friend, war-time colleague,' part. The doctor offered no sugar coating.

"Three months is our most optimistic prognosis, I'm afraid, Mr Margrave. The end may come much sooner."

* * * * *

Some memories we cherish, reminding us of better times, best times, of life, and joy, and tenderness. Some we have to bear, either to punish ourselves or because we cannot stop those endless ruminations over pain and failure. And then there are those memories which are simply uncomfortable.

I had shuffled the details of that night in early 1944 away, not caring to dwell on it, but Peter's presence had reminded me of what I had *felt* at the time—my selfish fear of being trapped under falling beams, the choking smell which lingered around the rubble, frustration at how the hydrant fittings were different from those I knew, how I would look a fool to the professional firefighters...

And worse, a sickening urge, as the last bodies were carried away, to try and snatch a glance at what lay beneath the canvas. At sixteen I had never seen death, or the dead, close-up.

It was the only 'official' time Peter and I met. We were short-handed because of a warehouse blaze by the river, and I had been delegated to help make a quick search of the bombed premises, whilst others extinguished the last flames in the area. I'd been told that half a dozen kids had died inside. Although the victims had been removed, we were supposed to help by recording what sort of bomb had been used, and any other relevant details—especially unexploded ordnance, if a stick of bombs had been dropped. It wasn't unusual for the Germans to simply release what was left in their bays quite randomly, just to lighten the load for the flight home.

Peter was already inside, and I remember being puzzled that he was in a Civil Defence uniform—I was sure that wasn't his regular job. I remember finding him in the main school hall, its roof open to the night, and how he pointed out a clutter of characteristic metal fragments, still hot—the remains of the bomb. Then he paused, crouching, and he reached under a charred length of timber. I raised my flash-light, seeing his face properly for the first time that night. He was deathly pale.

"What is it," I asked. "A body?"

"N-no, it's all fine."

One of the regular fire fighters shouted that they needed more help the river, and had to pack up here. Peter followed me outside, and pressed a metal disc, quite hot, into my hand.

"I say, Margrave, hang on to this for me, will you."

I couldn't really see what it was, but it was the size of a half-crown, unusually heavy.

"A Jerry device? Part of the bomb?"

"It's a... a keepsake. Someone probably dropped it," he replied. "Just... put it somewhere safe for now, eh? I'll square it with the authorities later."

I was distracted—this was only my third incident on the job. Assuming it was a medallion or locket, maybe a St Christopher, I slipped it into my pocket, and went to join my colleagues.

About a week later, the scowling, chain-smoking Grace said there was a note for me behind the counter. She passed it over, spilling my mug of tea as she did so. Handwritten, it said:

'Sorry, Margrave. Won't see you for a while. Keep your head down, and remember, never serve a Rioja with fish.'

One of the regulars at the cafe thought that Peter might have been transferred to Naval duties on the coast, but that was it. And I was a teenage boy with his own problems. I never enquired further.

After the war, I overheard a chance mention of his name at a party. It wasn't complimentary. They said he'd been sent to the States in disgrace. His sin? Getting 'too close' to a Naval attaché—it had been America, or the police cells, said the empty-heads by the punch-bowl. We all knew what that meant. Homosexuality was often tolerated in the forces, as long as it couldn't be seen.

But Peter had been seen.

* * * * *

MY FIRST ACT when I got back from St Leonard's was to go into the room set aside for oddities—curios, unusual *objets d'art*, the less savoury mementoes of various trips, and the like. I do have a system, but it is not always immediately recognisable. After half an hour, I turned up an ancient shoebox with a few war-time trinkets in it. The metal disc in question was at the bottom, thrown in there the day after Pimlico.

Its surface was duller than I remembered, but I was fairly sure it was solid lead, and this would be the patina of age. Back then, I had noticed the curious markings on one face, but had concluded it was Hebraic script, something along those lines. Not German, anyway.

Re-examining the disc now, in good light, the script—etched into the metal and inlaid with a dark lacquer—certainly wasn't Hebraic. A much older and wiser Margrave had no difficulty in recognising that the inscription was in Enochian, of all things—that tongue conjured up by Dr John Dee and his friend Kelley, centuries before. The language of angels.

Do not misunderstand me—I sincerely doubt the existence of angelic beings, and I consider Enochian to be a complete fiction. The Elizabethans were obsessed with ciphers—at times, the upper echelons of the Elizabethan world seemed to be populated by regiments of spies and alchemists. They loved secrets.

No, what affected my digestion was the thought that Section Seventeen had any truck with that sort of thing. In my experience, such pursuits tended to throw logic out of the window, and then break the window frame for good measure.

I put the disc—amulet, medallion—away, and turned to Peter's dented and flaking tin box, which wasn't locked. Inside it was...

A single black and white photograph of eleven young men and women standing outside an Anderson shelter, all in civilian clothes. One of the women's faces had been circled in ballpoint. Three addresses for an Edith Raines, each annotated with the date she left them—no suggestion of a current location. The last date was seven years ago, so might possibly help me. A war-time forage cap, with a brass '17' badge upon it, and an old service revolver.

I slid the gun aside—I dislike the things, except as collectibles—and found underneath it a buff manilla envelope which was more recent, with 'To Edith' written on it. I left that unopened.

On the back of the photograph was written 'The Section, 14th Aug. 43'. That would be around five months before Pimlico.

A half-bottle of Malmsey helped me organise the pieces in my head. Before I sought out this Edith Raines, I wanted to know more, to feel I had some sort of handle on this business. So Peter had been in the military, yes, and Army by the look of the forage cap and revolver. I could just make him out in the back row of the photograph, next to the person he'd highlighted. I didn't recognise the background—it could have been anywhere, though the shelter suggested it was taken in Britain. Seventeen. The Section.

My best guess was Military Intelligence. Peter never spoke of combat—he seemed to be involved in more intellectual activities, from what little he had said at the time. So had there been a Section Seventeen? I was wondering what mystery lay behind Peter's request, and wanted to be better informed before I went to ask favours of a stranger.

I have never had any real interest in the military—one of the main reasons I had volunteered for and served in the Auxiliaries was to do what I could without having to kill—but after too many days, and nights, of careful enquiries, I discovered that Section Seventeen had indeed existed. It had functioned under the umbrella of the Special Operations Executive, that peculiar organisation which dealt with sabotage, infiltration, spying—the 'ungentlemanly' side of war. Even today, some of its operations were classified, and there were few accessible records that I could find. The libraries were silent; old friends were genuinely ignorant, as far as I could tell.

A continental colleague finally put me on to an SOE veteran, Pierre Caslet, now retired and living in Brittany. He was a relict of the Free

French, and on the telephone with me, was willing to talk.

"Seventeen? I knew of it, *Msieur* Margrave. It was, eh, formed well before my time, many years before the war. There was an officer, Blake, Redvers Blake. He had been there a long, long time. He was there in forty-two, forty-three, a colonel, but I heard that he left before the end. I did not, eh, meet him, *Msieur*—I do not think that many people did."

"Is he still around to talk to?"

"He died a few years ago. *Merde*, he would have been ninety years old by then, peut-être more."

That was disappointing. A line of enquiry closed.

"But what did they *do?*"

"Seventeen? We called them *Les Effrayantes*—the Creepy Ones, the Scary Ones, you would say, I think. Secretive. It was not a large section."

"Eleven or twelve of them, maybe?" I suggested, thinking of the photograph.

"*Oui*, it could be so. I never heard talk of a single successful operation of theirs... but I never heard of a single failure, either. *Rien*. Nothing."

And Peter Carew had been one of them.

Un effrayante.

* * * * *

FINDING EDITH RAINES was my easiest task, because the pleasant couple who lived at her last known location, in Purley, had bought the house from her.

"Oh yes," said a Mrs Rutherford, "We have a forwarding address. Her friend Miss West wrote it all out for us—poor Miss Raines was not a well woman, you know, poor soul. Arthritis, I think. They moved to the coast for the air."

She copied out the address. No telephone number, but I had always preferred to meet people face to face. And Miss Raines might not welcome the contact—I was harder to close the door in someone's face than simply put the phone down.

Assuming that Peter was correct, and she was still alive.

The place I sought turned out to be a converted two storey farm-house, set back from the cliffs near that well-known Sussex town, 'Bug-ger Bognor'. Or Bognor Regis, as the locals preferred. I had hired a car, and driven there on my own—it did no harm to escape the city for a while.

The woman who answered the door was in late middle age, plainly dressed, with the look of a matron about her—in control, efficient.

"Yes?"

I took off the broad-brimmed hat I was wearing and held it to my chest, trying to signal both a polite demeanour, and the possibility that I might be allowed in.

"Good afternoon. I was hoping to speak with Edith Raines."

"Why?" Not aggressive, but as crisp as her blouse.

What a terribly good question.

"It's a little awkward, I'm afraid. I'm here as a favour to a man called Peter Carew, who knew Edith during the war."

A tilt of the head, a sharp appraisal from small grey eyes.

"I see. You'd better come in, Mr...?"

"Margrave. Justin Margrave."

She showed me through to a small, tidy sitting room, and indicat-ed a chair. No offer of refreshments. The house smelled of bleach and camphor, and seated across from each other, I felt that I was attending an interview.

"How is Peter?"

She didn't seem the sort of person who required small-talk.

"He's dying, I'm afraid."

"I see."

"Did you... know him?" I asked.

She had offered no name, and I had to wonder if she *was* Edith Raines. On balance, I thought not.

"I knew of him. And Edith speaks of him, occasionally. From our time in the SOE."

"You were in Section Seventeen with her?"

That provoked the first visible emotion she had shown—a glare.

"No." The glare faded. "I met Edith whilst I was doing SOE administrative work—supplies, logistics. We have been companions ever since, Mr Margrave."

I stared at my fingernails. "Then I imagine that speaking of Peter may be unwelcome."

"It depends what he wants."

There seemed to be no point in being oblique with this woman.

"He believes that Miss Raines has something in her possession, something he needs to see before he dies. Before you ask, I don't understand the significance of it, nor what he intends. But he has only a few months left, at best, and as an old acquaintance, I agreed to help him. If I could."

"I see." Which appeared to be her standard response to receiving information. This one was followed by an over-long silence, and then: "Do I assume that you, like Peter Carew, are a homosexual, Mr Margrave?"

She said as if stating I must be a bus-driver, and I could not help smiling. Had she reached this conclusion from my association with Peter, or were my crimson cravat and the cut of my shirt betraying me?

"Unrepentantly so, Miss West."

"Then I need not be coy about our situation. Edith and I are a couple in all sense of the word. We have no secrets from each other, but she has long been haunted by what they had her do back then. She has long suffered terribly from depression, nightmares, and agoraphobia. Sadly, these have grown worse over time. I love her dearly, but these last few years... I sometimes think that it would be better if she were released."

"I was given to understand that she had arthritis."

"That as well, yes."

"If I should come back another time...?"

She shook her head.

"There is no good time to revisit Section Seventeen, Mr Margrave. As far as I am concerned, it destroyed its own people—killed them, or drove them towards insanity." She brushed a hair from the arm of the chair. "I am Harriet West. Westie, as Edith calls me. I care for her, as best I can, protect her if necessary."

"It must be difficult for you."

"I manage. It is more difficult to believe in a God who allows such things."

Hard to answer that one.

However, I did at least feel we had the measure of each other.

"What Peter seeks," I said, "Is an object which was relevant during the war. I'd like to say that it's a keepsake, but I suspect matters aren't that simple. A small lead disc, of which I have the identical twin—apparently—given to me by Peter in 1943. He believes that Edith might know more about it, or its whereabouts."

Her response came with a frown. "We do not know you, Mr Margrave, nor have we any guarantee that you are serving Peter Carew's best interests. I think it would be foolish of me to say more at this stage."

"He expected as much."

I took out the buff envelope in my jacket. She saw the name on the outside, but had no hesitation in opening it. A rapid scan of the note within seemed to suffice.

"We are to trust you, it seems. The Enoch Coin. That's what she calls the dull little thing."

That would follow, from the script on the one I had. "Then she has the other disc?"

"You had better come upstairs."

The main bedroom was large and well-aired, but it retained a subtle hospital odour. Surrounded by dark, ancient furniture which would certainly have given me nightmares, Edith Raines sat facing the window, as if she peered out at a world which might assault the house at any moment. Although clean and neatly dressed in her wicker chair, her face was haggard, blotched, with limp grey hair and thin, dry lips. I wondered at 'Westie's' devotion, and how these two might have been, over thirty years ago—lively, attractive and in love? It was, in a way, more depressing than my first sight of Peter in his current state.

Yet Harriet's hand, gentle on the other woman's shoulder, and the soft nod at the gesture, the relaxation of Edith's posture... we judge too quickly, we who live alone. I stayed back in the doorway, letting a murmur pass between them.

Harriet straightened.

"Edie wishes me to tell you. She will correct me if I stray."

She dragged another wicker chair forward, but stayed on her feet herself.

"Neither of us wish to discuss the finer details of Section Seventeen activities. We could be prosecuted for doing so. But in essence..."

And she gave me a brief, clipped account, one which raised its own questions.

Edith Raines had been an operative for the SOE, but not one of the sort who parachuted into France, or smuggled radio transmitters to Norwegian informants. If the SOE tried to remain a shadow organisation, then Section Seventeen was a shadow's shadow. This was not because of its 'dirty tricks' or unorthodox proposals for warfare, said Harriet—it was because no one else in Government or the military believed it to be of any real value.

"Lunatics and fakers," said Harriet. "That was what they said of Seventeen in the corridors, if anyone mentioned us at all. Creepy, into occult nonsense. But none of that was true. They worked hard for the war effort. And contrary to later public chatter and the imaginations of writers, the British never had a secret organisation to oppose Himmler's supposed occult plans, or frustrate remnants of the Thule Society. That was all nonsense, invented after the war."

Les Effrayantes. Rather less scary that I had expected—so far.

"Yet Peter and Edith did work there. It might help if you told me something of their duties, in general."

"The same as the rest of the SOE, but exploring different routes. Psychic research, not field operations." She glanced at the unmoving Edith. "They were looking into psychics, and trying to conceive of how they might be used for the war effort. Telesthesia was one of their aims. Sensing hidden things at a distance—enemy troop movements, key placements of armaments, and so on. And telepathy, for interrogation and communication."

I confessed myself to being curious. "And did any of that work?"

"Do you believe in paranormal phenomena, Mr Margrave?"

What a question.

"I believe... that the world is stranger than we would like. Less orderly, less certain. That there are undercurrents we cannot understand—we must simply learn to swim, and avoid going too deep."

"Then my reply to 'Did it work' is—occasionally. But unreliably."

The other woman stirred; Harriet nodded, as if listening.

"I'm getting there, darling." She sighed. "Edie threw herself into Section Seventeen's activities with enthusiasm, volunteering for any project, however dubious. It was what I loved about her, when we met in the garden or the naffy. She embraced every possibility."

"And Peter...?" I was hearing no explanation of why Edith Raines was especially relevant, or of what the discs represented.

Inside Seventeen, Peter had worked alongside Edith as an observer. He was assigned to the collation of results, if any, from experimental projects, and attendance at tests. A watcher and recorder. They had been amicable enough, though Peter appeared to have no pretensions to 'gifts' or abilities, beyond having sharp eyes and being good at statistics.

"He knew about our relationship, and helped cover for us, as we covered for him on occasion."

Three or four operatives were considered to have a genuine psychic or paranormal ability, to be able to connect with matter at a distance.

Enough to be of interest within the section, but not reliable or repeatable enough to be presented to the Brass. Thus, in the early days of 1943, the section devised a new experiment, one which might make their point to someone more important. This experiment involved a matched pair of objects, especially made for what was planned—the Enoch coins.

Edith, considered one of the genuine talents, was picked to take part. At that point, Harriet's face darkened. "For the truth about that particular operation, you must ask Peter Carew."

I remembered my conversation with the Frenchman on the phone.

"Did you know a Colonel Redvers Blake?"

"The Colonel? Yes, we knew him, from afar." There was a long pause. "He resigned, you know, over the direction in which Seventeen was going. Mr Margrave, Edith came away a damaged soul at the end of the war. I have been beside her for thirty years, Mr Margrave, and given her such love as I can. I blame Section Seventeen for her condition. Perhaps taking that coin away will help her forget it all—I would have thrown it away years ago."

The window panes shone in the sunlight, one thrush sang to another—or sang simple because it wanted to; Edith Raines lifted one gaunt arm, forefinger pointing to a book case.

"Yes," said Harriet, and going to the shelves—ugly dark mahogany—she retrieved a small, battered cigar box, which she handed to me.

"This is what Peter wants. Tell him that we will think of him kindly. He was a good man."

Two women, much the same age, surely only in their mid-fifties. One tall, straight-backed and clinging to purpose, the other exhausted, damaged by time and a war long gone.

"I'm sorry," I said, as she accompanied me down the garden path. "If there is anything—"

"We have what we need, thank you."

She did not wait to watch me drive away.

What had ruined Edith Raines? It might have been natural for Harriet West to resent what had happened in the SOE, but sometimes we suffer for no good reason. One of my cousins had passed away after a long battle with liver disease, despite rarely drinking—and he without an ab-natural bone in his body, or any interest in the subject of the paranormal whatsoever. For all I knew, Edith may just have been unlucky—but my imagination had been triggered.

It gnawed at me as I drove east, seeking London and my own comfortable rooms. The car rattled, disliking the pitted minor road beneath it; my stomach felt empty, agitated, despite the reasonable steak pie I'd eaten only an hour before at a roadside public house.

Parking in a lay-by, I had a shot from my hip flask, let the breeze ruffle my hair for a few minutes, and urinated behind a convenient hedge.

It was as if I was not alone. And as nothing had changed except my acquisition of the second Enoch Coin, it was hard to ascribe the feeling to any other source. It sat on the back seat in its cigar box, quiet, docile, and yet...

Undercurrents. That was the word I used with Harriet West. I never seek them out, but oh, how they do like to find me. Poor old Margrave.

Safely home, despite appalling traffic around Kensington, I settled into my favourite chair and browsed some of the latest art magazines, more interested at that moment in gossip than serious news. Edith's coin sat on the hall table; the one I had held for Peter all these years remained in the room I kept for such oddments, and all was peaceful...

Except for the boy in the doorway.

I am not easily surprised. I placed my copy of 'The Sculptor' back into the magazine stand, and smiled at him.

"Can I help you, young man?"

He wasn't there, of course. Not in any normal way. I don't generally believe in your traditional ghost, which is more the field of the over-religious and the gullible—people who spend too much time dwelling on various increasingly bizarre forms of afterlife. Or the cannier publicans and hoteliers who populated their establishments with nuns, Roman soldiers and Grey Ladies. At least their motives were understandable.

But there was the image of a boy, clear enough to make out considerable detail, tenuous enough that I could see the wallpaper and study door through him. He brought the terms 'ragamuffin' and 'street urchin' to mind. A shabby tweed jacket which did not fit, a dirty shirt which had once been white, and sagging trousers with frayed turn-ups. He had brought an echo of his own surroundings with him—hints of an entrance, a splintered door-frame around him.

The smudged expression on his small face was one of shock, perhaps a sudden realisation. He—the image—took a step forward, and...

And it was over. He had gone.

I poured myself a glass of madeira from the decanter, trying not to gulp it. Appraisal was one of the ways I earn a crust, and so I appraised what I had seen. Cast-off clothes, in the style of the nineteen thirties or forties, and rather worn; the boy himself was... twelve, thirteen, white, and cut his own hair. Thin-faced, but not emaciated. A utilitarian door-frame, neither shanty-built nor of any prosperous home—a council office or other municipal building?—and an event or appearance which he hadn't expected. He had showed no sign of seeing me, or knowing that he was in a Chelsea flat in 1974.

A second visit to the decanter made me think that I knew what I had seen—not the boy, but the place. It nagged at me. And logic suggested that this had something to do with the two lead discs, with bringing them into proximity. The first one had certainly never prompted such an episode, in all the years I had possessed it.

What I had to do was obvious. I telephoned a close friend, and went round to his house with the intention of having vigorous sex, an activity which tends to clear both the mind and the heart for a few hours.

Or it should have. Strangely enough, the presence of the small boy in the bedroom doorway, however transparent, did not enhance my performance. This time, his head was turned as if to look behind him, and his right hand was raised, beckoning—but clearly not to me.

I made my apologies as Anthony buttoned up his shirt. Bri-nylon, drip-dry, the one aspect of the chap I found hard to bear. He may have been a theatrical set carpenter, but surely he could have sacrificed at least a basic cotton shirt or two for his art?

"Oh, don't worry, dear," he murmured, always the gentleman. "It happens to us all. Anything on your mind you need to talk about?"

"Not on my mind, no." I kissed him on the cheek. "But hovering around it, you might say. An old friend's problems—I'll tell you some time."

I wouldn't, though. I never talked to Anthony about the strange, the unusual. Despite his charm and genuine good nature, he leaked gossip like a sieve, and there was enough talk of 'that Margrave fellow' already in my various social and professional circles.

On the telephone again at home, I learned that Peter had been going through a bad patch—pneumonia again—but they thought had it under control. He should be well enough to receive visitors in a day or two, said the nurse on duty. I had the feeling that it was, and that time pressed, but said none of that to her.

I had my regular work to do, which kept me busy for a while. A concerted effort the next afternoon yielded a passable review of some new slate installations in one of London's smaller museums, a piece which allowed me to show off my modest knowledge of the Welsh tongue without resorting to grammars or dictionaries.

After meeting this humdrum obligation, I sat again, facing the door to my study, and waited—an Enoch coin in each hand. I felt nothing peculiar from them, but then I am not especially 'sensitive'. Nor did I want to be.

I must have dozed for half an hour or so, when I felt an unexpected heat in both palms. I opened my eyes, and...

The far side of the room exploded into a roiling hell, into fire and confusion. I flinched at that, I admit, even though I knew that this wasn't real. Not real *here and now*, I should say. I was beginning to consider another interpretation.

No boy accompanied the blast, and the apparition vanished as quickly as it had appeared; the coins held no more than the natural warmth of my hands. I put them away, and sank into thought. Had Peter, had Edith Raines, seen what I had seen? Was this what troubled them both?

Ah well, I had both the Enoch coins, and I'd spoken—in a sense—to Edith. It would soon be time to return to St Leonard's.

* * * * *

IN MANY STORIES, Peter would have died during the interim, leaving me with some dreadful puzzle to solve on my own, no doubt with more mysteries and ghastly encounters to come. Fortunately I do not inhabit stories, and so when I went to his private room at the hospice, he was still there, propped up but looking worse than ever.

I helped him sip at a cup of orange juice, and told him of my visit to Sussex, after which I brought out the two coins.

"You want to know." He held them in shaking fingers, as if torn between caressing them and throwing them across the room. "What they are, what they mean."

"I know the symbols are Enochian," I said.

"That was our poor joke. It doesn't matter that the symbols are Enochian—the markings could have been Gaelic or Swahili, for all the difference it would make. It was just that one of the chaps was an enthusiast of occult oddities, and said it would be appropriate. The supposed symbol for a divine being, if you get me? But the one I gave you—it had to be identical to the other, the one held by the operator. That was the important part."

"Because...?"

He explained, between rasping coughs.

Section Seventeen had been developing their own detonator, one which required no timer, no wires, one which would work with any explosive or combustible material. A psychic detonator.

"It was codenamed Project Gohon, which became its own joke inside Seventeen."

"Gohon?"

"It means 'They Have Spoken' or something like that in Enochian, but we all pronounced it Go On, as in 'Go on with you, this'll never work'. There was a lot of black humour in the section back then—had to be, given that ninety nine percent of what we did failed utterly. You see, Justin, most of this stuff is nonsense, wishful thinking. The true paranormal, psychic, ab-natural—they don't fit science, and probably never will. They don't *want* to be measured or harnessed."

"I know."

"I had a feeling you did. That's why I can talk to you, old chap. As for Project Go On..."

It was ludicrously simple, according to Peter. Two identical objects, nice and simple, not too large, no working parts. One was placed, dropped, inserted, wherever there was something which would combust; the other was held by an operator with supposed—hoped for—psychic abilities. The operator was to concentrate on the disc they held, and set up a resonance with its far-off twin, a resonance which would produce a surge of mental energy at the other end.

"Apart from having trouble with this 'mental energy' thing, how would that be different from just having a saboteur place a bomb?"

"Don't you understand? We could detonate anything, in theory. Enemy munitions dumps, petrol and oil stores, their explosives—simply by getting one of these little discs near enough. A kids' catapult could be used, if you got close enough. We had them made in lead so that any investigation of the blast area would yield nothing more than a blob of melted metal—if anything was noticed at all.

"We even had a couple of physicists interested—something about tangling particles, that any effect on one Enoch coin changed the state of the other—but that wasn't my area. My job was to observe, and analyse any results—timing, yield, and so on"

"Results?"

"It worked once, twice in every ten tests, set up in disused country barns, away from the public. Scotland, mostly. Absolute concentration, the most able operators, no other people around—perfect conditions. They had to know if Project Go On could be used in crucial ports, packed cities, busy factories. Where, the theorists said, there would surely be unintentional psychic interference. Too many other minds, and all that. But let's face it, we were almost all theorists in Section Seventeen.

"I was the spotter, the observer, for Go On, first in the countryside and then for the main test. They chose Pimlico for that, because the area had already sustained considerable damage from the Blitz, and people were used to such stuff. All they needed was a decent-sized, unimportant building, not too close to occupied houses, and an air raid. Nothing spectacular, just one of those sporadic raids that Goering threw at us to try and keep in favour at home. We were used to being patient—had to be, given our limited results up to that point.

"The Brass located a disused school, already damaged, and the mechanism creaked into play. One of the coins was placed under rubbish, lumber, next to a cache of explosives—nothing too extreme, and no detonators. The usual clues—fragments of a German bomb and so on—were planted nearby, just in case anyone spent too much time poking around in the ruins afterwards..."

I recalled him conveniently pointing out those very things, on that night in forty four.

"The 'usual' clues?"

I began to wonder about the 'bodies' that had been on stretches, being taken away, when I arrived. Had there really been any casualties? My tone may have been sharp, for Peter looked faintly embarrassed.

"Standard SOE practice, Margrave. Not everything that blew up during the war was down to the Germans. Politics, and all that."

"Wouldn't it have been easier to attribute any explosion to an unexploded bomb?"

Prompting a faint smile. "It would. But SOE as a whole was a nest of paranoia and over-complexity. Things were always done the hard way."

"All right, so the Pimlico test was set up..."

"We waited, until at last we received advanced notice of a raid from contacts in the French Resistance. A night-time sortie, only a dozen or so Heinkels hoping to hit the docks. We had to hope that they wouldn't all be shot down before they got over London."

"A pretty damned cold approach," I said.

"You didn't get far in the SOE by speaking up about fair play."

"I suppose not."

He shifted in the bed, trying to find a comfortable position.

"I was rushed over to Pimlico, kitted out as a Civil Defence spotter—tin hat, gas mask and binoculars, you know—and installed myself on the roof of a local church. We'd had a telephone line installed up there, specifically for this op. Meanwhile, the operative took up her position in a small Whitehall shelter commandeered by Seventeen. She—"

"Edith Raines."

"Yes, Edith. She had the other coin, and one of the Johnnies with her was ready by the telephone. It was cold up on that roof, and a damned long wait, but the ack-ack started up around midnight; searchlights swept the sky, and all was going according to plan. Most of the Heinkels had made it that far, though they were dropping some of their loads a bit further east. Nevertheless, they would pass over the Pimlico area before they turned back for France. That would have to have to do, I was told.

"Picture me, Margrave. Crouched with my binoculars aimed at the already-battered school, the sirens starting up further west in the city; ice on the lead roof, my mittens doing bugger all to keep my fingers warm. Away from the searchlights, all I could see were shadows and deserted streets. There might have been no other humans in the world—the distant bombers empty, on predestined courses with their throttles jammed, our lights and anti-aircraft guns driven by clockwork and elastic bands. I felt very lonely, in short.

"Then the line came to life. 'Ready.' One of the chaps with Edith. I had one last check to make sure that there were no civilians in the area. Nothing in sight. 'Ready,' I answered. I imagined Edith there in the shelter, an Enoch coin on a table in front of her, and her eyes fixed upon it as she concentrated, focussed her mind. In the next couple of minutes, either there would be a bloody great explosion down there, or, well, absolutely nothing would happen. I wasn't putting money either way on this one.

"I remember checking my flask to see if there was any cocoa left, and feeling, very suddenly, that there was something terribly wrong. I picked up the binoculars... to see the faintest of lights from the now-open door of the school. The entrance with 'INFANTS' carved over it. Not a lantern or electric light, but a candle, perhaps—a candle flickering inside an empty building.

"And there he was. A kid, about twelve, thirteen, his features barely visible, black smudges for eyes. I thought that I saw two or three small figures behind him, though I couldn't be sure. Horrified, I grabbed for the telephone, one of those olive-drab field affairs; my cold fingers dropped it twice, and I know that I was shouting, yelling, down into the street, trying to warn them...

"The boy looked directly at me, a shocked expression on his thin face; he made as if to run back inside, and all the time I was screaming 'Get out! Get out!' It was useless. I never got to make the call, to tell them to abort. Project Go On had worked, you see, for the building erupted at that moment—a white flash, and then a sullen blossom of orange flame and black destruction, tearing open the damaged roof, outlining the boy in the doorway for a heart-beat, only a heart-beat, before he was consumed."

Peter coughed, began to sob. "His face, his face..."

I stood and went to his night-stand, unsteady as I poured myself some water from the glass jug. I didn't feel able to speak. The bodies...

they had not been faked.

Perhaps Peter saw some of this in my expression.

"There were seven of them, none out of their early teens, two or three much younger. Runaways and homeless scavengers, we assumed. The police tried to match bodies to names in Missing Person reports, but with no luck—the charring, and a lack of papers. Maybe no one ever missed any of them. There had been no sign of anyone at the school the day before, when our people did a last-minute check on the place—no sign that anyone had been there for weeks."

"It must have seemed somewhere safe," I said, my words flat, dulled. "Somewhere to shelter." I had realised what the outline was around my visions—the doorway to the school, a doorway I had stepped through just before I first met Peter.

"Yes. It must." He winced, not with emotion this time, I think, but at physical pain.

"Do you want me to ease you back down, make you more comfortable?"

"No, I'm fine. Justin, his face has never left me. I tried to drink it away here in Blighty, but that didn't work. A crank doctor in New York said that I'd suffered psychological trauma and needed to use psychedelics to flush it out; a woman in Atlanta said I was carrying a haint, a ghost, and needed an exorcism."

"And did you try those things?"

"No." He flexed his wasted fingers, tried to pull the sheet closer to his chest. I helped him. "I don't believe in ghosts, Margrave, and according to the many tests we ran at Seventeen, I'm not in the slightest bit psychic, or gifted in the paranormal sense—

"But he was." It seemed the obvious conclusion. "The boy himself."

"I believe so. I believe that in that dreadful moment, his mind met mine, knew everything. He was turning to try and get the others out... too late. But he remained, scorched into my being, buried in the folds of a damaged brain."

I was struck by a sudden, worrying thought.

"Peter, the coins—they worked. What in God's name did you tell your superiors?"

"I lied. I even used your name—well, the good name of the Auxiliary Fire Brigade. I said that it was a tragic accident. That the children had lit fires in the school for warmth, and inadvertently set off the cache. Heat, or sparks, had triggered our arrangement of explosives. It was bad luck. Project Go On hadn't come off."

"Edith—"

"Heard of the deaths, and she went along with my story, despite some of the others being suspicious. She reported that she couldn't make a proper psychic connection, and she wouldn't be swayed. Operative and observer had spoken. The Enoch coins didn't work. If they ever had, no reliance could be placed upon them."

"And did you ever talk to her properly about that night?"

"I couldn't. I couldn't bear to think about, admit, any of it. I resigned the next day, went to work with the Navy on analysis of U-boat patrol routes and patterns. Outside London, far away from Pimlico. It was as if... it felt as though Edith and I had conspired in some terrible, shameful crime. Seven, Margrave. Seven innocent children..."

"Neither of you could have known."

"That doesn't help. But you can finish it now—you can destroy the Enoch coins, and when I'm dead, then it will surely all be over."

I wasn't sure if that last part was a statement or a question. If the latter, I couldn't give him an answer. Although I wanted to tell him that I had seen the boy, I couldn't bear to do so. If it were a psychic photograph, a series of stills recorded in the coins like images on celluloid or photographic plates—imprinted, possibly—then their destruction would indeed end it.

I had only one question left, and wondered how to put it.

"You gave me one of the coins that night," I said.

"It hadn't melted—I don't know why. Shielded by timbers, or something along those lines."

"Yes, but why didn't you ask me, or someone, anyone, to destroy them both, years ago?"

For a few seconds, I saw a deep, heart-wrenching sorrow in his face.

"I kept meaning to. Initially I wanted to forget it all, and then... you can't see how it was for me, Margrave. You're single, alone by choice; you've prospered, and have no shame as to who you are, what you are. You've defied the world around you, done so well for yourself that society can't quite find a way to spurn or scorn you. It probably never will. Few of us are so fortunate.

"But I... I stumbled from one poor choice to another. I fled the SOE, then I was cashiered by the Navy for loving another man, exiled to a country which I did not know. At first I hid and did my job—the Navy's single kindness was to make no note of my proclivities on my record, because of my war work. I did paperwork for British trade delegations, nothing with any importance for the homosexual who might be blackmailed any day.

"America... it's an alien world, Margrave. Brash, reaching, demanding, where sex is reviled and worshipped at the same time. Nowadays there are clubs, communities, where our sort of people live as if there is no tomorrow. I never got my head around it. I never found love again; I never fitted in.

"Over the long years, there have been times when the boy... the boy was all I had. My only companion, the only stable thing in my life..." He choked, coughing bloody sputum into his handkerchief. "He and I have been alone, together... for thirty two long years."

"But—"

His eyes pleaded with me to understand.

"I found... Justin, I found that I couldn't bear to lose him."

* * * * *

I NEVER GOT TO SPEAK to Peter again. He died the day after I showed him the coins. I wasn't able to be with him at the end, which came suddenly. I expressed my sadness to the nurse that he had passed on without anyone there, except for strangers, if I might beg her pardon.

"He wasn't alone, Mr Margrave," she said, trying to tuck a lock of hair under her nurse's cap. "Someone was with him, for a while."

I wasn't aware that he had any living family, and asked her who it was.

"Oh, a quiet boy in his teens. I didn't catch his name, I'm afraid, but he stood by the door, waiting, until it was clear that nothing could be done."

The official cause of death was pneumonia with complications. When I asked for more details, the doctor added that, in view of the sarcomas, which had spread to Peter's internal organs, and the compromised state of his immune system, it was a surprise that the poor soul had lasted so long.

"Sarcomas?"

"You must have seen the dark growths at his neck—we call it Kaposi's sarcoma. I'm sorry that we couldn't do more for your friend."

I was the only person at the cremation. No boy, no terrible soundless burst of flame and destruction. I didn't inform Harriet West and Edith Raines—hard to see what comfort it could have brought them. I paid for a bunch of fragrant white lilies, and for an urn. Afterwards, I went and emptied it into the Thames, kissing the mud-scented air.

Brooding that night, I wondered at the course of Peter's life, of my own life. In the morning, slightly hung over, I begged a favour from my friend Anthony—without explanation. Puzzled, but as affable as ever, he introduced me to Lauren, a welder who worked on stages and sets for a number of the local theatres. It didn't escape me that her work was currently on the set for a performance of *The Tempest*—some said that Prospero was based on the Enochian John Dee.

Lauren's acetylene torch was quite enough to reduce the Enoch coins to unrecognisable slag, which I threw into a skip by the nearest building site.

It was only some years later that I realised what had truly taken that sad, haunted effrayante from us. Peter Carew had been one of the first—unrecognised—victims of a monstrosity which would take many more friends from me as the nineteen eighties sloped into view. And that monstrosity would soon become well known.

They began to call it AIDS.

STILL SHE STARES

TWO

It is several days since they heard of the fate of Peter Carew, and yet the mood at *The Hummingbird* remains sombre, constrained. Perhaps the dull weather is to blame; perhaps both of the men are remembering the loss of Stefan's uncle a few years ago. 'The compromised state of his immune system'... but no one in Stefan's family would ever speak of awkward topics such as HIV. In much the same way, they still liked to refer to Marcus as their boy's 'business' partner when outsiders were present.

"Oh, of course there's nothing *at all* wrong with being gay," Stefan's mother would say, avoiding their eyes as she arranged another vase of silk flowers, "But there's no need to dwell on it, is there?"

Followed by that little laugh of hers, as artificial as the roses and poppies in her hands...

Margrave comes the next evening, blown in by a brisk, rain-spattered wind, and like an old comedian who can read the mood of the room, draws them into a star-studded tale of pompous painters and exhibition mishaps—no mention of the weird or the unnatural.

"These canapés," he murmurs, "Are frightful."

And he pops another into his mouth as he examines a modest Jamaican oil which Marcus purchased earlier in the week..

Marcus has to agree. "An excess of basil—in everything. I don't think we'll shop there again."

"I had an excess of Basil once." The old man wipes the corner of his mouth with a burgundy handkerchief. "Basil Lehrer, during one of the miners' strikes. Never date a journalist, dear boys. You must endure either endless chatter, or that silence which indicates they are only there to see if you slip up on some juicy, newsworthy point."

There is wine, naturally, followed by a slow digestion in the flat upstairs.

Stefan flicks back his long blonde hair.

"You've been telling us tales of the seventies, Mr Margrave, but how did you survive the fifties and sixties, when you were much younger? Being gay back then—it must have been very difficult." Stefan seems to be searching for the right phrase. "I mean, it can be difficult even now, but..."

It is a long time before Margrave blinks, his dark eyes fixed on Stefan, and Marcus wonders if this is a question too far.

"Survive?" The word is drawn out, each consonant and vowel enunciated, even the final 'e'. "A strange word, that one, with so many connotations."

A faint blush touches Stefan's cheeks.

"If it's too personal—"

"No, it's a reasonable thing to ask." The old man smiles, and turns the onyx-headed cane in his hands. The room is scented with the subtle bergamot he is wearing today, reminding Marcus of Earl Grey tea. "Any answer I could give you, however, would not be terribly helpful, I fear. It was different for each of us, ameliorated or worsened by social class, occupation, family, or sometimes simply how much money you had."

Marcus is ready to change the subject, but Margrave leans forward slightly.

"You must understand, my dears, that in those days, you did not 'come out', unless you had the protection of fame or great facility—such as a few of the more influential artists. Warhol got away with it, for example. It was in general a time of secrecy, misdirection, and deception. Even self-deception."

"Self-deception?"

"Church and State were against us—and their stale dogma had been hammered into most of us by previous generations. Some of our persuasion took themselves wives, fathered children, and lived as 'normal' men until the grave, their natural feelings buried under the same tombstones as their mortal shells. They lied to themselves, and perhaps lost what might have healed their hearts. There was a degree of love, of course, in some of those arrangements—the warmth, if they were fortunate, of companionship, of genuine friendship, but still..."

"You don't—you didn't—approve?" Marcus shifts, uncomfortable. More than one of his uncles had insisted it was what he himself should do—find a 'nice girl', and bury his true feelings. 'Even a *white* girl,' they added, as if that was the wildest compromise they could imagine...

"My dear boy, how can I judge? If anything, I feel compassion for them—especially as I know what they faced. I was there, after all. Besides, one did not need to be queer to end up in a loveless marriage—or, for that matter, in a partnership where neither parties really had much time for the whole business of fumbling with damp genitalia."

"You never thought of going down that, er... road?" Stefan, never easily distracted from a topic.

"A marriage of convenience? No. That wasn't the only ploy, though. Take Mallory Charles, the actor. You may have seen one or two of his films from the late fifties. Not an attractive man, not in the usual sense— his long hair was clearly bottle-blond, and his eyes too closely acquainted with the bridge of his nose. He did, nevertheless, have a powerful physique and a robust sexuality which caught the attention of many men."

"And he was gay?"

"Irrevocably. Remember, to be so inclined on the art scene and in theatrical circles was often tolerated, even feted by some—until you were caught mid-liaison by some particularly vicious gossip or dutiful policeman. The Law still had its lizard eye upon us. One overt incident of spite, one single oh-too-public misstep could bring a man down.

"But I was speaking of misdirection, was I not? You see, the bread of social functions was leavened with a scattering of young women (I dislike that term 'ladies', used so disparagingly by many), who were happy enough to mingle and hang on one's arm if photographers pounced. The press would hint at titillating threesomes or awkward rivals, where in fact they were witnessing two men with a tactful girl in tow. Charles utilised his sister Millicent for such a purpose, as it happens."

"That seems cold."

"Oh, it fell apart when they both developed a passion for the same man. I comforted her, poor darling; he flew to Corfu with his lover, and they died when their two-seater went down in the Med. In fifty seven, I think."

Stefan puts on that pondering face that normally amuses Marcus.

"Nineteen fifty seven? So you would have been about—"

"About town," says Margrave, clearly teasing. "Making my way writing copy for the art journals and the dailies. *Sculpture Review*, *Apollo Magazine*, the odd piece for *The Times* and the *Mail*, whoever would pay a decent rate and spring for the odd outing. Not that I'd use that latter rag to wipe Archie Crane's arse these days. I even wrote restaurant reviews, occasionally."

"Quite acid ones, I imagine," says Marcus, topping up their glasses.

"Occasionally." Margrave smiles. "I was... a tad more tactful in those days. And careful. As I was in my personal life, going back to young Stefan's question. I had seen comrades fall in the trenches—too many gay men scarred by one unjust, pathetic criminal charge after another; ostracised by neighbours, shunned by family. Beatings were not unknown, thought that hasn't entirely changed, I'm afraid.

"There was no 'gay community' in the post-war period, not on the scale of nowadays. If we did gather in any number, doubt, fear and jealousy could so often be fellow-guests, however much some ignored them and indulged in private revelry. And even though my 'artistic' circles were the more privileged, there were still police raids, remember, unless you had a senior politician or judge to shield you. For most men, the dangers of exposure to wives and workmates, arrest, or the risks of rough trade, these were constants..."

Margrave stands. Abandoning his cane, he walks to the window, to gaze out over the capital as the night tries to possess it. London blazes back, defiant.

"I was determined not to be another casualty," he says. "I was... how can I put it? Careful, yes, but measured might be a better word. In short, I refused—politely—the offers of older men, even when genuine and well-meant; more than one of my college tutors was disappointed in me. I never splayed myself on a cheap hotel mattress, or indulged in cottaging. I have always thought that, apart from the obvious hygiene issues, public toilets were best used for urination, not ejaculation."

"Close friends—and a few scribbling colleagues—knew that I was homosexual; anyone outside my immediate circle might well have thought so, but gathering any substantial proof would have been a tiresome business for them. I was relegated to being 'flamboyant', and people left it there."

He turns to look at them.

"A coward's path, do you think, my dears? Simply existing as I was, not making a huge fuss and getting in the papers, having my day in court?"

Marcus and Stefan stutter out denials; Margrave shrugs.

"Perhaps it was. Two, three decades later, I might have been wearing outrageous spectacles and holding up my banner at some march or other. And even so I did my part, at times, as the years passed, though more with carefully placed words and quiet influence than placards.

"But in those years of black and white television, with ration cards a recent memory, before decriminalisation, we kept our heads down—to keep our heads, so to speak. Poor Alan Turing—you must have heard of him, the computing and cryptanalysis chap—received chemical castration in nineteen fifty two for having a male lover. Nineteen fifty two!"

His tone returns to its usual low rumble.

"Besides, as might be said in these slightly more enlightened times, queer is a spectrum, not a single pot of paint to splash on every wall. I myself was not possessed of an especially rampant libido. I saw physical relationships as rare treats, like marzipan at Christmas, an ice-cream cone in high summer." He laughs. "Sometimes that cake in the shop window is better left there, to be admired only through the glass."

Stefan looks to Marcus, brushes his fingertips against his partner's.

"So you had no... no *one* love back then, sir—no special person without whom—?"

"Stefan!" Marcus is horrified. "For God's sake!"

Their guest appears unperturbed, even amused.

"I had passing fancies, naturally—a night, a few weeks only. And there was an Italian, a glorious fellow who worked in white marble. *Mármaros*, 'the stone which gleams', and yes, he gleamed, he positively shone. We met when we were in our early thirties, when I first—no, I shall save him for another day, possibly." He takes his seat again, and wets his lips with dark, gleaming Puglian wine. "As for this evening, I think, we have had enough of Margrave himself. However, as I find *The Hummingbird* conducive to storytelling, would you care to hear another rather odd tale of mine?"

Relieved at the change of topic, Marcus finds himself nodding enthusiastically for once.

THE SMOKE MARKET

Morocco, 1977

I CONSIDER MYSELF, in fanciful moments, to be akin to a fine wine, or even a vintage port. That is to say, I improve with age, but I do not travel well, and if I must be moved far, I need time to settle and recover.

That latter point was much on my mind after a long train journey from Casablanca. The carriages were awash with Moroccan soldiers in transit; there was war in the Western Sahara, now that the Spanish were gone, and we civilians crouched out of the way as rifle butts jabbed— by accident, I hoped—into innocent ribcages. Already feeling harassed when I stepped outside the railway station, I descended like Lucifer into more chaos and heat, a Pandemonium of croaking beggars—'*Baksheesh*! *Baksheesh*!'—steaming taxi radiators, and tourist guides... endless guides to the reputedly endless pleasures that awaited any foreign visitor.

Fortunately, I had been here before.

"*Je ne suis pas américain*!" I yelled, and the herd thinned, for the dollar was a sacred animal in these parts. Of the remaining candidates, I picked out a rather plain Arab boy in djellaba and scuffed baseball boots, a teenager scratching at pockmarks on his face. He appeared charmless and practical, which was all I required.

"*Tu parles anglais?*" I asked.

"*Bialtabe*," he replied in Arabic, then kicked his own ankle in annoyance. "I do. I am Salim."

"Excellent. I am Margrave." I drew out a wad of dirham and handed him what would be two week's pay for the typical guide. He took the notes, squinting at them.

"This is much money, father of generosity," he said.

I noticed his suddenly averted gaze, and I knew what he suspected, for there were many types of white men who visited countries like Morocco. Including quite unpleasant men, who thought nothing of preying on and using young Arab boys.

"*Jeune*, I am a tired old man, with only a small bed," I replied.

Reassured, he asked where I needed to go, instead of launching into a torrent of advice on the bargains which his myriad 'uncles and cousins' had to offer. And there was no mention of what his 'sister' might do for me.

I decided that Salim would do.

* * * * *

I WAS IN MARRAKESH to assess a range of local sculpture and ceramics on behalf of my wealthy friend David Causton. David's interest was in importing unusual pieces to give inspiration to artists in the various studios he ran. To bring vitality to tired European styles. Put that way, it sounded close to intellectual theft—which is common enough in the art world, of course. Personally, I preferred the idea of finding Moroccan-born artists who would consent to doing a guest circuit in England, but I would have to sell that little scheme to David after the fact.

The city was awash with history, with a scent, a feeling, a mood. Here you were open to both Arabic and Berber influences, intertwined with French and Spanish colonial history. And the Berbers, who I should properly call the Imazighen—for the B-word was imposed upon them—were here first, long before the Arabs.

Salim knew his city. He found the less-frequented galleries, the right people at local museums and innocuous-looking carpet stalls which were only fronts for more expensive goods; he calmed bad-tempered gendarmes and suspicious dealers. In the first couple of days I was eased into bars where the artistic and political gathered, with few other Europeans in sight. It went well; a tall, dark-skinned painter even offered a much larger bed than the one in my hotel, but I declined his offer, tempting though it was. The indulgent pleasures of the flesh and the acid eye of art criticism do not mix—that's how my colleagues in London so often end up praising absolute stinkers made by pretty people.

It was whilst seeking out sustenance one afternoon that I noticed an iron-studded door in a mud-brick alley wall, not that far from the Medina. It reminded me of monasteries and castle sally ports, of hidden places; it spoke under my skin.

"Do you know what's behind there, Salim?"

"You do not go," said Salim, tugging at my sleeve.

"No?" I raised my eyebrows. "Why not, dear boy? Is it illegal, or forbidden?"

"It is... strange place. Not safe."

This was Marrakesh, not always the safest of places itself, yet 'strange' was such a delectable word.

"What is it called?"

Salim shuffled, picking at his spots, until I offered him a few dirham notes.

"It is called Souk al-Dkhaan, the Smoke Market," he muttered. "A place of the Berber women, who make pots. Only women."

The twitch of his eyelids showed fear... and fear has been an altar boy to me for many years (not that I was ever High Church, mind you). It has brought me many rare moments. I knew that, somehow, I was meant to see this door.

That feeling was amplified later that day, on the edge of the Djemaa el-Fna, when I spotted a woman squatting behind a wealth of interesting pottery—starkly-decorated urns with bold black geometric patterns, plates with cunningly intertwined threads of red and blue.

"This is Berber—I mean Amazigh—work, yes?" I asked.

She nodded, but made no sale pitch.

"And you are the potter?"

Again a nod, but her henna-tattooed finger pointed at a particular group of platters, wide enough to hold a family meal. The outsides were plain, but the glazed interiors were rich with blue and grey geometries which confused the eye. I was impressed, and bought a smaller example of her work.

"Do you have a workshop I might visit?"

Her eyes narrowed, and she turned away. I was dismissed.

* * * * *

I T WAS INEVITABLE that in my hotel that evening I thought of the Souk al-Dkhaan and the Amazigh women. Holding the plate I bought, I was reminded of an occasional market outside a Welsh town (I will not name it) where women from the hill farms come to sell their weaving—blankets and cloaks which last for lifetimes. The women are short, dour, and darker hued than the townsfolk, a strand of the Celtic past in a larger tapestry. And they rarely speak, except to state their prices.

I had felt something of that here, under the commercial bustle of Marrakesh.

I needed to know more.

Salim had the night off (I believe that he had family on the edge of the city), so I made my own way into the alleys around the Medina, taking many wrong turnings until, shadowed by the late sun, I saw at last the scarred, studded door again. It had a small iron grille, a wooden hatch obscuring any view inside.

I rapped on the door. Twice, three times. After a few seconds, the hatch slid back, and brilliant blue eyes met mine.

"I believe... I believe I am meant to be here," I said, struggling with the Arabic.

The eyes blinked, puzzled wrinkles forming around them. What I said must not have been expected, for although the hatch slammed shut, a moment later hinges creaked and the door opened, revealing a short, robed woman with those blue eyes set in a dark, weathered face.

"Come," she said, gesturing with a crooked finger.

I followed.

Inside was an open square which apparently served as both souk and workshops, surrounded by thick walls which rose ten, eleven feet from the ground; pungent smoke drifted from large kilns at the far end (perhaps why it had its name?). A colonnaded two-storey building rose behind these, a place such as a rich official might once have owned, hinting at former splendour. Eight or nine people, all women, worked under drooping date trees, and the doorkeeper pointed to the oldest potter, who had those faded blue tattoos you rarely saw in Morocco any more, running from her lower lip to the tip of her whiskered chin. She was grinding pigment, and looked up at my approach. I felt the lowered gazes of the others were quite deliberate, so I walked over to her, hands held out, open.

"*As-salaam alykum,*" I said, and then in French: "Forgive my presence. I believe I saw your ceramics, your pottery, laid out by the Djemaa el-Fna. My name is Margrave. Justin Margrave."

Her deep-set eyes appraised me, and she replied in the same tongue, heavily-accented. "English. You are a merchant?"

"Not exactly." I couldn't think of a suitable word for a critic and valuer. "I travel, and I look. Sometimes I see."

That seemed to please her.

"*Wa alaikum salaam.* I am Dihya." Her voice was sand-dry, almost a whisper. "Margrave. A good name, not unlike *al-maghrib*—'the West'.

Nadia," she gestured to a younger woman, "You shall show al-Maghrib here what we do."

Nadia, it turned out, was the woman from the Djemaa el-Fna. Dihya shrilled something to the others—in Amazigh, I thought—and so it came about that I was allowed to explore their small souk.

This time Nadia was willing to talk—a little. In her thirties, she spoke some English, but we continued in French. I was told that women could come here to buy directly from them, but men were not welcome. She offered no explanation as to why I had been allowed in, and I decided not to ask, just in case doing so had me ejected. I tried to confine myself to the art—for art it was.

"How is it," I asked her, "That you produce such incredibly fine, fired pieces? I am told that such work was done by men, that women in this area usually confine themselves to domestic ware, pots for the home."

The spouted jar I held was a masterpiece, heavily glazed, with dots and lines in black and red, patterns which drew the eye back to them again and again.

As Nadia took it back from me, I saw that, underneath the henna pattern on her left hand, the skin was scarred, as if by acid.

"We are not the same as others," she said. "We are unwelcome in our homes, and so we work as we choose." She lifted up a broad plate. "This may please you, al-Maghrib. It is one of mine."

It pleased me greatly—a rich green glaze with intricate black lines intertwining along the rim, and in the centre, a symbol that I knew from across North Africa, one to avert the Evil Eye.

"The *khamsa*."

"The Hand of Fatima," she agreed.

"To protect you from... what? The evil that drove you from your homes?"

Nadia's brows tightened. "From men. Most evil comes from men, al-Maghrib."

Perhaps I had been too direct, for I was soon handed over to another women, Ghanima, who was content to discuss pigment-grinding and kiln-temperatures at length, but would say nothing about the souk. When my 'tour' was done, I knew only that there was much more I wanted to discover about this closed community.

"May I return?" I asked Dihya.

"With others?"

"Alone."

She put down her mortar and pestle, and closed both her hands over one of mine. Callouses rasped against my soft skin.

"You have seen darkness, al-Maghrib," she said at last. "More than most of your kind."

Well, yes, maybe I had... but what was a fellow to do if such things kept coming his way?

"I am only what I am, mother." I shrugged. "And half the world is dark, however many lights we carry."

That brought forth a thin smile.

"You may come again."

* * * * *

Salim was disappointed that I had no need of him for a few days, though I paid him a bonus and said I would use his services again before I left. I didn't mention my visit to the Souk al-Dkhaan. I went in the evenings, when the street was either quiet, or too busy for anyone to notice me.

Trust came slowly, but over the grind of pestles, and whilst I watched strong fingers shaping pots for the kiln, I learned more from Dihya, Ghanima, and eventually from Nadia.

The souk was an unofficial refuge. These were women who had been mistreated or abandoned by husbands—or had incurred the anger of their families, their communities. Some were Arab, most Amazigh. Nadia had refused sex with a police captain, the cost of protection for her village, and been shown what her lack of 'respect' meant.

"My father did this," she said, holding up her scarred hand. "To him, I had failed to do my duty. My family was weak... and I heard of the Smoke Market..."

Some tales were of physical violence, others of mental cruelty. Dihya, who had been there many years, would not speak of what had happened to her, but she did arouse my curiosity when I asked why she didn't fear the women being found by those who had abused them.

We were drinking mint tea in the courtyard, away from the bags of pigment and the half-finished goods.

"This was a palace, once," she said. "It saw lords come, and lords go. One day, however, in the time when France chose to punish us and bombard our coasts, a French column came to Marrakesh. They sought one of the 'Alawi chieftains who had interfered in their wars in Algeria, and they found him here, in this place."

"Was there violence?" I added more sugar to my already sweet tea.

"There is always violence. The French troops broke down the door through which you come, and let their guns speak for them; as men lay dying, the Amazigh women who served in this place turned on the French using whatever tools or weapons they could find...

"The women did not win. Some were killed, others made captive. And afterwards, the French officer let his men do what they would with the survivors—mothers and daughters. The tearing away of undergarments... you understand?" She saw that I did. "Those women, al-Maghrib, they are here."

"Their spirit of defiance, you mean?"

Reaching down, she picked up a broken tile, which might have been from the eighteenth or even seventeenth century. Deep red and polished by so many feet, it shone in the lamplight.

"In the clay, in the tiles beneath our feet."

She bade me press my hands to the mud-brick outer wall, and I humoured her. The wall held the warmth of the day, and... something else.

I am not, to the best of my knowledge, a psychic or sensitive, yet when I touched the rough material, a mixture of clay, straw and dried camel dung, I had the oddest sensation, that of fierce, embracing maternalism, of anger and nurture which swirled in and out of each other...

"They are here," she repeated.

Perhaps she was right. It could always have been my imagination, though, after the power of her words.

On other nights, one of the potters played a two-stringed *rebab*, and I listened to her songs—some Arabic, some from the Imazighen. The women occasionally smoked hashish, though I refused it; it always gave me indigestion, which in your fifties becomes a constant obsession.

There was a hypnotic tranquillity to these times at the souk, especially compared to my work during the day, which consisted mostly of arguing over figurines and artisanal work in cramped backrooms or offices.

"You have no heat for women, al-Maghrib," Dihya stated as she threaded a last few silver beads onto a wire.

"Mother, I barely have enough heat for men these days."

She laughed, and gave me the slender necklace she had made.

* * * * *

RETURNING FROM THE Smoke Market on the fifth evening, I saw Salim outside my hotel. The hood of his djellaba was up, and he gestured to me.

"Some men wish to meet you." He sounded rather awkward. "They have much art, and an offer they wish to propose," he added. "But not... not where others might see, yes?"

Ah. Well, we had already been to many dubious nooks of the city. Short of a kidnapping, I should be safe at least until I arranged for money to change hands. Robbing me of what little cash I carried seemed unlikely. And as my grandmother used to say, a cow that will deliver buckets of milk for a month is better than a stolen cupful.

He led me back towards the Medina, and I started to lose track of where we were.

"Salim—"

"Almost there, Margrave."

Around the next corner, a group of men were smoking cigarettes under a street-light. My heart sank (as they say), for they didn't look like patrons of the arts, or the usual middle-men. They looked like rather more like peasant farmers, about to beat up a passing traveller.

I turned, but there was another man there, a curved blade in his sash belt.

"You are a friend of the Souk al-Dkhaan," he stated in guttural French. "We have heard how you come and go among… them." His dismissive tone left little doubt as to where he stood.

I looked to Salim, but he was cowering across the street; his djellaba hood had fallen down, and I could see the ugly bruises across one side of his face, the left eye almost closed.

"Whatever your argument here, it doesn't involve Salim or me." I tried to get my muddled brain to work. "Let us alone, let the women alone, and I won't report this."

"Oh, I know you will not. You will speak at the souk door, and they will open it for you. After that… you will know to stay silent."

"Please, *afak*, I cannot do this. It's their place, not yours, and—"

A dirty hand clamped over my mouth from behind; the man in front of me slid his knife from his belt.

"You prefer we find some woman who can be persuaded? Someone who is even less of a man than you?" He moved the knifepoint close to my crotch, and mimed the act of procreation.

Another men, who had only one eye, came closer. His breath smelled of neat alcohol.

"My daughter is in there, English, but their door is barred against me. It seems that you are the key."

My protests were ignored; with a blade at my back, I was bundled down the alleyways, and into the passage at the side of the Souk al-Dkhaan.

"Go, say your words," hissed the knife-man.

There were seven of them in all, and there was nowhere to run—not that I could have outpaced any of them.

I stepped up to that scarred door. One knock.

"It is al-Mahgrib," I said, and then, with a sudden courage which surprised me, I added more loudly: "But do not let me in—evil follows!"

Despite my warning, the door fell open. There was no sign of the doorkeeper.

I turned to try and block the way, perhaps slow my abductors, but my resolve had come too late. They thrust me ahead of them into the souk, with knives, cudgels and unlit torches in their hands.

Dihya was standing in a circle of lantern-light, the other women behind her. My attempt to grab the *djellaba* of the nearest man was met with a blow which sent me crashing into a stack of unfired pottery; I tried to rise, but Dihya called out that I should be still.

"This is not a place of men," she said to the one-eyed intruder.

He laughed, humourless. "All places belong to men, as do all women, to treat as we will. To use or cast aside. God made it so."

"Then you have not met God," she responded.

She sat down, settling herself cross-legged on the cracked tiles, followed by a rustle of robes and clink of jewellery as the other women did likewise.

And this is the point where you stop believing my story—of which, after all, I have no proof. For the moonlight dimmed, and I caught a scent of blood on the air, blood and ancient perfumes, the smell of fresh henna...

They came from the earth walls, from the ground beneath us; they were were smoke, *dkhaan,* and glints of fire. Some had obvious wounds, and some had not. The main door to the souk slammed shut, though no one was near it, and the courtyard filled with these wraiths, these women from another time.

The dead of Souk al-Dkhaan.

Terrified men cried out '*Ghūl!*' and "*'Afārīt!*" They yelled for Allah, even for the police—ironic, given their original intent. No aid came. As mist and smoke, the women were among us, brushing past Dihya and her sisters, and a *rebab* which was not there played an angry tune upon the night air.

The spirits of the souk were upon the men in a heartbeat.

I saw One-Eye fall, his face contorted, a mask of bloody gashes as if clawed by an animal, and I saw him drawn, impossibly, into the wall of the souk, half flesh, half shadow now. The smoke-wraiths surrounded, enveloped, each man in turn—xtheir bodies were insubstantial, and yet their nails were iron, hot iron which slashed and seared mere flesh—and dragged them to, no, *into*, the fabric of this place. Flesh met clay, and flesh was overwhelmed.

The screaming did not last long, lost in a swirl of dust which obscured my view. I rose to my feet, trembling, as vague figures closed on me...

Dihya spoke out, gentle words in Amazigh, caresses between mothers, daughters, sisters—women's words—and the figures slowed. Hands, insubstantial hands, plucked at my hair, my clothes, but did no harm, and at a further word from the old woman, something again in her own language, they withdrew.

"God is merciful to fools, and to those whose eyes are open," she said. I wondered into which category she placed me.

By the light of torches and lanterns, I could see only the residents of the refuge. Those sturdy walls had perhaps more cracks and buckled places in them than before, but of the men who had forced me here, there was no sign, save scuff marks in the dust.

"Souk al-Dkhaan remembers," said Dihya. "And that is why we do not fear. So, you look—and sometimes you see. What did you see this night, al-Mahgrib?"

If I had been younger, if I myself had never suffered scorn and abuse simply because of what I was... maybe then I would have demanded answers. But I was not that man.

"I saw nothing," I said. "Nothing of worth came here this night, and nothing of worth has left."

I spoke in fractured Arabic, and my words drew a soft ululation from those around me.

"Margrave," said Nadia. "It was willed."

Generous words, since it was through my weakness that the men had come here. Or perhaps not—perhaps Nadia knew better than I did.

With that—and the blessings of Allah—I took my leave of Souk al-Dkhaan.

I never saw Salim again, though I held no rancour, and would have paid him recompense for what the men had done to him.

Nor did I forget why I was supposed to be in Marrakesh. Making a few telephone calls, and further hurried visits to certain local artists and dealers I had already met, I gathered together enough over the next day to earn my fee from David when I returned to England.

* * * * *

I HAVE BEEN BACK TO Marrakesh since then, but never to that particular alley, however tempting. The Smoke Market needs little from men, and men do not belong within it, whatever those scarred mud-brick walls may hold.

I do still have Dihya's necklace, though.

THESE PALE AND FRAGILE SHELLS

East Yorkshire, 1978

PAUL ISCARIOT WAS AN ARTIST—or an artisan. The point was moot. None of us believed 'Iscariot' to be his real name. His supposed upbringing on the Sussex Downs was unlikely, given his vague Northern accent (acquired, he said); Oxford had no details of his graduation, though he insisted that he had attended there; the St Martin School denied he had ever been with them.

We did believe his stories of India, on the other hand, because he'd been seen there, at a village of artisan sculptors who worked only with chalk. For over a year he learned the finest techniques, carving devotional figurines and temple adornments alongside men who spoke no English and worried at first that a Westerner would corrupt their daughters. I imagine they soon realised the irrelevance of that particular fear.

We called him the Artist of the White Powder, for he ran on chalk and cocaine. I encountered him for the first time in seventy three, when he was being thrown out of a Soho gallery. Recognising him from the magazines, I plied him with questions in a wine-bar; we met again the next day and had sex at my flat that afternoon. Or we would have. Not only had I begun to sense that an ungenerous spirit dwelled within him, but his approach to lovemaking was as bedevilled with minutiae and self-concern as was his work. I abandoned ship after half an hour.

I did subsequently write a couple of articles on his work. 'The confused child of netsuke and scrimshaw,' I said of one of his pieces, in a leading journal. Iscariot, in a drunken rage, threw stones at their offices, yet the next day he insisted on taking me to lunch, during which he talked of nothing but Celtic knotwork. After that our contact was as intermittent as I could make it.

I was surprised, therefore, when his name came up again one summer afternoon a few years later. I was up North because an editor fancied a piece on Hepworth. Dear Barbara had been dead three years, and people were beginning to open up. My work was done, and I had gone to York station to catch the London train, but then I spotted an old friend, David Causton, on the station forecourt. David was about to get into a huge black Mercedes, but he waved, his plump figure almost toppling from his wheelchair.

"Justin! How very nice to see you again. What brings you up here?"

I explained my recent commission, and we exchanged pleasantries. David was, by nature, an affable fellow, but there was an awkwardness about him that day. Eventually he ran one hand through thinning hair, and came out with it.

"Justin, could I persuade you to visit us?"

I confessed there was nothing to drag me back down South immediately. He was delighted, inviting me to share his car and accompany him back to Torwick Hall.

"I enjoyed your latest article in 'Masonic'. Very to the point." David had one of those collapsible chairs, and swung himself into the car as he talked. I slipped in next to him while his driver dealt with the chair. Once we were inside, David looked at me with some intensity.

"Look, Justin, you know Paul Iscariot."

Both the sudden mention of that name—and the nature of David's expression—threw me off balance. I recalled an announcement in the press the year before, something about Iscariot having a possible residency at Torwick.

"I used to," I said.

David nodded. "My brother... Philip is spending a lot of time with him."

"Wouldn't have thought Philip went that way."

"Oh, he doesn't. This isn't a bed-hopping situation, as far as I know. I can't explain, really, but I feel... uncomfortable. For Philip, and for the way things are going. When I saw you, I thought you might be just the chap to soothe ruffled feathers."

"I have no influence on Iscariot, I'm afraid. What's the problem? Drink, or the white stuff?"

His gaze dropped. "Come and stay a couple of days. We have your friend Yevgeny Petrov with us, and something big coming from Iscariot. Something important..."

We said no more on the matter of Iscariot as the car sped eastwards, seeking the coast. At least I would have the pleasure of seeing Yevgeny again.

Back then I never tired of seeing Torwick Hall appear on the horizon. The land rose towards the cliffs, farmland with few signs of human habitation except for the hall, a giant's skull cast down amidst the gorse and stunted hawthorn. The white chalk ashlar of its facade shone in the late afternoon sun, hiding the fine detail of Torwick's Regency construction—three storeys and at least two dozen rooms. Behind it, the barns had been converted into studios—'The Artist' had done a feature on them and their judicious use of glass to bring natural light inside. Iscariot would have one, I imagined, as would Yevgeny, and there were always other artistic transients, picking up loose change dropped by the Caustons.

The car stopped not far from the main entrance.

"Don't say anything to Philip yet," said David as he manoeuvred himself into his wheelchair. "Get the lie of the land first."

There were messages and an urgent phone call for him; I was whisked up to a large, panelled bedroom by one of the staff, a diminutive red-headed girl, who was keen to explain the layout of the house.

"I have been here before," I said, smiling.

She almost curtsied. "Yes, Mr Margrave."

"Justin." I sighed. "I'm nothing important, my dear. An ageing critic, an occasional queen who couldn't sculpt an ashtray."

She giggled, and backed out of the room, leaving me to unpack.

Unemployment was at a post-war high, and strikes were spreading across the nation. The Winter of Discontent was on its way, but here at Torwick the order of the day was opulent comfort. There would be dressing for dinner, and each dinner was served in surrounds clustered with the creativity of centuries. The brothers were neither married nor available, except to the offspring of the Muses and their wares. They saw only art, not life; I crept between the two, never certain as to which of them mattered most.

I took a stroll around the grounds in the early evening, and came to the conclusion that something had changed at Torwick since my last visit. More than once I heard a low hooning, and other tuneless sounds on the breeze, sounds with no obvious source. They jarred with the landscape, and puzzled me, as did the lack of the usual gulls, which seemed to be keeping well away from the hall. I watched them sweep across the darkening sea, but none came inland.

When I returned, only one of the studios was lit, and that one held a cursing Russian bear.

"Yevgeny."

He threw a wax model of a half-eaten apple to the floor, and embraced me.

"Justin, *tovarisch*."

I eased myself from his great arms. "Are you well, Yevgeny?"

His face became a pantomime of woe. "Justin, I have lost my soul, my art. It has fled these clumsy fingers! It is the chalk." Pacing the airy studio, he frowned. "It does not like me."

I accepted plum brandy from his flask, and immediately thought of the chalk sculptor.

"You've fallen out with Iscariot?"

"No, I mean land... this land." He stamped on the floor. "Is very hard. Unforgiving. You can taste in water, feel when sea hits. These cliffs... I do not go off path."

Given that we were only half a mile from a three hundred foot drop into the North Sea, I sympathised with him on purely practical grounds.

"How are things here in general?"

"In general? I eat, I make art. There is girl..."

"Red hair, small and pretty?" I knew his type.

"*Da*. Melanie. Her father catches lobsters." He laughed, as if this was uproariously funny. "Lobsters and crabs. He is worker."

"Someone has to be. Do you see much of the brothers?"

"David, yes. Philip—he is always out, plotting with little stick man."

A fair description of Paul Iscariot. The hulking Yevgeny could have strangled Iscariot using only one hand.

"Odd sounds out there tonight," I said.

Yevgeny stiffened. "Da. That is him, Iscariot."

I pressed him for more details, but apparently no-one apart from Iscariot and Philip Causton had access to whatever was underway. When last we met, Iscariot was working on small, intricate carvings in that most difficult of materials, natural chalk, which might crack or crumble to dust at the slightest misplaced pressure. Chalk was clearly still his obsession. How he might be responsible for the unpleasant noises on the wind, Yevgeny had no idea.

I left the Russian to his work, and walked around the studios, curious as to who else was in residence. The Caustons were patrons of Papal dimensions, able to draw in or reject the finest talents as they chose. Henry Moore had spent time at Torwick, leaving behind the undulating masses of stone which flanked the doors. I had brief words with a ceramicist by another outbuilding—I remembered her work from an exhibition in London—and decided that I would put my feet up for a while. Matters would unfold, no doubt...

Dinner that evening was held in a room dominated by Tisanetti's *Giants Under the Snow*. I heard that it cost them two million, and that Tisanetti himself had reworked part of it in situ. It was blasphemous and beautiful, with the curious effect of making every course taste better than it should, the last meal before the hangman's smile.

The talk was of art. The talk was always of art. Others of the Caustons' set there, including a couple of major dealers—and Alastair Routh.

"I thought you were in Marseilles, Alastair."

Routh sneered. "The Vermeer was a dud," he said. "Simply a van Meeren, 'in the style of'', part of their little game. I bought it, and paid off Suki with it. Glad to be rid of the girl."

I remembered her, daughter of a wastrel duke. Her father was facing several indecency charges, and her mother was in hock to a Harley Street doctor known to be generous with his prescriptions.

"What brings you here?"

"Iscariot."

"Ah, yes." Which made me sound as if I knew more than I did.

The feel at the table was brittle. Yevgeny was drunk, which rarely impaired him; the ceramicist, Marguerite, argued with two minor sculptors about Hepworth's legacy. David Causton slipped in and out of all the conversations; Philip Causton, tall, dark-haired and with his brother's plumpness beginning to show around his waist, was at the far end with a muttering Iscariot.

"Are you well, Iscariot?" I interrupted at last.

He turned to me. The years had tightened the pale skin over his cheekbones, his eyes darker and more sunken as a result. His dark blonde hair was oiled back, like a greasy helmet.

"Well enough."

"So this piece of yours—something quite new, I understand?"

Philip smiled. "You'll be... surprised, Justin." He and Iscariot shared a glance.

"Rare enough these days," I said, sliding smoked salmon onto a bed of buttered samphire.

The Tisanetti did not sit easily with the desserts, and so after the main dishes I wandered off to smoke in the billiard room. David wheeled himself in a few minutes later, and accepted a Sobranie.

"So Philip's commissioned a piece from Iscariot, eh?" I lit his cigarette, and drew myself another one from the silver case, a present from a lover long dead.

"He's been at it for almost a year now. They took over one of the old chalk pits, fencing it off." He ground his cigarette butt into the wall, twisting his wheelchair so he faced the open window. "Do you hear that?"

Going to the window, I smelled the furnace from Yevgeny's studio, a waft of cow-dung from the farther fields. I heard chatter from the dining room, and outside, a discord on the air again, nagging at both the outer and the inner ear.

"That is Iscariot," said David, gloomy.

As I closed the window, others joined us—Philip and a high-placed dealer arguing over a bottle of brandy; a sniffing, wide-eyed Iscariot.

"Philip has an eye for the future," said Iscariot. He had obviously been to powder his nose, literally. I wondered that I had ever shared a bed with this gaunt figure. "Margrave, I want you for a moment. A special viewing."

"I thought you and Philip were working on the headland?" I said as he dragged me towards the main stairs.

"Oh, we are."

He took me up to the third storey, and into a long gallery which faced the sea. The Regency windows had been torn out and replaced with panels of floor-to-ceiling glass. One panel was open. A curious sculpture stood by it, and all around us there was a dissonant whistling. I went closer, at Iscariot's urging.

The sculpture was an assemblage of delicate carved tubes which rose from a block of rough-hewn chalk. The night breeze played over them and through them, creating that sound.

He caressed the curving tubes, which had a strangely organic look.

"Imagine what made this possible, Justin. So many millions of coc-coliths, their tiny symmetries pressed together by further millions of years of history. These are voices from the Cretaceous—"

"Dead shells." I peered at the carvings. "Many, many dead shells. If there's a voice, it's yours."

He squinted at me, unable to work out if this was a dismissal or a compliment.

"Pity the critic," he said. "For he can only glimpse the edge of won-ders. I am teaching here, you know?"

"Teaching who?"

"That, my dear Margrave, you will learn—shortly."

I was tiring of him already. More importantly, I was finding the sounds from his piece increasingly disturbing. Where a sympathetic sculptor might have enhanced the natural harmonies of the material, Iscariot had somehow found discord within the rock.

We rejoined the guests, and I sat at the back of the room with the Russian.

"You don't really like any of these people, Yevgeny, apart from the Caustons. Why do you stay?"

"I have studio, my *krasnaya devushka*, and Melanie, my red-head." He shook the flask. "I have my *slivovyy* to keep me warm." His broad face, pocked with small scars from furnace and forge, held sudden sadness. "I complain, but I belong here more than you, my friend. I read your words. You should write your soul, not waste it on praising yet another magnificent Petrov bronze."

At that, we laughed together. There was no attraction, no bond be-tween us save the absurdity of genuine friendship.

Iscariot was holding court under a massive John Martin of dubious provenance. It was *Solomon at the Abyss*, the usual monumental stuff; Is-cariot's arms were those of a marionette, jerking as he regaled the others.

Most of the guests had indulged in lines of cocaine in between drinks, and had the same dilated pupils, the same over-excited look.

"I am the chalk," he said. His high-pitched voice attacked my fillings. "It inhabits me, my very bones, and I inhabit it." He held up one arm. "You see, a veneer of flesh, laid upon the chalk that gives it form, structure—"

"Apatite," I said.

"What's that, Justin?" David glanced at me.

"What bones are made of. It's a sort of phosphate, I believe. Nothing to do with chalk, apart from a calcium atom or two. Might as well compare table salt with sodium cyanide."

Yevgeny rumbled with amusement. "Be careful what you put on your food at Torwick."

Iscariot advanced, eclipsing Solomon, his head thrust forward on his sinewy neck.

"I spoke with an artist's heart."

"One has to know one's chemistry," said the ceramicist with a giggle.

"A joke," I said, holding up Yevgeny's flask. "I drink; I joke. Apatite and appetites. To the chalk!" I took a long swig, and the mood of the room shifted back to inconsequentials. I had broken Iscariot's flow, though, and displeased him.

After half an hour, I drifted away for a more pleasant encounter. The Caustons' estate manager, George Calvin, was a solid, handsome man only a year younger than myself, and we had a relaxed arrangement. If I had a bed at Torwick, he would inspect it and make sure that it was comfortable. Neither of us had other ties, and so George and I usually removed each other's tensions for an hour or so before drifting into a sound sleep. Sex without huge passion, I suppose, but with affection, and certainly without unnecessary later complications.

This visit was different. There was something wrong at Torwick, he said. He was sworn to secrecy over the unveiling due later in the week, but it sat ill with him. He told me of heavy machinery which had been hired a few months ago, and an increased tension around the place. He didn't know if it was Iscariot's presence or what the man was working on, but the brothers were frequently at odds, and as for the animals...

"Animals?"

"We have a herd, but the milk yield's dropped, and they cluster together when it's windy, or around high tide. That's when those damnable sounds come. The farm cats left as soon as it started."

"Iscariot says that he teaches here."

George shrugged, and said that he had never seen him doing so.

* * * * *

BREAKFAST AT TORWICK was always a moveable feast, with guests and resident artists flitting in and out, but the company this morning was picky and argumentative, to a degree which was slightly alarming. Minor discussions grew close to fist fights; scurrilous remarks went beyond the usual gossip. I slid into a seat opposite Philip, who was engaged in a staring contest with a kipper.

"The herring," I said, "Eats much the same miniscule beings as form the cliffs around us."

Philip ignored that. "Justin, you and David are fairly close. Put in a word or two, if you get the chance. We are... how can I put it? In dispute. And this place could be so much more. We're on the verge of creating a central pillar of the British art scene. We've been on that verge for almost ten years now."

"You've never fallen out before, and you've an impressive set-up."

"It is. But I want to take that further step. Iscariot... what I have him doing will make all the journals. It's a headline winner."

"And David objects?"

Philip pushed his plate aside. "No, he wavers. He's a collector without that vein of ambition, Justin."

"There's probably a compromise. You want me to see if I can sow a few seeds?"

Philip relaxed back in his chair. "That would be... appreciated. Iscariot says that if I leave it much longer, Torwick will be relegated to a provincial oddity—Arts and Crafts, God help us. Hammered copper tea trays for the middle-classes."

"That's only his view."

"Wait until you seen what he's done. We unveil the day after tomorrow. It's monumental, like nothing he's ever managed before."

Yevgeny and I walked the cliff path after breakfast, and I satisfied myself that I hadn't been over-imaginative—the gulls kept more than a mile from the vicinity of the hall, nor was there any sign of the usual rabbits and jackdaws. It was as if some malign presence crouched within the headland, waiting to be unleashed. The sea was high, and I watched for a while, grey-green waves collapsing into white foam as they slammed into the cliff-face.

"I do not care," said the Russian. "I do not care for chalk or Iscariot. The rock is cold, unreliable, and so is he." He pointed out the site, half a mile away.

Two men with dogs were engaged in a solemn progress around the high plywood panels which surrounded Iscariot's site. I knew that the lads from the local villages occasionally dared each other to 'improve' outside installations at Torwick, usually with spray cans.

Nothing could be seen of the actual work—tarpaulins covered most of it, billowing gently, and as we approached I heard an unpleasant thrumming, up and down, minor keys. The dogs, young German Shepherds, kept close to the watchmen's heels, turning their heads uneasily, and I remembered what George had said about the livestock.

"Some sort of soundscape, perhaps," I said as we strolled back. "Synthesisers and sculpture."

Yevgeny rolled his thick shoulders in disinterest.

There was blood at the hall when we returned. Iscariot was high, screaming at George Calvin. George had a cut to his forehead and red furrows where it looked as if fingernails had scraped his cheek. Philip was having to restrain the sculptor.

"He went to my site!" Iscariot kicked and struggled in Philip's arms.

"I went to reset the alarm system on the fence, when we changed the codes" said George. "For God's sake..."

"Paranoid little wretch," I muttered, staring at Iscariot.

Fevered eyes shifted, the pupils like pinpricks. "Justin Margrave," said Iscariot, stretching the syllables, a sneer contorting his white face. "Licker of boots, and—"

Philip hustled him away, looking apologetic. As more guests arrived, David Causton retired to the decking beyond the French windows, wheeling himself up and down.

"Are you all right, David?"

"No."

He halted on the edge of the rough pasture. A large Venetian sundial stood alone in the field, surrounded by thickets of gorse, yellow flowers bright in the afternoon sun. Beyond that, half a dozen cows huddled by the fence, heads low. I could feel their misery.

"I loathe Iscariot," said David. "Do you remember Cheyvis?"

I remembered 'Bonny' Cheyvis. Twenty two years old, deft with file and chisel, he had dared to venture into carving chalk. Dropped by Iscariot after a drug-fuelled argument, the boy committed suicide—a razor blade to each wrist.

"It'll be over tomorrow," I said. "Unveiled to much chatter and far too many misjudged articles in far too many journals." The wind had risen, and was making me uneasy again.

"Philip has the advantage over us," said David. "He's almost tone deaf. Justin, I don't think this should go ahead."

"Can it be stopped, now? Philip seems very determined."

"Perhaps it can't. But Iscariot has to go after the unveiling, even if there's a scene. I want Torwick cleansed, freed from his influence. Old friends barely speak; others sharpen their claws. And those damnable sounds..."

I left David to his troubles, and went to mingle with the usual horrors.

Dinner that night was dark and disturbed—wine and white powder in abundance. There were more than twenty fragile, fractious guests at table. David was right—Iscariot had become the malign, self-obsessed centre of the place. Arguments abounded, until a dissipated Cornish poet rose and held up her glass of d'Yquem, swirling the golden wine.

"Of Bacchus, and of Circe born, great Comus,
Deep skill'd in all his mothers witcheries,
And here to every thirsty wanderer,
By sly enticement gives his banefull cup."

"Milton," I said to Marguerite. "The Masque of Comus."

Eliane Frost, a critic from *The Times*, saluted me with her own glass. "To the noble rot."

I laughed; Marguerite was puzzled.

"The grapes for d'Yquem have to be infected with a fungus to achieve such qualities." Eliane leaned closer. "From decay comes the finest honey."

Philip called for attention, and informed the company that the unveiling of Iscariot's great creation would be at half past one the following afternoon.

"High tide," George Calvin whispered into my ear as he passed behind the chairs, carrying a case of brandy.

Iscariot, at Philip's side, had the look of a spoiled child whose over-extravagant birthday party had been announced. It was his expression then that decided me. His eyes were damp pits above high cheekbones, his lips were parted in a self-congratulatory smile, and there was a drip of mucus from one coke-reddened nostril...

I, too, loathed Paul Iscariot.

And I had the feeling that something dreadful was coming.

I took a half bottle of Bordeaux up to my room. The lift shaft whirred as I passed it—David Causton going up to his quarters, I presumed. When I opened my bedroom window, I found a dead gull on the outside ledge. Its yellow eye was veined with blood, and I pushed the body off with a rolled-up magazine, apologising to whatever spirit saw to the souls of gulls. Afterwards, I stood there and made myself listen to the night.

A plaintive piping rose for a few minute, and then there came a sound which I could only liken to a diseased calliope, the pitch wrong, fairground music warped into noise. There was something mean-spirited on the air. A full moon shone; a stiff breeze assailed the headland. Surely Iscariot's carving in the gallery above could not account for what I was hearing?

From here I could see across fields and paths, small stands of trees twisted by the blast from the North Sea. I scanned the curving chalk track which went down to the installation, out of sight from my room...

Along the track, a dark figure wheeled another towards the site. I checked my watch. One in the morning, almost high tide that night. Philip, taking his brother for an early peek at Iscariot's creation? The sound of the custom-installed lift could have been David coming down, not going up.

I slipped down the stairs and left by the side door. I am not an especially brave man, and so I barged into Yevgeny's studio and dragged the Russian out, making him bring a torch.

"They go to check the site," Yevgeny complained. "It is first night nerves only, *tovarisch*."

"I hope so." I hurried him, our boots crunching on the track, and tried to explain the complications between Iscariot and the brothers. The long curve drew us over a ridge in the headland and down to the fenced site. The gate was open.

A deep hooning welled across the fields, followed by a rising discord of other tones. Schoenberg played on broken flutes. This close, the sound was more than irritating—it burrowed under the skin. If the Russian hadn't been with me, I might have gone back.

"Peh," said Yevgeny, slapping at one ear. "This is not good."

We strode though the opening. Some of the tarpaulins had been removed, and we saw, for the first time, the bulk of Paul Iscariot's creation.

The former quarry had been re-modelled into a shallow bowl of striated chalk, fifty yards across. Nodules of black flint emphasised the pallor of the base rock. The focal point was at the side nearest the cliffs, where a single, wedge-shaped chalk promontory, perhaps twenty feet from base to tip, had been left to jut out into the bowl.

This prow of living rock arrested us. It had been carved on a scale which I would not have believed of Iscariot. Gone were his miniature curiosities—here were faces which varied from a few feet high to almost as tall as Yevgeny, distorted faces which thrust from the chalk around a large central aperture.

'Bonny' Cheyvis was there, a slack-faced carving which showed none of his charm or wit, and George Calvin, made Neanderthal. I saw Yevgeny's face, carved into a brutish caricature, and others from the past, some of whom were dead now. Near the far edge I spotted the relief of an Italian who Iscariot had discarded a while back—it was a vile depiction, emphasising every flaw.

In each case the chalk lips were wide open, showing only darkness within, and dreadful sounds emanated from each twisted mouth.

"My masterpiece, Margrave." Iscariot emerged from behind the promontory with David Causton. David was slumped in his wheelchair—unconscious or drugged. "Is this the 'idle scrimshaw' you once described?"

A larger opening at the tip of the wedge boomed, alarming me. "How..."

"Wind and tide, my dear Margrave. I experimented on the Downs, but was booted out for damaging heritage, as they put it. Heritage, eh? I am creating heritage. Here, there are caves and deep fissures, faults and vacuoles which run down to the cliffs. The air is driven through such channels, creating a unique effect. A high tide adds its own weight as it beats against the rock, though I had to abandon and refill some of the initial bores. Philip was very patient."

The Russian stared at him. "It is clever, *da*, how you use the stone. But there is no harmony. This music is sick."

Iscariot drew his lips back in a sneer.

"You wouldn't understand, either of you. See, I included you, Margrave." He gestured to one of the far faces, and in the moonlight I saw myself, a sly apparition, cheeks swollen, eyes narrow and judgemental. Each face was how Iscariot saw us, his work corrupted with his own tempers and whims.

"This is the Voice of the Chalk, which has been waiting for millennia to be released by Paul Iscariot. I haven't opened all the mouths yet—I left a wooden plug in some of them." He tittered. "I told you I was a tutor, Margrave. I am teaching the land itself to have a voice, to sing its soul. It is learning."

"But David? Why have you brought him here?"

Iscariot sniffed. "He's drunk, and nicely coked-up. I thought I might leave him for the night, to enjoy the music, and maybe in the morning he'll understand my significance. I'm told that some find the Voice of the Chalk disturbing."

My mind flashed back to Milton's Comus.

"The wonted roar was up amidst the Woods,
And fill'd the Air with barbarous dissonance."

David Causton moaned, and I moved forward.

"I heard your little 'chat' with the cripple the other night, Margrave" said Iscariot, "But I will remain here; Philip and I will achieve glory, and the rest will bow their heads to me. Including you and that drunken Russian oaf."

Yevgeny rumbled; I looked at Iscariot with disgust. "I'll take David back to the hall, Iscariot. I think I'll also tell Philip a few home truths about you."

A wave, or a sudden gust, must have hit the various cracks and openings in the chalk beneath us, for many of the faces protested, creating ice-water in my belly. As I hesitated, Iscariot lurched at me. He had an archetypal wiry strength, and he clawed at my throat.

"You're deranged," I gasped.

"I am art," he said, his breath hot and sour on my face.

I lashed out, more to get him away from me than anything, but loose debris moved under his feet; unbalanced, he staggered, and the side of his head slammed against the rock. I went to grab the wheelchair before he came at me again...

But Iscariot did not get up. A dark smear marred the chalk, one which glistened wetly, and I could guess its true colour.

"Oh God." I stood back, confused. "Yevgeny?"

The Russian went over to the body. He examined Iscariot, searching for a pulse at neck and wrist.

"Is he... is he dead?" Unused to physical violence, I felt sick.

"Soon, I think. Skull is broken."

"I should run back, call an ambulance..."

Yevgeny stared at me, like someone appraising a painting, and then he did a terrible, unexpected thing. He took the unconscious man's head in his huge hands, and to my astonishment, he wrenched it round—I heard the crunch of vertebrae, even over the noise around us.

"Too late for ambulance."

"But—oh God—"

"He will not be missed, tovarisch."

I watched Yevgeny pick up Iscariot's corpse as dismissively as he would a failed casting from the studio. Before I could speak again, he strode over and pushed the body into the largest of the openings in the promontory. The limp sack that had been Iscariot slid into the depths; for a brief moment the sound from that orifice was muffled, and then it resumed as before...

"You... you killed him."

"I finish job; I save you much time—doctors, policemen, questions.

Now we take Mr Causton home. We see no one in this pit."

"Iscariot..."

"We see no one here. Iscariot is gone. Who knows where? Maybe he has cold foot at thought of unveiling. He is not reliable man."

We wheeled David up from the site, slowly so that I could breathe and think. He stirred a couple of times, his pulse fast but steady.

"You did that for me." I was shaking.

"*Da.*"

"It doesn't bother you?"

Yevgeny gave one of his massive shrugs. "You think it is first time I have done such things? You are good man, Justin. I am man, not so good. I was child in Stalingrad—but not for long."

It was starting to rain, that slicing rain which whips the East Coast at regular intervals, and we headed back, David insensible to the jerking progress of the wheelchair. Inside the hall we found a couple of the guests wandering around, unable to sleep because of the sounds.

"Ought to have the place double-glazed," said Routh, then realised that David was out of it.

"He overdid it at dinner," I said. "We took him for some fresh air. Don't want to spoil tomorrow."

With the Russian next to me, it was surprisingly easy to lie.

Routh nodded. "Tried to get a word with Iscariot, but his studio's locked up. You seen him?"

"*Nyet.*" Yevgeny's eyes were wide and guileless. "He is very asleep, I think."

* * * * *

Yevgeny PERSUADED MELANIE to unlock Iscariot's studio during the night, so that the Russian could remove a few personal possessions. They arranged everything to seem as if the sculptor had left in a hurry during the night. I was told about this part later, of course, and what exactly Yevgeny said to his girlfriend, I never knew.

David woke mid-morning, with a pounding headache. I helped him down in the lift, and into a comfortable chair in one of the lounges, keeping my thoughts to myself. He remembered only a vague sensation of being out in the open with someone. Gulping down a mug of black coffee, he frowned.

"George tells me that Iscariot's disappeared."

"Done a bunk. Some of his stuff's gone," said Philip, crestfallen. "Nerves, maybe. I half expected it, the amount of coke he was using, but thought he was too proud of his work to actually do a runner." He looked at his brother. "Didn't like what he was saying about you yesterday, David, old chap. I may... I may have been rather carried away with this whole thing."

"Never mind." David put on a pair of dark glasses. "I'm not unhappy to be shot of the devil, at least for a few days." I could see that reconciliation between the two was on the air. "Philip, we might as well go ahead with the unveiling. You masterminded this, after all."

The assembled crowd of twenty or thirty headed along the track to the chalk pit. I was propelled by Yevgeny and shots of plum brandy. A cold wind scurried across the open landscape, bringing an unpleasant thrumming noise with it. Before we entered, Philip paused at the site entrance, and asked us to wait whilst he 'awoke the land', as he put it.

I was trembling, but he came out shortly after, and two unhappy farmhands tugged away the final tarpaulins.

"Here we go."

Philip ushered us in to the Voice of the Chalk. I could see a number of polished wooden plugs piled neatly to one side—others occupied the mouths of many of the smaller carved faces. Like the rest of the onlookers, I was caught between staring at the physical work and listening to the rising sounds, from the low hoon of the central orifice to the toneless hisses and piping from the other mouths. I looked to where we had been the night before—there was no sign of blood on the rock there. Perhaps the rain had washed it away.

"The full effect comes quite quickly," said Philip, "When the tide hits the higher apertures in the actual cliff face. What you're hearing now is the result of spray and wind entering the holes down there. Iscariot could have explained it better."

He hauled on a length of chain, helped reluctantly by George, and as a plug came free, the mouth of 'Bonny' Cheyvis added a shrill, plaintive sound to the chorus. One after another, mouths were allowed to give voice.

In the daylight, in a crowd, the sound was bearable at first. It was much as I had heard before, but was being amplified minute by minute as more and more plugs were removed. Someone gave a cry of surprise as the chalk faces began to truly sing. Harry Mountford, who played the piano as well as he did the City markets, rattled on about minor chords and harmonics, but soon few could hear him, for the song was turning with the rising tide, swelling into a wall of sound. A more powerful surge of waves hit the cliffs below—all I could hear now were anger and malice, no longer pretending to have any musical form at all.

And as the clouds parted and allowed the sun to play across the whole work, I saw what I had missed the night before. Only with daylight and from the correct angle could you make out that interwoven with the other carvings was the face of Paul Iscariot, far larger than the rest, cut in shallow bas-relief on the leading edge of the promontory. He had dealt more generously with his own features than with others, as you might expect, but what I noticed was that despite all his work, it was the face of a monster—gaunt and pitiless, caring only for its own supposed genius.

It was then that I stepped back, trembling. For I had the sudden realisation of what the Russian had done when he lifted up the sculptor's body the night before. The largest orifice was also Iscariot's own mouth, the lips cut from the living chalk...

Yevgeny had fed Iscariot to himself.

The sound grew louder, more insistent—the high notes were wasps at our heads, and the low ones rumbled inside us, stabbing at our bellies. A woman next to me went pale, holding onto her companion, whilst others fell back in confusion. The chalk had found its full voice, and begun a discord—that 'barbarous dissonance' of Milton—which threatened to burst ear-drums, to boil the thoughts within our thin skulls.

I grabbed David's wheelchair and pulled him back, jostled by fleeing guests whose screams provided new notes for an insane instrument to twist and throw back at them.

Philip Causton was trying to force the wooden plugs back into some of the smaller apertures, and I was horrified to see blood trickling from his ears—Yevgeny took hold of him and dragged him away. I had David, and the four of us struggled across rough pasture, too disoriented to bother with the path. The others ran in any direction, seeking only to put distance between them and the pit.

Two hundred yards, perhaps, and the sound was bearable, though no less malign. The Voice of the Chalk sang on, a warped and terrible thing.

"This... this is what Iscariot taught the land?" I sank to my knees by the wheelchair.

Philip shook his head, indicating that he could not longer hear; his brother stared down at the installation. The plywood barriers around it had buckled, opening the great bowl to anyone's view.

"I feel as if I dreamed this, last night," David muttered.

Yevgeny pulled me to one side, and pointed.

"There, see? Song was already wrong, but we, tovarisch, we finish it. We give it... final touch."

I made myself look back at the exposed site, its vicious caricatures of the living and the dead, singing out whatever madness had seeped into the chalk below. Paul Iscariot's likeness dominated, and now I saw that one temple of the huge face was cracked and broken, as if it had suffered a powerful impact. Or as if if a fatal flaw had finally exposed itself...

I was physically sick then. The damage was a mirror of the bloody wound on the sculptor's head the night before.

"We must get Philip to a hospital," said David, gripping the wheels and beginning to make his way back towards Torwick Hall.

"What will you do?" I asked, trying to keep up with him. "After that?"

"Do?" David kept his eyes on Torwick. "I shall destroy the monstrous place. As soon as the wind drops and we hit low tide, George can bring the heavy machinery up. Crush it, bulldoze it, make it as if it had never existed."

I do not truly believe in God, but I spoke to Him that evening, as Iscariot's creations came crashing down; as gulls, still wary, wheeled like silver crescents across the sky.

And I asked that the chalk might forgive us, all of us...

AT THE COURTLY PLACE

London, 1977

I HAD HEARD PASSING MENTION of the new Italian restaurant, *Il Posto Cortese* at the Manningley, a few times that spring, but I had seen no reason to go there until fellow critic Jenny Fuller-Smith raised the subject. The Manningley was only a minor hotel in Hammersmith, and besides I disliked the common kind of Italian cooking on offer in Britain—the commercial pizzas were poor, the pasta tedious, and most risottos clung to the stomach lining. But she was full of praise for the place.

"Fresh seafood—*polpo, vongole,* the lot. Chaps from the City visit regularly. That ghastly cousin of mine, Gerald, for example."

We stared at the lacklustre offerings in Archie Crane's gallery—a casual Hockney sketch was the best Archie could offer at the time. Jenny was clad in her usual tight dress and purple tights, ready to dismiss every work she saw. She was rather fun, really.

"They go for the sardines?" I made a note of a watercolourist who might yet amount to something. A token gesture—my field was more ceramics and sculpture—but might suggest a line or two for an article.

"For the... what's that awful word, ambience. That's it. I'm told the staff at 'The Courtly Place' are terribly obliging."

"Courtly?" It sounded like a euphemism, one of those establishments where pretty young men and women were available after the dessert trolley, whether you called them 'escort' services or simply prostitutes. I was too old, too fastidious, to be looking for cocaine-fuelled boys with eyes only for your wallet and watch. Jenny saw my expression, and laughed.

"Not like that, Margrave. No, I hear they are simply very helpful, polite, in a quite proper way."

"That seems admirable."

"Most things are admirable until taken to extremes. You should visit the place."

I thought nothing more of this until an old flame was passing through, a few weeks later. Cesare Gallo, a Puglian sculptor with whom I'd once had a torrid fling—yes, the Italian maestro of marble I mentioned a while back.

Dear Cesare had a Moorish look which was always been enough to intrigue; not only that, but we shared an interest in the potent wines of his home region. And though the allure of the bedroom had faded somewhat since our earlier encounters, we had remained close friends through letters and telephone calls.

"Try the Manningley," I suggested when he telephoned about accommodation. "I'm told their Italian restaurant is of interest."

Duly installed, Cesare invited me to join him there for a late dinner the next week.

The hotel itself was nothing special—three stories, a Victorian stone facade—set rather too close to industrial wasteland, but this was offset by a red and white striped canopy across more than half of the frontage, a sign above announcing '*Il Posto Cortese*' in neon crimson. I paid off my taxi, and stepped inside...

Bold columns, muted colours and room for thirty, perhaps forty covers; tables well apart, simply draped in white. A smiling maître d', clearly of Mediterranean stock, strode up to greet me.

"For one, *signore?*"

"I'm the guest of Mr Gallo, I believe."

"Of course, of course—forgive me, *signore.*"

There hardly seemed anything to forgive, but I let him direct me to a corner table, where Cesare was smoking a long, thin cigar.

"Justin!" My friend rose and hugged me, smelling of tobacco and limes. "A long time since we sat together at the same table."

"Fourteen years," I said, taking my place. "I was almost young."

"You were insatiable."

"Once."

The wine waiter was there before I had settled, and a waitress was at his heels, eager to assist us with our selection. When she realised that my companion was Italian, she apologised effusively for any assumption that we would not be able to navigate the menu on our own.

Cesare ordered for both of us, avoiding the denser dishes. He remembered my tastes, then. We shared a light starter, then a *brodetto* piled high with mullet, sole and prawns; I requested more wine. The wine waiter was again eager perhaps over-enthusiastic, and we settled for a *primitivo* which was a little strong—but I did not see Cesare often, after all.

"*Piemontese,*" said my friend.

"Sorry?"

"The chef, I would say he is from Piedmont. You see the menu—the use of cream, some of the dishes. Very Northern."

He caught the attention of the maitre d', who was pleased to confirm Cesare's notion.

"Si, our chef de cuisine, he is Enrico Grimaldi," he said. "He is the foundation of *Il Posto Cortese*, since we open last year. From a fine *ristorante* near Asti."

Although the place was filling up, the service was not the usual robust 'get them in, fed, and out' of a busy London establishment. Diners lingered; we ourselves were encouraged to take our time, with staff always ready if there was anything else we required. I watched, curious, as staff flitted from table to table—slight bows, constant attention, almost servile.

Cesare waved one hand vaguely. "They are so helpful, all the time. Look at them—nothing is too much trouble for them." He grinned. "And there is no bellowing from the kitchen. It is not natural—imagine if you had a family like this? You would have to go into the hills and shriek at trees, be *irragionevole*, unreasonable, or you would go mad."

"All rather British."

"But not Italian, my friend. And half of the staff, I would say, are from my country."

I did not stay the night with Cesare. Perhaps I was conscious of being more corpulent than when we were closer, certain that my performance would disappoint. In the end, we simply embraced, kissed, and I promised to show him one or two sculpture galleries whilst he was here.

It had been a curious evening, though.

* * * * *

IT WAS A BUSY WEEK for me—deadlines for *Modern Sculpture* magazine, and a shipment of oddities from Rome to appraise. A small marble satyr—attributed to a young Bernini—lacked a certain grace to its limbs, and I decided to disqualify it. In my field, you begin to suspect the slightest chisel mark, the least imperfection in the base of a bronze; you become a detective.

And so when Cesare invited me to dine at *Il Posto Cortese* again, I admit that I was already in a generally suspicious mood. The maitre d' greeted me as if I were a wealthy, long-lost aunt; the wine waiter remembered my tastes and had further recommendations. I was chatting with Cesare about Brindisi, where he was currently living, when new arrivals were ushered into the restaurant.

"Brokers and hedge-fund thieves," I observed. The six young men had that look about them, and I thought I recognised Gerald Fuller-Smith. "City yahoos."

Cesare looked blank; I explained the Swiftian origin of 'yahoo'—the coarse, materialistic men from 'Gulliver's Travels'.

"Ah, *si*."

The staff of *Il Posto Cortese* were as always so very polite, ushering the newcomers to a large table to one side, at which point the men insisted on a centre position; accordingly, two tables were made one in the middle of the room. The City men wanted more candles, and bottles of 'the good stuff' brought immediately. The wine waiter's suggestion of the house red (very decent) was met with scorn—'Something expensive, Giovanni, and pronto.' The wine waiter's badge said 'Marco', but what did these idiots care?

Cesare growled and examined the menu again; I tried to keep my own counsel. The banking types were loud, and possibly already half-cut, yet the restaurant staff proceeded as if they were honoured guests, taking every slur and unreasonable request in their stride. '*Si, signore.* Our apologies, *signore*.'

My friend called out suddenly.

"Julia!"

A petite waitress with long dark hair turned, and her eyes widened.

"*Zio* Cesare!"

"You have a niece in London?" I asked.

"I am not her uncle really, Justin—a family friend. I did not know where she worked."

She was a fine-looking girl, eighteen or nineteen years old, with what books call olive skin, though I could never understand why. Someone the colour of most olives would probably belong in a hospital.

"*Zio* Cesare, you should not be coming here." Delivered low, in a husky voice.

I thought at first she meant because both Cesare and I were of a certain persuasion, but after a stream of Italian too purely Puglian for me to understand, Cesare turned to me.

"Julia is leaving her position here at the end of the week. She says there is something, *come dirlo*, dangerous. Beneath the smiles."

The girl left; I looked at the *primitivo* as if it was corked. I had heard of restaurants where awkward customers received urine, spit, even semen, in their dishes, or were served whatever fell on the kitchen floor. Unpleasant, but not really 'dangerous'—unless the staff suffered from a range of communicable diseases.

Cesare filled our glasses. "Julia is young, too easily alarmed."

I had a different reason for wanting to leave. The young yahoos were now intolerable—loud, unsparing with their crude language and brays of laughter. The more polite and punctilious the service, the more offensive the men became. Soup was too cold, wine too warm; there was gristle on the veal (which I doubted very much), and the pasta was undercooked. We tried to ignore them, but when one of them deliberately tripped a passing waiter, causing dishes to clatter to the floor, I rose to my feet and strode over. The waiter—astonishingly—was apologising for his clumsiness.

"Enough," I said, pinning my gaze on Jenny's cousin. "There are people here for a pleasant evening."

My voice is relatively deep and strong—I may be an ageing queen, but I have never been 'affected' in my speech, though it was admittedly fashionable in some of the scenes I frequented. Their laughter paused.

"What's it to you, you old queer?" said a wispy blonde thing at the end of the table. "Chaps need their fun on a Friday night—no harm in a laugh with a few Eyeties."

I was about to respond when the maitre d' touched my arm, a soft gesture.

"*Signore, per favore*—this is our concern. See, we have *limoncetta di Sorrento* for you, on the house."

I looked to Cesare, who looked ready to join me.

"But—"

"*Per favore.*"

Shepherded gently back to my seat, I tried to apologise for the behaviour of my fellow British diners, but the maitre d' would have none of it.

"You are not such people, *signore*. We deal with these things, always."

The mood of the evening was somewhat spoiled. Cesare was returning to Brindisi the following day, and after our *limoncetta* we ended with a prolonged handshake, a promise to keep in touch more.

The yahoos were still creating when we left...

* * * * *

WHICH SHOULD BE THE END of my story—a minor incident, to be forgotten—had it not been for two chance meetings. The first was with Jenny Fuller-Smith, who was trying to put an article together on landscape art. I was happy enough to advise her.

"I saw that cousin of yours, Gerald, a couple of weeks ago," I said, as I hunted for files on my desk.

"More than I've done. He seems to have run off, probably with one of those silly bints who will bed anything that drives a Jaguar."

"Run off?"

"Well, no one's seen him in the last eight or nine days. This time he'll probably lose his position, which serves him right."

I couldn't think of anything to say to that, and returned to the topic on hand.

And then, a mere day later, I was dining in an unpretentious bistro off Wardour Street when I realised that I recognised my waitress. It was Julia.

"You remember me, a friend of Cesare Gallo?"

I thought for a moment she was going to run, but she swallowed, came closer.

"*Signore* Margrave."

Her shift was finishing, and I insisted that she join me for a drink after my meal. Reluctantly, like a doe fearful of the hunter, she agreed. Was there something that she wished kept from her 'uncle'? We exchanged small talk over a bottle of some thin French red—I sipped, she gulped—and she relaxed a little.

"Tell me, what was so wrong with *Il Posto Cortese*. Bad pay, tempers in the kitchen?"

A nervous laugh. "Oh, there were never tempers, *signore*... Justin. It is always as the name, so courtly, so polite..."

A second bottle encouraged her to be more forthcoming. 'Something odd' happened occasionally at *Il Posto Cortese*, behind the scenes. A party, an event—she wasn't sure. Only the Italian staff were invited. Officially, it was announced as stock-taking or deep-cleaning, the restaurant closing for two days. All under the authority and guidance of the chef de cuisine, Enrico Grimaldi.

"Don't tell me he's secretly a bad-tempered ogre?"

"*Un orco*? No, he is so calm, pleasant. He does not shout at the waiters, the other chefs... it is not that."

"Perhaps they get very drunk, a two day binge. I would, if I had to be so dreadfully polite."

Hesitation; another great gulp of wine. Her dark eyes would not meet mine.

"There was a commis chef, Aurelio, a Portuguese." Her voice was scarcely a murmur. "He told me that he had overheard... he understood some Italian, which they did not know."

"Overheard what?"

"That on these closed days, *Signor* Grimaldi invited a special guest, maybe two, to dine. But this time when they are closed, they call it *Il Rilascio*, the Release."

"Chefs can be characters. He probably wants to impress other chefs, or newspaper critics by making a special effort."

She shook her head violently. "No, such guests... there was something wrong with it all. My friend found another position once he had spoken to me—he was the one who advised me to look elsewhere also. Before I might be asked to a *Rilascio*."

A chill settled in my abdomen. I remembered a curious story I had read, by an American called Elling or something like that—a story about a restaurant whose speciality, served only a few times a year, was intimated to be the flesh of hapless diners. I was hardly, however, going to suggest cannibalism to the girl. Too ludicrous.

"Restaurants, Julia. So many wild tales, some spread by the owners to make their establishments seem interesting. Ghosts, murders, wild parties, famous guests, secret recipes... it will be nothing, I'm sure."

"I would not go back there."

I smiled—or my face did, at least. "I doubt I will either, my dear. You look after yourself, and," I took out my card. "For *Zio* Cesare's sake, should you ever find yourself in serious need—money, accommodation, feel free to contact me."

We parted amicably, both a little drunk, in the early hours of the morning. On a whim, I took a taxi to Hammersmith, asking the driver to wait. *Il Posto Cortese* was dark, only a few lights showing in the upper storeys of the Manningley. Head low, I strolled past the restaurant front, an idle pedestrian. By the simple card in the window with the set menu, another notice had been posted:

Il Posto Cortese regrets that it will be closed on the 14th and 15th for staff training. Light meals will be available at the hotel bar.

Five days away. I returned to my bored taxi driver, and went home.

* * * * *

I AM, IT IS TRUE, something of a meddler. It irked me not to know what was really going on at 'The Courtly Place'. I didn't for a moment believe they were butchering guests to bulk up the *pecora e verdure*—lamb wasn't that expensive. More likely, I supposed, was that Signore Grimaldi was part of some Piedmont equivalent of the Mafia, using the restaurant to launder money. Which was not my business, not unless it involved interesting *objets d'art*. And yet there were some curious undercurrents in my field that year—the fake Berninis, for starters. Could it be that—by one of those quirks of fate which *did* happen—the two were connected?

Thinking of what Jenny said, I spoke to a friend in the Met, who confirmed that Gerald Fuller-Smith was now a missing person—but there was no indication of foul play. One of his colleagues, Max Johnson, was also unaccounted for. The company for which they both worked was investigating internal discrepancies. So—probably the usual tale of botched fraud, so common in the City.

Even so, I booked a room at the Manningley for the 14th of the month.

* * * * *

A ND THAT WAS HOW I found myself creeping through an almost deserted hotel late at night, seeking entrance to the back of their restaurant. There were always many service corridors in such places, and I found one easily enough, a passage which wound its way into immaculate kitchens. I was in the secret places of *Il Posto Cortese*.

I might have had a chance of quiet observation, were it not for the fact that as I slipped past one of the commis chef stations, my jacket caught on the handle of a huge frying pan. Before I could catch it, the iron vessel clattered to the floor, resounding like a church bell.

A swing door opened; a small, neatly-moustachioed man regarded me with interest. One hand held a plastic container which sloshed with some dark liquid.

"*Che cosa vuoi, signore?*" The enquiry was polite, delivered with a gentle smile.

What did I want? That was a hard one. Claiming that I was lost, as intruders do in stories, was so feeble that I chose half of the truth.

"Forgive me—I am a slave to curiosity. There was a rumour that when the restaurant is closed, you serve, um, *pasti molto speciali*, meals that exceed your usual fine fare."

He blinked, his smile growing wider. "Ah. I recognise you now. *Signore* Margrave is it not? I have seen you at dinner. You have a fondness for seafood, for which you have a palate *eccellente*. Your Puglian friend..."

"Returned to Italy."

Rather than eject me, or protest at my presence, he beckoned me forward.

"Come, come, *signore*. A man such as yourself is always welcome. If you like, I will show you our *pasti speciali*, although I fear I cannot invite you to dine. I am Enrico Grimaldi, who is honoured to do some of the cooking here."

This was not what I had expected. He was neither threatening, nor was his voice edged with that false note which people use before they do something unpleasant. In short, he seemed friendly and entirely genuine.

"It is... your restaurant, *Signore* Grimaldi, is it not?"

"*Si, si*. But there are many who help me. Come now."

He led me down the corridor to an open service lift, beckoning me in with him and pressing the single down button. Basement.

When we stepped out, I could see a large storage area to one side, including what must be a cold store; to the other side, a heavy wooden door, closed. He saw my hesitation.

"No harm will come to you here, *Signore* Margrave. You are kind, and considerate of my staff—I hear from Paolo, my maitre d', that you attempt to assist my people the other day. Perhaps you will appreciate *Il Rilascio*."

I was shown through into a room smaller than the storage area. Along one side sat nine or ten members of the restaurant staff—a few of whom I recognised—and on the other side...

Two men had been seated at a solid pine table. I say 'seated', because heavy ropes were tight around their waists and legs, and their current position was clearly not voluntary. One of them was Gerald Fuller-Smith, the other the vapid blonde man from my dinner with Cesare—Max Johnson, I guessed. I suspected they had been drugged, because although they called out to me, their words were slurred, unintelligible.

"What... what are you doing to them?" I managed to ask.

Grimaldi sighed. "Ah, *signore*, we Italians, we have long memories. I myself am from the Piedmont, of a people who have for centuries sought to pursue quiet lives in the villages and small towns of the region. Farmers, artisans, merchants, and yes, cooks. Do you know our history?"

"Not especially," I admitted. It was insane to be talking so casually, but I was trying to think of what to do—if I had any choice at all.

"Brutes and barbarians—coarse, demanding, greedy... these have all trampled our roads and taken what they wanted. The Franks and the Saracens; the French, the Austrians, and the Germans. We *Piemontese* are a decent people—we tried to be hospitable, to be generous, but if we offered a little, they took all, and were abused all the same. Our men were beaten, our women used..."

"*Signore* Grimaldi—"

"And so *Il Rilascio* was born, long ago. A folk custom, you British say. At certain times, we crept from our cellars and lofts, and we took from them—we took *them*. Just a few, every season. Our... what is it, *falci*, scythes slit them; we made them eat the ordure of our pigs, we taught them manners. It was fair, no?"

"But for God's sake, that was in the past—"

"The past? Here, here are the brutes once more." He gestured to the seated men. "I must ask my staff to swallow their pride every day, to listen to abuse, to deal with petty complaints and drunken threats. How are they to deal with such rudeness, and not grow bitter? *Il Rilascio!* It is their release, which allows them to continue, to serve good people like yourself, who appreciate us."

Appalled though I was, I also knew of that under-life, of the Julias who hoped for tips, who fended off crude advances, and had to bite their tongues at quite unreasonable complaints and demands. Waiters, bar-tenders, servants and shop-girls, all manner of souls who fuelled this city.

He noted the conflict in my face.

"You will see," he said, and if I did not want to see, if I wanted to run, two tall, black-haired waiters appeared at my side.

"Will they have to hold you, *Signore* Margrave?" asked Grimaldi. "It would cause us all much regret."

Bereft of options, I stood there, to watch *Il Rilascio*.

I suppose I must hint at what was done. Bluntly, Gearld Fuller-Smythe and a man who I presumed was Max Johnson were made to take dinner. I almost fainted at one point, much to the dismay of my host, who enquired with genuine concern as to how I felt. I was offered wine, which I refused, and a chair, which I had to accept before I fell down.

I do not ever wish to know what the two were served. Some of the dishes simply stank; others were rank and dripping with the foulest decay. One decanter, when opened, filled the close air of the basement with a harsh, acidic edge, and none of the liquids they were given were wine. If they would not take what they were offered, they were made to open their mouths, made to swallow.

"Yes, *signore*, there we go," murmured a waiter.

"A little more, perhaps?" said another, feeding a difficult but much-loved child.

The staff of *Il Posto Cortese* remained agonisingly polite throughout—the two victims were even asked if everything was to their satisfaction. There was no rage, no shouting of abuse, as I might have expected.

A physical beating would have been far less painful to watch. In the wide, eager eyes of the gathered staff, you could see the feverish emotion which the scene aroused them. I was shocked to realise that some of the men clearly had erections; one of the waitresses was touching herself under her skirt. This moment, this night—this was their release from every indignity they had taken with a smile.

I turned away many times—but not as often as I should have. Too often we are ghouls, voyeurs, when we should be angels. In this situation, I had no choice on the matter.

By the time the 'dessert' course was over, the men's lips and chins were hideously blistered; bloody vomit soaked their shirts, and their fingers were ulcerated, the skin peeling away, from whatever was in the finger-bowls they were forced to use between courses. Fuller-Smythe was wracked by convulsions which threatened to break his restraints; Johnson gasped and screamed for most of the session before slumping, silent.

"Ah, almost done," said Grimaldi, as if describing a normal evening in the restaurant above. "After another day's rest, we will open again, and all will be well."

"These men..."

"Forget them, *signore*. They will not be missed."

I shuddered. "And me?"

Dark eyebrows shot up, as if I had suggested something dreadful. "*Signore* Margrave, you are our honoured guest. It is, *naturalmente*, necessary that you return to your room until morning. After that, you must do as you please."

"Even if that involves going to the police?"

"If you so wish. But this is a fine *ristorante*, *signore*, with very high standards." His smile was proud, relaxed. "Do you think there will be a single trace of tonight, the smallest drop of blood, for others to find? I am Enrico Grimaldi—I demand such perfection."

I thought of the London police, who were—for the most part—singularly unimaginative. 'You say that an Italian chef is force-feeding junior stockbrokers in a hotel basement, sir. Why, we'll send our best officers immediately!' Followed by a knowing chuckle between the desk sergeant and his juniors.

Escorted back to my room and locked in—with Grimaldi's apologies—I could not sleep. The lock clicked open around nine in the morning, and I staggered into the daylight. Everything looked horribly... normal.

* * * * *

I DID NOT SPEAK to anyone of what had occurred. Not a word. I had seen many strange things over the years, but this... this was simply humanity doing what it sometimes did. However...

Critic, appraiser and *bon viveur* Justin Margrave, devoutly gay and slightly flamboyant, is considered to be rather a sweetie by some. But he has his moments—and connections not written down in any address book. A week went by, a troubled, restless week, and finally he picked up the telephone.

The following Friday, the local newspapers had a headline to break up the usual talk of strikes and inflation. A terrible fire had raged through a small part of Hammersmith in the early hours, gutting the Manningley Hotel and its restaurant. Only a blackened shell remained. There were no reported fatalities, thanks to an anonymous warning.

The entire affair was—in the end—nothing to do with Berninis or the art world. It was merely what it was. Nothing was ever heard of the fate of Gerald Fuller-Smith or Max Johnson, who were assumed to have run off with someone else's money. Enrico Grimaldi left for America soon after the fire. Where the other staff went, I do not know, but Julia prospers, engaged to her Portuguese. I send them an engagement present—black truffles in extra-virgin olive oil. Portuguese oil, in fact.

But I rarely visit Italian restaurants these days. Not in England.

STILL SHE STARES

THREE

THE *HUMMINGBIRD* is at rest for the day, its owners in retreat from the unexpected chill breeze which has nosed its way into the city's byways, offering a taste of the autumn to come. The flat above the gallery is warm, their sanctuary.

"So now do you believe him?" Stefan puts the last of the plates in the dishwasher, wiping a spot of horseradish sauce from his shirt sleeve. "The stories he tells?"

There's no need to clarify the 'him', though Marcus wonders at the tone Stefan is using—almost challenging. Margrave has visited several times, and each time he tells them another odd or unlikely tale. Stefan remains fascinated by it all; Marcus listens, but doesn't always like what he hears.

"It's... it's how he remembers things. Who's to say?"

"I'll tell you what," says Stefan, "There *was* a hotel fire in Hammersmith around that time; there *was* a disastrous installation at Torwick Hall, and Paul Iscariot *did* disappear after the fiasco, apparently. I checked. And if you were able to use Google Earth—you Luddite—you'd see the scar near the cliffs, where something big was filled in. Yevgeny, the big Russian sculptor Margrave talked about... he was real. Died in ninety eight. Fell out of a third-floor window, trying to get away from a jealous husband. It was in *The Times*—his death, not that last part."

Marcus bites back a sharp retort. "Come on, Stef. The best lies come from twisting the truth, messing with it to suit you. It's how politicians survive. And storytellers."

"I don't think he's lying."

"Oh? Because lonely old people never try to spice up their memories, so that someone pays attention to them? So that they get free wine and an audience who isn't bored with them?"

"I wouldn't say he's lonely at all—he's pulled himself back out of choice, withdrawn. You saw how he was greeted when he turned up that night. And from what I hear, he's not short of dosh. He could buy his own vineyard."

Not only is Marcus not winning, he doesn't even really subscribe to his own scepticism. He suspects that his hesitancy—no, his fear—stems from the possibility that everything Margrave said is true. That such things happen, had happened, and would happen again. It is the sort of knowledge which give you no reassurances, offers no comfort. What use is that, unless you're another Margrave?

"Does it make any difference what I believe?"

"Of course it does. To me," says Stefan.

Yes, it would. Ever since Saanvi's party in Camden, ten years ago, when the cheerful white man spilled korma sauce down the grumpy Black man's front, and tried to wipe it off with the nearest chapati. Korma and carbonised flatbread, the perfect combination to destroy a new silk shirt. Stefan and Marcus, who had first made love in Saanvi's spare room the same night night, as they wrestled to rip that shirt off and make it part of their shared history...

Marcus closes his eyes.

"You remember the card he left, with his address, the one he'd written on? He obviously knows something about me. About Brixton, when dad was alive, and we were struggling. And I don't want to hear it." There. Out in the open, at last. "I don't care about the past, Stef. I don't want to be dragged back there."

No, he doesn't want to dragged back into his own past, being raised by an atheist bus driver with a drink problem, barely getting by until the rest of the family forgave what had happened to his mother, drew him back into the fold. That was what part of the funding behind *The Hummingbird* was—an apology, reparation, or something like that. Maybe even penance.

"I've made my own way. I got though art school, made decent money, got together with you—I've shown them all."

He knows immediately that he's said the wrong thing. It's an old argument, a crusted wound. The dishwasher whirs and gurgles; Stefan taps his fingers on the edge of the sink, his eyes averted.

"Is that why you're with a white boy, instead of back in Trinidad with a nice Black girl? To 'show them all'?" Sudden, sharp.

"Oh God, no! I didn't mean..." Marcus is on his feet, halfway to the other man.

"I'm bushed," says Stefan. "See you later."

The door to their bedroom bangs shut behind him.

* * * * *

B Y TWO IN THE MORNING, Marcus has worked his way through a bottle of the Salice Salento that they keep aside for their visitor. Ten minutes after two, he takes out his mobile phone. The response comes after only two rings.

"Margrave." Crisp, no 'I was asleep' befuddlement.

"I'm sorry to bother you at this time, sir, but—"

"I was sitting with Celine."

"With the painting? After what you told us?"

A slightly hoarse laugh. "Oh, that sort of thing doesn't bother me, not these days. No, I wondered if I could perhaps bring her some peace. If companionship would settle her soul. I read a little, smile at her, put out an extra wineglass, you know? We all hope to wanted, to be genuinely wanted, in one way or another. I'm sure your Stefan feels like that, sometimes."

Marcus bites at his knuckle.

"Is Auntie Vi still alive?" He didn't mean to voice that thought, but now it's out there.

"No. Cancer took her, five years ago."

"But you're hiding some weird, horrible secret about her—and me—I suppose?"

That receives a dry chuckle. "You should have been a dramatist, dear boy. I doubt I know anything which would shatter your life, unless I misjudge you. Call it instead a closing scene, to set the audience at rest—or to make them more certain of which show they want to see next."

"Maybe I don't like this play of yours. Maybe I feel like walking out."

"Oh, I've been there, Marcus. Trust me in that. I have refused my role, stormed off stage, at times."

"And...?"

"And nothing, usually. Few of us are so terribly important that we can't simply leave. But to stay... ah, sometimes it helps, just a little."

"Like sitting alone by the picture of a murdered woman, with two glasses of wine?"

"Very much so, as it happens. Very like that."

It is impossible not to imagine the old man by the telephone—it will be one of those seventies-style landline phones—with 'Who Doh Hear' propped in front of him, and the painting's dead, pinpoint eyes watching him. The promise of release...

Stefan loves both histories and mysteries, and makes that obvious when Margrave calls round—but how can clever, know-it-all Justin Margrave really understand what matters to Marcus Evenche? Or where Marcus comes from, what he is?

"I'm Black." Blurted out, the result of all that wine. "Black and queer. Is that the sort of person who should be on your stage?"

He never says this sort of thing out loud. Or hardly ever. The gloss of metrosexual times, the pretence that you can be whatever you wish, and no one else minds. A queer, Black gallery owner, respected in his immediate society, but likely to be kicked and spat on if he walked the 'wrong sort of" streets, met the 'wrong sort of' people; Stefan's mother always by his shoulder: 'Oh, of course there's nothing *at all* wrong with being gay... but there's no need to dwell on it, is there?' And yet her evident little thrill at being able to introduce a *Black* man to her social groups, a prize taken under circumstances which one doesn't discuss...

A cough, on the other end of the line.

"I had noticed, my dear," says Margrave. "I was acquainted with the Caribbean Artists Movement, if you remember—there were those beneath its umbrella who found themselves in the same situation, in far crueller days."

Marcus feels irritated. "So you're saying I should count my blessings, that it's a different century, I've done all right for myself, and—"

"No." Abrupt, for Margrave. "But I imagine that's what you tell yourself, in those bleak hours which fall upon us all from time to time. You hardly need me to repeat your own thoughts."

"I..."

"You are an interesting young man with a good eye for art. You have the blood of Africa within you, the cultures of England and the Caribbean at your hand, and you are a lover of men. Is there anything there, within your essence, that brings *you* shame?"

Alcohol fights with intellect, achieving at best a draw. "There... I mean... well, no. I suppose not."

"Quite. Now, dear boy, I imagine that your real question, the one which drove you to the telephone tonight, is 'When are you going to tell me what happened in April, 1981, you garrulous old bastard?' Am I correct?"

"I want to... I think I want to hear it." Not Marcus in command, exactly, but Marcus trying to open up, trying to bear the thought of opening up.

"Then indulge me just a little longer. I find that I enjoy sitting with the two of you, telling my ridiculous tales. No, please don't argue. Soon, I promise you, I will answer your question, or leave you be—as you decide. By then, you will feel more comfortable with what I have to say."

"I doubt that."

"A little doubt is always good for the soul, dear boy," says Margrave. "Even for mine. I will see you next week, then."

The connection goes dead.

ELK BOYS

THREE

Sussex, 1976

DROUGHT—PROLONGED, uninterrupted drought—is a gift to the archaeologist. Rivers, lakes and reservoirs fall, revealing damp histories; fields grow strange shadows which suggest the delvings of the past. I am not one of the trowel and arthritis brigade, thank the gods, but I do have acquaintances who are, and I have seen their eyes glitter as they abandon the trenches for long dawn walks, eager to scan the new landscape. If their institutions have money, then light aeroplanes soar beneath the clouds, cameras clicking. Are those the marks of a Roman villa down there—or the abandoned layout for a post-war sewage works? Such a game.

The remarkably dry time we were having in the March of seventy six was on my mind when I received a telephone call from Emilia. Professor Emilia Foxton, I should say, and you will then recall how she was noted for her archaeological successes across the South of England, including the great dig beyond Amesbury.

"Justin, I'm so relieved you're in town." Her voice was thin, as desiccated as her many finds. Deceptive, as she was a solid woman who ought to have bellowed like an opera singer. "I'm out at Abbot's Elk, and I need you."

"Never heard of it, Emmy. Is it one of your sites? I'm not picking up a shovel, if that's what you think."

"Dear Lord, no. It's about Adam. At least, I think it is. He and his boyfriend are with me, and I'm at my wits end."

I remembered her son Adam. A tall boy with blonde hair and a gentle manner. He had his mother's robust physique, but not her weight.

"What is he now, nineteen?"

"Twenty. In the second year of his degree. But Justin, listen, there's something wrong."

"Call a priest; call a doctor. Bribe the police, tell the barman it was all a misunderstanding."

"I'm serious. Please. I can't explain you over the blower, but if you could come out here..."

We had been friends for years, and we both knew that I owed her. The year before she had proved the true provenance of some Bronze Age pieces I had been considering for a feature in 'Masonic'. They had been copies—good ones—and I had been saved a lot of embarrassment.

"Where is this place? And how soon?"

"It's a village, north of Chichester. And, well, as soon as you can."

"Is there a passable inn near you? One that doesn't only use wine bottles as candle-holders?"

"The *Grey Horse*, in the village. That's where I'm staying."

I sighed. "Book me a room there for tomorrow. *En suite*, or I walk."

"Done." There was a moment's silence, and then, "I'm out of my depth, not just with Adam but with this place. I wouldn't ask, Justin, if it wasn't important."

"I know."

I put the receiver down, and sighed again. Was I being summoned as an avuncular family friend, an art critic, or a moral compass? In other circumstances I would have pleaded pressure of work, but Emilia—she had not sounded herself.

Not at all.

* * * * *

THERE ARE MANY MISCONCEPTIONS about dear Margrave. Some I do not correct, but I do wither when people corner me and ask if I investigate what they call 'peculiar' instances related to the art field. Just because they've heard unreliable gossip here and there. No, I tell them, and mean it. I don't investigate anything except the provenance of *objets d'art*, developments in modern sculpture, and the telephone numbers of men who appeal to me—interesting, not necessarily handsome, independent, preferably in their forties, if you need to know.

Most artists, like my good friend Yevgeny Petrov, are hard-working men and women with a tendency towards depression, alcoholism and periods of unbearable self-confidence. They have no time for 'peculiar'. I am merely easily persuaded to poke my nose into other people's affairs.

The trains were punctual, and the taxi ride from Chichester dull. I don't think the driver approved of a large, softly-spoken man in a red shirt, black silk cravat and panama hat. I am, after all, an unrepentant cliché.

Abbot's Elk, when we arrived, was much as the gazetteer said—small and unimportant. I'd read up on it before I caught the train. It's only oddity was the name, which had apparently been Abbot's Encester until the seventeen eighties, when a number of carvings had been unearthed whilst a well was being dug. A few were crude stone figures—Neolithic—but some were carved from antlers and bone, and according to the book I had, rather fine examples. The Elk part had gradually replaced the Encester, the result of over-imaginative Victorian collectors. Those digging vicars have a lot to answer for.

Emilia was at the bar in the *Grey Horse*, which was old in a tired rather than historic way. When she saw me, she abandoned her gin and tonic to rush over and hug me.

"I have fragile ribs," I said, and gave her a peck on the cheek.

"Let me get you a drink, Justin."

I wanted to confirm the driver's suspicions and have a campari, but I hated the stuff, so I paid him off and agreed to sample the wine list. A Sicilian Nero D'Avola turned out to be a surprise, in that they had it, and that it was drinkable. I'd expected the usual half-empty bottle of overpriced Nuits-Saint-Georges behind the pumps, so symbolic of the seventies.

"I think," I said as we settled down in one corner of the room, "That you had better explain what this is all about."

She turned her florid face to me, and there were bags under her grey eyes.

"If I could explain it, I wouldn't have called you."

The dry autumn had exposed a set of lines in the fields beyond Abbot's Elk, and a local historian had been curious. He called in Emilia, who advised the Sussex Archaeological Society, and she drove out for a cursory look. That was last October.

"The lines connect with what locals call the Greenway, which may or may not have been a processional route in the Iron Age—but if I'm right, it's a Neolithic cursus."

"Which is, when it's at home?"

"A length of parallel earthworks. No one knows what they were for, and they're uncommon. They can run for over a mile, the banks or ditches marking a clear path. But portions are often ploughed out." She stared at her gin. "I hired a chopper, and saw that some earthworks had survived, dotted across various stretches of grassland. With the markings exposed, I could see how they all lined up. It was quite a moment—"

I held up one hand. "Emmy, this isn't why you dragged me here. I know how to use a library."

She nodded. "Alright. I decided to do a series of small digs. Adam is studying Archaeology, and his college gave him permission to get some fieldwork in, along with a young man he's seeing, Malcolm Tate."

"A gay outing sponsored by the bursar." I chuckled, but she wasn't amused.

"They set up a tent near the end of the cursus; I felt too creaky for roughing it, and came here. The landlord lets us use an attic room as our headquarters..."

"But?"

"I don't know. Adam is... out of sorts. They both are. They stayed with me last summer, and everything was fine. Nothing's gone wrong between them since, as far as I can tell. It was only after they came to Abbot's Elk that it started. And I... I found something last week which made things worse." She reached into her canvas shoulder bag, and took out a heavily wrapped bundle.

I waited as she peeled back layers of polythene and hessian, to expose an object which had me leaning forward. It was six inches long, a piece of bone or antler carved into the most wonderful resemblance of an exhausted deer, possibly even an elk. I picked it up, and held it to the dingy light, trying to see the detail. This was more in my line.

"How old?" I traced the haunches with one fingertip, gently, and it felt... it felt of deep, deep history.

"Four thousand years, at least. The style, finds in France and Spain, the deposits around it. It was in the boundary mound at the far end of the cursus, two and a half miles north of the village. No one had realised until now that the mound was part of the whole thing. It had been written off as yet another Bronze or Iron Age lump, of indeterminate purpose."

"This was in the earth, alone?"

"It was in a stone cist—no bones or funerary material, simply this— right where the cursus ends and the mound rises. I found a few Iron Age odds and sods in the layers above it, nothing important. I'd made an exploratory cut to see how the strata lay—hadn't expected to find anything."

The weight, the density, all suggested antler, or tusk. I knew my raw materials when it came to sculpting, and I favoured antler. I didn't want to put the figure of the elk—it had to be an elk—down. You had that feeling that it might have been alive the day before—a beast at the end of its strength after the chase, flattened antlers lowered, needing to settle and recover...

My chest constricted for a moment, and I gave the elk back to here, making myself breathe in and out, slowly. It passed within seconds.

"Are you alright?" asked Emilia.

"Old age." I sank half a glass of the Nero D'Avola.

"Justin, you're in your late forties."

"Didn't you know? That's about one hundred and eighty in gay years."

She almost laughed as she wrapped the elk up again. She didn't look quite so grim now.

"What has this to do with the boys, then?"

"Meet them. They'll be over for a pint around seven. And you can see if I'm getting worked up over nothing."

It was two in the afternoon, so I explored Abbot's Elk. It took seventeen and a half minutes. The village shop was closed; the pond needed ducks. The church was Victorian mock-Gothic, and almost painful. A glass display case inside the church held three pieces of Bronze Age bone sculpture—deer or similar—found last century. They were not Emilia's elk, though they might have been very poor copies of it.

I found the Greenway, though, and walked a mile of it. Normally I prefer a landscape which has coffee shops and wine bars, but this was a fine place—partly an open bridleway; partly one of those classic sunken lanes, lined with oaks and with elms which had survived where their sisters elsewhere had not. Along certain stretches, a natural canopy made the Greenway into a tunnel of branches. Fat buds held promise, and some had already burst. The hedges were greening around me, rushing towards the spring equinox; you had a sense of imminent growth that could overwhelm a world. Had I not been a cynical old critic, I would have been moved.

Emilia had shown me aerial photographs of the cursus, and with some squinting, I could see what she meant. A gently rising field beyond the Greenway had a suggestion of two straight shadows beneath the rough meadow, lines which continued the sunken lane. I assumed these were the Neolithic ditches. They were ten yards apart, lost here and there under hillocks or a row of animal troughs, but back again further on, occasionally augmented by short raised banks which had been co-opted into forming a field boundary.

I could see how the dots might never have been connected before, and I had a sense of the long 'road' which might once have started at the beginning of the Greenway and taken men into the hazy distance beyond the next rise. I would wait until tomorrow to get a lift out to the terminus, as Emilia called it, and where she had found the elk.

Back in the village, Emilia nibbled cheese sandwiches in her attic war room, and I sat in the tiny dining area, eating a rabbit stew which did reasonable justice to the unfortunate bunny. I thanked it for its sacrifice, and checked that the landlord had more Nero D'Avola in the cellar.

"Most of a case, sir," he replied in a good Sussex burr. "No real call for it. You'll be beasted after being along the Greenway."

I think he meant tired, so I nodded and ordered a bottle, along with the oldest cheddar he could find, preferably some that had never seen cellophane..

Adam and Malcolm walked in as I was finishing the cheese crumbs. They brought a certain agitation with them, faces turned away from each other, but Adam came over at once, managing a smile.

"Uncle Justin—I didn't know you'd be coming." His handshake was oddly vigorous and emphatic.

"And?" I tipped my head towards his friend, a tousle-haired young man with a gypsy look about him.

"Oh, yes. Malcolm."

Not the way you introduced your lover to a family friend in the know. I stood up and shook his hand as well. The same grip, too intense for the situation.

"Two ales, landlord," I called out, and insisted they join me. I might have been sharing a table with two prizefighters, sizing each other up before the bout. It was uncomfortable. "Your mother's beavering away upstairs, Adam. Go and say a quick hello, there's a dear boy, and ask her if she wants a gin sending up."

He moved with reluctance, but did as he was bid; I looked directly at Adam's boyfriend. Dark eyes, a strong nose, and lips which should have held an easy smile.

"So you're another one of these chaps who likes to rummage through ancient middens, Malcolm?"

"I... suppose so." He did smile, but it was weak and awkward. "Foxton and I met on the course at college."

"And are you having any luck at Abbot's Elk?"

He muttered something about ditch layers, and contamination, which I let pass.

"I walked the Greenway today, most of it," I said.

And oh, the lifting of eyelids, the shifting of small facial muscles, at those few words.

"It's magnificent." He leaned forward. "The whole thing, I mean. A genuine cursus, the long journey to awakening. What it must have seen, Mr Margrave."

"Awakening?"

He swallowed. "There's a theory that it may have been a sort of trial course, or a ritual procession, from one end to the other. I sort of... sort of imagined how they might use it."

"Is that what Adam and his mother believe?"

A door closed.

"I wouldn't know, sir," he said, and turned to his pint.

Adam and Emilia came down a minute after—Adam reserved, Emilia trying to look bright.

"There's a moon, Justin," she said. "Walk with me, and we'll leave the boys to relax."

That didn't seem likely, but I accompanied her down the street and down a path to the start of the Greenway. We paused by a Victorian mounting stone.

"Is this where it begins for them?" I asked, looking up at the waning full moon. "Or where it ends?"

"What do you think?" She sounded very unhappy.

"From such a brief meeting? Tension. I would have said a lovers' tiff, but you wouldn't have asked me here if that was all that was bothering you. Trouble with the locals, but I doubt Abbot's Elk is up to that. The village itself seems rather devoid of character, including any of a malign nature. It would surprise me if they have a single folk myth or legend."

She offered me a roll-up, which I declined.

"They say that a witch once haunted the lands around here, that she could change herself into a white deer."

"And?"

"Oh, that story was made up in the eighteen fifties by a parson who was short on local colour for a book. So, yes, a point to you. But the cursus..."

"Malcolm seems taken with it."

"They both are. I can't get them to focus on simple tasks like recording finds properly or taking measurements, but I also can't get them to tell me what is... infecting them. That's what it feels like. Infecting. They were so close before."

I softened, because Emilia loved her son dearly, and wouldn't have minded him going out with an Aberdeen Angus if it made him happy.

"Were they like this when they arrived?"

"No. It grew, and it grew fast after I found the elk figurine. They treat it like it's a holy relic. What I thought would be a relaxed preliminary investigation has become a bit of an obsessional thing for them."

"Well, it's quite a fine piece, but I do hope that you're not going to suggest it's cursed, Emmy. I have too many boxes of supposedly jinxed pieces of art in the basement already. People dump them on me, and few have lived up to their reputations—although I did think that a certain ebony framed mirror made me look far too jowly."

The end of her cigarette flared, a hot, orange will of the wisp in the night. The smell—an acrid tang like bonfires—was far too strong for such a little roll-up, but I couldn't see any fires nearby.

"Cursed? No, of course not. I just don't know why the boys are like this. I suggested they go and stay at my flat in London for a few days. They wouldn't hear of it—said they wanted to be sure that they'd covered the whole cursus."

"Is there more of it?"

"I'm sure there isn't. It starts outside Abbot's Elk, obviously, and ends at the mound by a copse of alder called Bright Woods. There are three mounds, actually, although the other two might be mistaken for spoil heaps left by labourers. I can see evidence of quarrying not that far from there."

"Tomorrow," I said. "Tomorrow you must show me that section. With the boys present—I might be able to get a better feel for what's eating them."

She squeezed my hand.

"I knew you were the right person to call."

We went back to the inn, and I did my best to engage the boys in conversation. Emilia hadn't exaggerated—they were quarrelsome. It was a quality I had never seen in Adam before, nor could I blame his boyfriend in particular. They both argued over who would buy me a drink, over who had the longest fingers, anything that presented itself. Yet whenever I introduced the topic of the elk figurine, or the Greenway, their eyes brightened; I could feel the blood pulsing in their veins.

After all three had left for their various beds or sleeping bags, I had a late night drink with the landlord—a sweetheart who obviously felt awkward as to what he should say, given my unshaded homosexuality, but who was too nice to pry. I mentioned that the boys were argumentative, and he cocked his head to one side like a dog who was suddenly listening.

"Aye, they are, but they weren't, when they do come. And, Mr Margrave, I can't say as others are settled. A lot of the young lads around here seem a bit off, to me. Had to chuck three out of the snug last Thursday, hadn't I? Argimentative, aye."

Interesting, but it was late. I bought him a last whisky, and went upstairs.

My room was bearable, and I had perhaps hit the wine more than I should. I kicked off my brogues, and lay back on the narrow bed. As I watched a spider traverse the ceiling, making for a somewhat incompetent web in one corner, I drifted off.

Jemison is leading, beautiful Jemison with his smooth thighs, and long feet as slender as a princess. Barefoot and fey, he surges before the pack, but I am close behind, so close that if I draw in one more great breath, I might be on him. Then the blows, my fists pummelling the side of his head, and the masters by the course urging me to be merciless.

I hear Mr Croker, who taught French and Classics, shrieking that I should finish him, leap the body and take the cup, for the glory of Edgeton House; other boys fall back, wary of me...

I stumbled to the tiny bathroom and held on to the washbasin. The taps groaned, and I splashed my face with ice cold water. The mirror showed me a Margrave I did not know, a visceral, panting stranger.

Sitting on the edge of the bed, I reminded myself I was at the *Grey Horse*, in Abbot's Elk. Harrington School and Edgeton House—those were before the war. And I had worshipped dark-eyed Jemison. I could never have considered striking him, not under any circumstances. I was not a violent man, nor had I been a violent boy. I had hated Sports Day, and had avoided every race, drawing on a collection of pretended injuries and complaints to be excused. It was a disturbing, vexing dream.

The spider flicked one leg as it managed to get tangled in the edge of its own web, then free itself. It knew no more than I did.

* * * * *

EMILIA'S BATTERED 2CV managed to make it over the rise beyond the Greenway, and rolled downhill with more grace. An unmetalled road followed the rough direction of the cursus, taking us past a farm gate or two; at ten in the morning in an obscure part of the Downs, there was no traffic. The folded landscape consisted mostly of pasture land and abandoned fields—this was before the surge to build on any square yard of free space.

"No one even knows exactly who owns some of this," said Emilia, stripping gears as she turned slight west. "There was a Manor of Abbot's Encester once, and I think it technically belongs to a family somewhere up North. I had permission from the Sussex Archaeological Society to do my preliminaries—they have some sort of arrangement."

She took one hand off the wheel to point to a long slope in the distance. Some of the cursus shadow could be seen, and by a stand of trees, a long, low barrow. The beige blotch of Adam's large tent sat by a diminutive stream.

"Chalkland," said Emilia. "These streams sometimes disappear, but there are pockets of greensand and gault clay where the chalk has been worn back,"

"I prefer my geology carved into a handsome form and put on a shelf. Too much of it in the wild can be tiresome."

We pulled up near the tent. Malcolm was crouched at the water's edge, dabbling one hand in the flow.

"Adam is... somewhere by the mound." He seemed distracted, though not hostile.

"Have you argued again?" asked Emilia.

"I suppose so." He would not look up.

"You two stay here," I tried to sound cheerful. "I'll go for a reconnoitre, and perhaps catch up with Adam."

They didn't disagree, so I stepped out in the direction of the trees.

Alder had flourished by the stream, and managed to form a thick copse to the east; I could see what Emilia meant about the two smaller humps in the land. The nearest was almost obscured by trees, and the other, no more than four feet high, sat unwanted in the middle of a ploughed field. But between them—no one could mistake that for an accident of nature. The main mound was a good thirty feet long and half as much wide, blocking any route further north. It rose gently, quite climbable, with the suggestion of a shelf or ledge on the southern side, facing the cursus and the far-off Greenway. Adam sat there, head low.

I walked over.

"Well met, young man."

He jerked, then relaxed slightly when he saw it was me.

"Oh, hi, Uncle Justin."

I clambered up and sat beside him. The world spread out before us; Abbot's Elk was hidden by the rise between, but it was just possible to see this end of the Greenway, heading towards us.

"Ēostre, Ostara. The dawn of spring; the awakening of the land." He turned to me. "We don't know what their name for it was, the people who built this. They were here before the Indo-European languages, and their words are lost."

"But not what they did." I wanted to shiver. "Do you dream, Adam?" It was a curious stab; I hadn't even expected to say it.

"Oh, I dream." His face was momentarily fierce. "I dream of this place, and of Malcolm. Of the wind scouring our faces, and our chests tight as drumskins..."

"The two of you seem to be at odds at the moment."

He shrugged. "I suppose it happens in any relationship."

I thought for a moment that I smelled burning again. If I was having a stroke, this would be a very inconvenient place to have one. The idea of being pawed at in a run-down Chichester hospital didn't appeal.

"It isn't always easy being of our... persuasion. People can be cruel. And you are on show, unless you are very, very clandestine. Do your friends at college know about you and Malcolm?"

"Most of them, yeah. They're fairly cool about it."

"I was assaulted, a couple of years ago. Three chaps saw me talking to a teenager down a side street, decided that I was preying upon the boy."

"God, that's awful. But what—"

"The spotty lad in question had approached me, to try and sell me drugs—a wasted effort, unless you can inject Malbec and Merlot. He was becoming threatening. These men didn't wish to hear the truth; they fractured my left wrist, and left me badly bruised."

"We've never had anything that bad."

He still said 'we' when he referred to himself and Malcolm. Perhaps this was a salvage job, not a crisis.

"You seem, how shall I put it, edgy with each other. If the three of us talked, privately..."

He stood up, as if bored with me.

"The year turns. *Oyn hner upyr. Oyn!*"

"What?"

"I'm sorry. I have to... I have to go."

And he went, running down onto the track of the cursus, legs pumping as he headed for the Greenway. Given my generous frame—not fat, I hasten to say—there was no point in pursuing him. I sat on the grassy ledge until Emilia came into view, ten minutes later.

"Where's Adam?" she asked.

"Gone, charging off along down the cursus." I was getting stiff sitting there. I rose, and looked around. "What does '*Oyn hner upyr*' mean to you, Emmy?"

"Absolutely nothing." Her broad brow furrowed to match the ploughed fields. "It sounds a bit like early Celtic, but not a branch I know."

"Hmm. Never mind."

Puzzled, she change the subject, indicating where she had found the elk.

"I put the turf back, but it was here, in front of that ledge or step in the mound. Deliberately so, I would say."

"Why?"

"I'm not sure. It's what Adam and Malcolm believe, and it seems reasonable. An offering, maybe, to the changing seasons, the wind, the moon. To propitiate the prey of the tribe's hunters? We don't know how Neolithic people thought, but they had rituals of life and death. The track may have been part of that."

We wandered back towards the car. I was tired.

"You say track. Malcolm says course, or a path for a ceremony."

"Theories. I spoke to Galton at Edinburgh. He believes there would have been times of the year when a tribe—or more than one tribe— would walk from the open end of the cursus to the mound. This one runs due south to due north, though that's not true of all of them. It could have been a symbol of unity, conducted at each solstice."

"How sweet. Like a peace march to Trafalgar Square."

She sniffed. "I didn't say Galton was right, Justin."

In the afternoon we discussed mutual acquaintances, Adam's late father—a reserved and incompetent financier who had been no great asset to the family—and Malcolm's people (who had no idea he was gay, but were very pleasant, according to Emilia).

"I don't think they'll be shocked," she said. "Confused at first, but kind about it."

"Ah, the kindness of strangers."

"Don't be a cynic, Justin. There are worse things."

We examined the elk together, and I had a second chance to stroke its smooth lines. The workmanship was guileless, rather than crude—a genuine attempt by the craftsman—or craftswoman—to draw out the characteristics of an exhausted beast without adding unnecessary drama. A Victorian sculptor would have added staring, alarmed eyes and senti- mentality in the pose; the youngsters of today would have reduced it to a vague form, and missed the inherent animal strength. This was perfect.

"It doesn't belong to me," said Emilia, watching me caress the long spine. "In case you were thinking about making an offer. The Archaeological Society gets it, and will then have to negotiate with the land owners."

I grinned. "No, just admiring it."

I took dinner at the *Grey Horse*—the alternative was a taxi into Chichester. Mutton pie, made with actual mutton, not a frozen lamb joint. It was rich and flavoursome, and invited another bottle of the Sicilian. At least I was doing well on that score—I offered the landlord a sum for the rest of the case, and we both came out of it well.

In a contemplative mood, I read a couple of recent art journals by candlelight in my room...

The boy-children, the great-fathers and every hunter, every fisher and planter, hold the torches high in the pre-dawn, and eyes weep with the smoke that lines the way. Some wear antlers, set in leather bands which encompass their brows; others have pipes of deer bone which pipe in plaintive disharmony. A drum is beating, an elm drum stretched with goatskin, the drumhead daubed with two long lines of green dye from the Women Over the Hill.

Jemison lifts himself up from the school sports-field on one elbow, his cheek split, mouth bloody. Mr Croker is beating on a tin drum by the finish line, a harsh, unpleasant rattle of a sound, and Matron is there, but she wears a rough hide cloak and she holds out a small, carved figure. Matron, a harsh woman who never tied a bandage without a vengeful twist, looks down on us.

Jemison is waiting. "You win, Margrave," he says. "Now you can have me."

I lean down to kiss those bruised lips...

* * * * *

I NEVER TELL ANYONE my dreams—it gets so tedious when people start on their own—and so I wasn't about to start. But I was willing to consider their role in that curious reorganisation of the subconscious that occupies the brain at night, and their ability to reflect less than obvious stimuli that had piled up during the day. When Emilia joined me for a late breakfast and told me Adam and Malcolm had been fighting, I wasn't surprised.

"It came to blows," she said, staring at her poached eggs. Nothing make an egg less appetising than poaching it to a soggy mass, slopped onto the plate. "They were here in Abbot's Elk earlier, buying supplies, and they argued outside the village shop."

"What was the cause?"

"Nothing. Malcolm had gone into the shop first, and Adam took exception, said he should be in the lead, that Malcolm could not pick before him. They were going to buy cheese and a loaf, for God's sake. Adam punched Malcolm in the belly, hard: Malcolm tried a right hook but missed. They're not speaking to each other now. It's getting worse every day, and I saw Adam's eyes. He really wanted to hurt his friend. If there'd been something heavy to grab nearby at the time..."

"I fell out with a boyfriend over crisps once," I said, chewing on a rasher of bacon. "I totally disapprove of flavoured crisps."

She gave me a glare, and I held up my hands.

"Emmy, I'm not taking this matter lightly. I don't even think it's our boys in particular—might be any or all of young men around here. And I have a most curious idea of what is happening, but you won't like it. I don't think I like it. At worst, it smacks of imaginative nonsense; at best it has a touch of Machen or his ilk which disturbs me."

She sat back, abandoning her food.

"What is it?"

I wasn't ready to answer her directly. "The elk figurine. Do you have it with you?"

"It's locked away upstairs. I can fetch it."

When she returned with the canvas bag, I took her by the arm and led her to the church. The studded door was open, and I showed her the display case.

"I've already seen these, Justin," she said, irritable. "They're far later than the cursus."

"Now hold up the elk."

She did so.

"And what do you see, Emmy."

She looked from one to the other until her eyebrows met.

"There are some similarities. Not in the quality, the workmanship, but in the prone position, the angle of the head."

"They're memories. Maybe a thousand years or more after the elk was carved, someone tried to make it again, but couldn't. They knew the general idea, but hadn't the gift."

"Uh, alright. I can almost accept that. Maybe they'd seen something similar, an elk carving which was handed around, whilst ours remained hidden away."

"That doesn't matter. What matters is the persistence—and the course. Come on."

We left the village, and stood upon the Greenway. In only two days, the buds on the trees had opened further, and the unmanaged hedges around showed green spatters of unfurling leaves.

"The land is waking up," I said. "Out of its winter slumber, and into spring. Tomorrow is the twenty first of March. The ritual is due."

"What ritual? Oh God, Justin—you haven't been sitting through screenings of that 'Wicker Man' film, have you?"

No point in stopping there, I decided. At the least she would realise I was trying to be helpful, even if she thought me deranged.

"Sit down and have one of your dreadful roll-ups."

She hesitated, but joined me on the grass verge and pulled out her tin of rolling tobacco.

"Emmy, there are male rituals, always have been. I don't mean the bullying, chauvinistic stuff so beloved of those insecure tossers who stand outside pubs and yell crudities—and no, I don't expect Christopher Lee to pop up in the church hall. I mean primal ones. Challenge and competition. That's what the cursus was for."

"Go on."

"My best guess, then. This was a running track, a very long time before little men in brown coats and flat caps trundled along marking out the lines on sports day with their whitewash machines. The young men of the tribe or gens or whatever used it to show off their prowess without anyone getting killed."

"A version of Galton's theory. And the elk carving?"

"That was the prize —reaching it first, touching it. Or it was the tutelary spirit for the ritual. I don't know. Perhaps a tribal elder sat on the mound, on that ledge, and held it out for the victor. And the boys feel it, feel the need to re-enact it, just as an anonymous carver tried to make the elk again. Echoes, dreams, memories. You dug out the trigger, days before the equinox, and placed fit, ambitious young men within its range. They have no choice."

She looked confused. "That seems... far-fetched, Justin."

"Emilia, I abandoned some pressing work, magazine deadlines and a degree of comfort, to stand around Abbot's Elk in the cold and watch your son and his boyfriend growing ever more agitated and angry with each other." I picked at my fingernails, wishing I knew a good manicurist out here. "Tell me your alternative theory, Professor Foxton."

"So we have to leave, that's what you're saying. As soon as possible."

"That, or see it through."

"See what through? I don't even know if they're safe to be sharing a tent after that fight. And—even if I credit your idea—what about any others round here?"

"We only need a symbolic act. Let Adam and Malcolm run. Let them run the cursus, at the right time and touch the elk. It's a ritual of green youths becoming men, not a bloodbath. I hope."

"And how did you come to this conclusion." She threw her half-smoked roll-up away.

I was going to cling to my dreams, as always, so I kept that part quiet. "Because I was a young man, once. And you were not. I don't claim to know anything about female mysteries, after all, so grant me this humble corner of the past."

She blew out her cheeks, stood up, paced. Her eyes were on the length of the Greenway, and I imagined that her mind was on that far mound.

"It starts in the dark, by torchlight," I said. "They must reach the mound with the dawn, and you must let the victor touch the elk."

"I can't..."

"Emmy, think about it. If nothing else, they'll run off some of this bloody aggression. Or would you like to wait and see if one of them has a steak knife to hand next time they argue?"

She pursed her lips. "You believe this, Justin Margrave? Honestly?"

I wanted to tell her that Matron had convinced me, but I don't think it would have helped.

"Yes."

"Then let's talk to Adam and Malcolm."

We drove to the campsite, and found the boys ten yards apart, staring at each other with what was now close to pure hostility. Emilia waited in the 2CV; I was her trusted envoy. Mostly trusted, anyway.

I got them to listen to my proposition not by any physical effort, but by going to both in turn and whispering a few words.

Oyn hner upyr.

Nonsense to me; ancient and important to them—I hoped. And it worked. They came willingly, hardly seeing each other. I stood on the western edge of the cursus; they sat cross-legged at my feet. All I had to do was to sound suitably wise and ritualistic.

"I know the last weeks have been disturbing. I know why, and I know what the elk requires."

"How can you?" Adam shifted, made to get up; I gave a sharp chop of my hand, bidding him stay where he was. It was like treading the boards in repertory; he sat down again as if it were scripted.

"An hour before dawn, where the Greenway begins," I said. Stern voice; Matron-no-nonsense voice. "The two of you will run the old track, for the same honour as was always given."

I held out the elk figurine, and Adam's eyes widened; Malcolm shivered. I could feel the urge in both of them to reach for it, grasp it. Thank the gods I was not a young man any more.

"Tonight you are kin and kin of kin, and peace will lie on you." That sounded a bit Biblical, but I must have caught the right tone, for angry and mistrustful faces smoothed. "We'd better have a few at the *Grey Horse* tonight, in preparation," I added more prosaically. "I'm buying."

That was an evening; Emilia nervous, fiddling with her tobacco, the boys shifting between commonplace talk and awkward glances. I told the landlord to put everything on my slate, and promised him I'd send a friend of mine along, a reviewer with a hearty appetite, to give the inn a decent write-up.

We talked of college, and anything archaeological that wasn't too far back—Greek, I thought, was a safe area, and Roman even better. I recounted some scurrilous tales of the art world and made a serious dent in the wine. Around ten, the boys hiked off back to their tent. They were speaking to each other again—not as they might once have done, but without evident animosity. I sensed excitement, anticipation.

"You must do it, Justin" Emilia said, when they had left.

"Do what?"

"Wait at the mound, with the elk. You're right—this is a male mystery, if it's anything, and I don't feel in touch with it."

I remembered my dreams, though I didn't want to go into detail with her. "I think the presiding part was probably a woman's role, Emmy."

"I'm delegating. You can feel what's happening—I've had too many years in academia, drying up. I'm not terribly 'visceral' any more. Besides, equal opportunities, remember?"

We argued, but she was firm. She would give me the elk figurine, drive the boys to the Greenway and start them off. Then she would return to the mound come to see the outcome.

"Will they hurt each other?" she asked as she rose to head off for her room.

"Probably. A little. Men are stupid like that, and have been since one man first saw another. Way before your Neolithic."

* * * * *

THE DARK MARCH MORNING was too dry for mist—chilly, but nothing that required an extra jacket. Emilia drove away from the tent with Adam and Malcolm, silent pillars of energy; I took out a hip flask which the landlord had given me, and sank a few mouthfuls of very strong, very hot black coffee. After that, I used a torch from the back of the 2CV to help me to the appropriate spot.

As I stood there, I felt it. I felt Jemison, and the race across the playing fields which had never taken place. A drop of cold sweat ran down the nape of my neck, and part of me saw the others, the men clad in hides lining the cursus, lighting their torches from an earthenware pot carried by children. The air rustled with movement, and smelled of burning reeds, animal fat. They were not there, and yet they were waiting. Not ghosts, but primal memories to which my over-active mind was giving a sort of form.

Where the writers in my circle would have inserted some unlikely supernatural cause of all this, I knew better. This was utterly natural, down to the wiry grass under my brogues and the soil which had known primitive mattocks, yielding as the ditches were dug, the banks raised. The cursus waited for those who would soon travel its full length again for the first time in millennia.

I took off my shoes and socks, a gesture to the land, and the vague figures gathered at the cursus were clearer, more present. Sweat and grease; stale furs...

Two yellow eyes in the distance would be the car, well away from the track. I waited, and wondered what the dealer Archie Crane or Felice at the Heystone Gallery would make of me if they were here—Margrave who once used a taxi to go from The British Museum to Praed Street, who prided himself on polished shoes and a perfectly-placed cravat pin. Yevgeny would have understood—he was Russian, and they knew the importance of the soil, and what lies within it...

Murmurs, a shifting in the onlookers. The car wasn't there for them, but the runners were. Over the rise from the Greenway, two figures brushed by the first grey light of dawn. Adam and Malcolm in shorts and T-shirts, running, jostling, swerving to the edges of the cursus and back again, always seeking an advantage. Four hundred yards away; two hundred yards. They seemed to be moving too quickly for mere men, and I saw Malcolm rise and leap, a deer's leap, as he avoided the remains of an abandoned tractor on the edge of a field. The present day was the shadow now, and I could see the entire cursus, turfed banks high and proud, narrow wooden poles set in the banks at intervals along the way.

Adam surged, lashing out with one arm as he passed Malcolm, who stumbled and was up again. I now knew that this was the way it had been done. Closer, urged on by those gathered around me, and I was a solemn silence in the middle of everything. Emilia, who had left the car and taken up position on one of the smaller mounds, was barely in this world of ours.

At fifty yards, both fell, gasping. Malcolm reached out to offer a hand, Adam pushed him away and charged towards the great mound, towards me. The other found his feet and made a late surge, legs flailing with less and less co-ordination; astonishingly, he passed Adam, broke three, four yards free of his rival—and stopped, in the middle of the trackway. Just stopped, hands on his knees, gulping in the cool air.

Voices gasped, swore, and torch smoke billowed across the two figures; Adam walking slowly forward, Malcolm motionless except for his heaving chest...

And I called out. Guttural, deep, in words which I did not know.

My hands held up the elk figurine, which felt alive, fur and muscle and sinew in my fingers, not a stained piece of discarded antler which a craftsman had worked.

I called out the heart of the elk, crashing through young trees; the deer in rut, and the wild boar grubbing the soil—no longer frozen—with its tusks. This was the Greenway, the first day of spring, and more, so much more that we had forgotten.

The boys were side by side when they reached me. History had gone, and we were alone, apart from Emilia, who started forward. I gestured that she should wait.

I don't know which of them touched the elk first. They might have done it in the very same moment, by chance or choice. But they both touched it, and when they had, they fell to their knees, exhausted.

I stretched my stiff neck, and then kissed each in turn on the forehead.

"Is it... is that..." Emilia couldn't get the words out. Her son and his boyfriend panted, eyes closed, before the mound. They were holding hands.

I passed her the figurine.

"I would bury it again if I were you," I said. "Somewhere off the beaten track around here, where only you and the boys know."

"You were right. At least, I think you were."

I frowned "I often am. Didn't you know that by now?" I say I frowned, but I am Justin Margrave, and I couldn't resist a sly smile.

"You see, Emmy? The old queen has blessed your children, and all is well again."

And there remained five bottles of Nero D'Avola waiting for me at the *Grey Horse*.

I really, really deserved a drink.

THE CHILDREN OF ANGLES AND CORNERS

Somerset, 1978

SCRAPE AND SCRAMBLE; *inside the pantry and under the damp sheets. Whisper and chitter, eyes in the angles, claws in the corners, always the dull-dark—ready, so ready.*
Close, so close...

My paternal grandmother, Eunice Margrave, lived to be ninety seven years old, a formidable relict of Victoria and a great source of both wisdom and prejudice. Curiously, she had a strong dislike of the West Country, which she never explained. I remember her refrain, often shared when that region came up in conversation:

Caught in Cornwall
Suffered in Somerset
Died in Dorset

Her views on Bristol I will spare you, as the language she used caused me to be banned from her house for a month. I should not, perhaps, have repeated it in front of my parents—not when I was only nine.

So when I found myself on business in that city of fat waistcoats and lean dole-seekers, Grandam Eunice was often on my mind. Bristol is, much like Liverpool, a place of such historical contrasts that one's head can spin—a place of slave manacles and Masonic handshakes, you might say. But it has its attractions, attractions which include a small restaurant on the edge of the St Pauls District, *Le Bon Couteau*, where cheap, wholesome French and Caribbean cuisine sit easy with each other.

My guest there, on one particular August night, was Margaret O'Leary, a St Pauls sculptor. Margaret, a thin and vociferous Irishwoman, was employing new techniques with the local Dundry stone—with some success. I rather liked her, but there was something off about her that night, a distracted note to her conversation. In the end, I gave in.

"A man, a woman; a block of stone that won't play nicely? Or, if you're having trouble with the studio rent, I could—"

"Ah, Jaysus, it's none of them usual fellers. It's a thing I was coming across, the other day. Stuck at the back of me mind, it did."

I waited for more, and if my heart rose at the very modest bill presented whilst we drank our coffee, it sank a little when she continued.

"You know of witch-bottles, do you not, Justin?"

I knew of them. They turned up on the antiquarian rounds now and then. An old practice—bottles and jugs, buried in walls or under hearths, as supposed protection against curses and sundry country annoyances. I'd never given them much thought.

"In passing," I said. "I did value some jugs once used for the purpose in Sussex, last year, as collectable items. Their bearded faces amuse me; their purpose doesn't."

Margaret squinted at me. "I'm thinking this isn't your ordinary witch-bottle. It has me itching. And then I thought to meself—wasn't Justin involved in that affair at Kemberdale...?"

I winced. It did sometimes seem that my lot was to be drawn towards unnatural events, regardless of my own preference for a nice wine bar and a catalogue of Venetian glassware. Or simply a nice Venetian.

"Margaret, I am a rapidly ageing queen, slightly too thick of girth. I really don't need to be caught up yet again in—"

"You'll not be coming with me tomorrow, then, when I go Dundry way to call on the woman who was finding one of them?"

My coffee stared at me.

Of course I would.

* * * * *

M Y IRISH TEMPTRESS—in matters strange, not in any carnal sense—drove at a speed which was suited to neither the lanes of her Cork youth or the byways of Somerset. As tractor drivers swore, and delivery vans swerved, she explained how she had been visiting several small quarries earlier in the week. And it was when she had paused at the sole tea-shop in Dundry village, that she encountered Mrs Judith Wheeler.

"You wouldn't have known her from a fighting cock," said Margaret, swerving round an alarmed bicyclist. "Calling such names, she was, demanding to know who had been at her hens and defacing her property. And while I like a bit of fire, she was in a state."

In short, Margaret ordered a pot of tea, and offered the woman a neutral and sympathetic ear. My friend half expected to get her own mouthful, but instead, the women burst into tears and began to talk...

"I told her about you on the phone this morning, and is it not better to let a cat catch its own mice?"

Which meant that she wanted me to hear Mrs Wheeler's story directly from the source.

We parked without completely destroying a stand of hollyhocks; Margaret was out of the car before I was sure it had stopped, and rapping on the cottage door.

If I had expected a termagant with rolling pin in hand, I received an awkward wave from a slight, pale-cheeked woman, and the indication that I should come in. So I levered myself from the car, and joined them.

"Justin Margrave." I bowed, and kissed her hand.

Mrs Wheeler—Judith, please—ushered us in to the parlour, and asked if we minded tea with lemon, as the milk had turned again.

"You've found what you believe to be a witch-bottle, I understand."

She glanced at Margaret. "My father did," she said, in a voice which had only a touch of Somerset in it. "Many years ago."

If that were the case, why was the thing suddenly of interest?

"Did you want it valued? If Margaret here hasn't warned you, I'm a critic and valuer—sculpture, ceramics, other fine art if I'm in the mood. Surprisingly trustworthy, they say, for one of my kind."

"Mr Margrave, I don't know what I want. I daren't keep it; daren't sell it, and daren't open it—not a third time."

A third time? Witch-bottles commonly contained all manner of things—urine, menstrual blood, iron nails, spit, hair and herbs. Whatever 'flavour' was popular in that neck of the woods. Opening them once was usually enough.

The tea, made with concentrated Jif lemon juice, was painful. I tried to smile.

"May I see the item?"

Margaret looked relieved, seeing that I had been hooked; Judith went to a rather fine Regency cupboard in the corner. A simple silver cross had been hung on the brass handles, the chain looped through both handles. She removed that, her hands stiff, and brought out a stoppered stoneware jug, which she deposited on the coffee table.

Some witch-bottles were simply that—glass bottles filled with all sorts of superstitious muck—but Bartmann jugs were a well-recorded alternative. This was at first glance typical of the late seventeenth century. Salt-glazed stoneware, with a surface like polished orange-peel, the colour muted to a pale russet. About nine inches tall, it had the usual bearded face at the neck, though there was something ominous about the mask on this one—rather than being an obvious application, the face flowed from the body of the vessel as if grown from it.

Why did it bother me? This was *like* the usual Bartmanns—but was it?

Candle-wax had recently been melted over the thick cork stopper, sealing it in place. Sitting back without touching it, I considered her nervous expression.

"The vast majority were simply used for wine, beer, or other liquids," I said. "The Rhineland potters produced them by the thousand. Why would you assume this is a witch-bottle?"

"Because there's *things* inside it, which clatter if you jiggle it. And because They want it. They... hate it."

Um. 'They' was said clearly, with a capital T. It sounded like the language of the isolated countryside, the folklorist, the aspiring Wiccan, and the somewhat deranged. Into which category did my hostess fall?

"Why do you say 'They', Judith?"

Witch-bottles were made to avert supposed curses, spells of misfortune and so forth. To stop a daughter's cramps, and relieve the sores on a plough-ox. To keep away a witch—rather obviously.

"I... it just feels like that. I hear... whispers."

She sounded entirely genuine. When some worried youth on a bleak housing estate grabs your arm and asks if you know anything about early Byzantine iconography, you stop to listen further. And when a sensible-seeming woman like Judith Wheeler offers a story like this...

Oh Margaret. Why did I linger over coffee in the restaurant; why did I stay long enough to let you drag me into this sort of thing? I shot her a rather venomous look.

"Judith, I want you to tell me the whole story. If you keep anything back, then I am Bristol-bound, and home in London by this evening, settled in my comfortable study. Do you understand?"

She nodded.

"It began with my father..."

Jethro Wheeler had a disappointing war. Asthmatic, he was refused by the Army, and of limited use on the farms. But he was first in the Local Defence Volunteers, and then the Home Guard. Dundry, Chew

Magna, Norton Malreward and many other small settlements were all on the flight path of the German raids over Bristol—and they suffered for it. Not as badly as central Bristol, but Dundry caught it a number of times, and there was always the worry of worse.

From the tower of St Michael's Church on Dundry Hill, to the flattened peak of Maes Knoll, Home Guard lookouts watched for the bombers, and for German gliders bringing paratroopers or infiltrators.

To their North, Bristol burned.

Yet the gliders did not come, and they could do nothing about the bombers; watch duty on Maes Knoll was long, and tedious. Each time he was on duty there he bicycled out, wheezing, and sat next to a small shed put up for them, watching the night sky. The other man with him usually dozed off, but Jethro didn't like to report that.

One night in 1941, after the luxury of a small piece of chocolate, Jethro went wandering around the knoll. A single German bomb had fallen nearby the previous week, probably a Heinkel getting rid of the last of its load after a run over the city, and the side of the tump, the highest point, was scarred by the explosion. Perhaps he wondered if there was a keepsake there; perhaps it was idle curiosity. Whatever the reason, he took up a spade from the shed, and poked around in the hole, his torch picking out fragments of burned and twisted metal...

Until the light reflected off something rounded, honey-brown, and intact.

The skies were clear, the Germans elsewhere. He got down on his knees, and with a piece of bomb casing he scraped away the soil until he could lift this odd object from where it must have been resting for many years. He knew Maes Knoll was old, and had hoped for something Roman, but this didn't fit the bill. A beer jug left by a Victorian farmhand?

The vessel swished and clinked. Beer didn't clink.

So he tugged at the thick cork, and slowly, very slowly, it came free...

Judith shook her head.

"I was fourteen, Mr Margrave, when he told me. He only talked about it because I'd discovered the witch-bottle in our air-raid shelter, buried under a loose plank. He was mad with me when he found out, and took it away to hide elsewhere.

"I pestered him and argued for a week, until he explained where it had come from, but he'd never say what happened when he opened it, just that he stoppered it again quick, and brought it home to keep it out of others' hands."

"Maes Knoll is..."

"An Iron Age hill-fort," said Margaret. "A few miles east of here. Nothing terribly spectacular, an elevated triangle of land with a mound one the top at one end, the 'tump'. They say it's the near end of Wansdyke—you know, the one which stretches from Wiltshire to here."

I knew Wansdyke vaguely, though not that it came so far west. An Anglo-Saxon boundary earthwork, broken in places. Later than Maes Knoll, which must have fallen out of use well before the dyke was dug.

"When my dad went into a care home, end of last month, I found the jug again. It was buried with a load of scrap metal under the old chicken run. I was digging, thinking I might use the run for potatoes, and there it was, cork and all. Well, I put it in the backroom, thinking I might get someone to look at it—one of them museum blokes.

"Then early last week, I decided to tidy the jug up, get the soil off. I swear I'd hardly touched it when the brush seemed to twist in my hand, like, and clean knocked the cork out..."

She shuddered.

"Did I get a fright? The smell, for one, like my Nan when she was in her last days, all bedpans and suchlike. And a touch of winter, though it was July. I even thought I heard voices, as if they came from far off, but now I don't know. Fair made me shiver, and I pushed that stopper right back in. Since then, nothing's been right. The house feels off; milk turns, the hens won't lay, and someone's been outside, scraping along the walls—like with a knife, scoring the plaster.

"At first I put it down to Bill Roughton's kids—bad'uns, the lot— and that was when I met Margaret here, and she asked me what was bothering me. The jug came to my tongue, and I told her of it, right out." She looked directly at me. "Margaret said you might be able to help. Are you a man who knows about... these things?"

I stood, and went to stare out of the window. A chicken pecked at the sparse grass in the front garden; a cat on a large log watched me watching the chicken.

"I really am an art critic. But I've come across some strange things in my time..."

"Ah now, these are the Summerlands, full of mysteries," said Margaret.

"Pshaw, as the writers used to say. Don't smear this with faux-Celtic nonsense—you'll be lecturing me on King Arthur, Avalon, and Tír na nÓg next."

The sculptor reddened. "Justin—"

"Mythology doesn't bother me, Margaret. It's what lies behind the myths I don't like. There are truths that don't tend to suit us."

I went and picked up the Bartmann jug. Moving it around, you could certainly hear the swish of liquid and the muted clatter of harder objects, loose inside. And there was that broad, crude face. When I looked more closely, it was clear that it had only one eye. There was no obvious damage—it had been made that way, which was certainly not usual for its kind.

"You could have it, if you like, Mr Margrave," said Judith.

I did not like, yet I was caught, unable yet to leave this mystery—if such it was—to its own devices.

"Might I borrow it until tomorrow? There are people I can speak to. I'm staying at the Royal."

She assented gladly; I took the witch-bottle, told her not to worry, and that I'd find out what I could. She seemed a little easier when we left. As we did so, I glanced at the limewashed plaster outside.

The scratches around the front door were deep, and to my untrained eye, they looked like claw marks.

Soon Margaret and I were back in Bristol.

"I'm going over the water to see me da in Kinsale for a few days," she said as she deposited me outside the Royal. "Will I leave you to it, then?"

I assured her that I would ferret up anything of use, and keep Mrs Wheeler informed.

"Good fortune, then, Justin." And she sped away, choking every pedestrian in the area with exhaust fumes.

In my room, I placed the jug on the writing desk, and stared at it. The Bartmann style had been copied at a number of English potteries from the late 1600s on, though I'd only seen examples from Derby and Staffordshire myself. Some clays worked better than others; there would be variations in the tone of the salt glaze, and in the devices on them—this jug had nothing but the wild, bearded, one-eyed face.

The theory behind filling a bottle full of your urine or whatever was, as far as I could remember, fairly simple. Either the contents lured in the offending witch and trapped her 'power' there, or they acted as a general charm, stopping the witch from having any influence over a particular person. Why such a bizarre act would work, I couldn't imagine.

I made a few calls to a ceramicist friend, an antiquarian in Bath and so on, but came away from them little wiser—except for the phone number of a contact who might be of use, and from another person, a thought about my one-eyed friend.

"End of Wansdyke, eh?" said Archie Crane, a London 'dealer' who, whilst being very irritating, was also reasonably experienced. "Obvious connection, old boy."

"Which is?"

"Odin, Woden. Wansdyke is Woden's Dyke. You know, the chap who gave his eye for knowledge, hung on a tree and so on?"

A witch-bottle made to invoke Odin, or warn him off? That was a new one on me. So I drank half a bottle of something which might once have visited Burgundy briefly, and fell asleep.

Tumble and scurry; scritch at the doors, and scratch at the keys. Chitter and whisper, down past-ways and thin-ways, peer through your dead hopes and out of the half-world, into the night-place, free of the day.

Hungry. Hungry for child-fat and sorrows; parched for the rattle of life in its leaving.

They are almost here, and They must play...

Margaret rang me at the Royal, the next morning.

"I'm off up to the ferry, but that witch-bottle, now—I was saying it was trouble, wasn't I? Well, there's the Divil abroad, and bad fortune laid on many a hearth round here. It's in the local papers, when you're looking for it. Sure, I haven't the Sight, but Mother of Mary..."

"Coincidence. The more you read these rags, the worse life seems."

"Ah, I don't know, Justin, I don't know."

When she rang off, I looked at my notes. With some reluctance, I picked up the telephone again and arranged to meet the local contact who'd been recommended to me. After which I went—with equal reluctance—to hire a car.

Beth Trethick was a short, round woman, maybe thirty years old, with tangled black hair and heavy eyebrows above hazel eyes. In corduroy trousers and a worn khaki army jacket, she was waiting on the roadside by Maes Knoll—waiting for me to rattle up in my car.

"Good of you to come," I said. I knew she was from Trowbridge, the other side of Bath.

"Choice is as choice does," she said, which told me nothing.

We strolled towards the knoll. Margaret was right—the knoll was scenic, but not spectacular. It rose from surrounding ditches like an enormous misshapen burial mound, most of its flat top about fifty feet above us and the 'tump' another twenty or so feet higher, one small mound on the back of its mother.

"Might I ask why you did come? Are witch bottles an area of yours?"

I had given her the gist of the matter on the phone.

"I've never seen one. But the rest, what's in the air... it feels wrong. The land here isn't happy. And then I got your call."

The climb was steeper than I'd expected; when we reached the base of the tump, I abandoned any shame and sat down on the grass, breathing heavily. To the north, the sprawl of Bristol lay in hazy sunshine.

"I don't suppose you feel like explaining what's going on to an innocent soul like myself?"

Thick eyebrows arched. "An 'innocent soul', Mr Margrave?"

"A figure of speech."

"You mean a lie." But there was a faint smile there as well.

"Art is a lie that makes us realize truth, at least the truth that is given us to understand." I returned her smile. "Picasso said that, a few years before I was born. But in Spanish."

She joined me on the grass.

"It's not a witch-bottle. Or, it is a witch-bottle, in its way. But it wasn't made to keep away the muttered curses of some mean beldam or local busy-body. It's a warding against something worse. I wasn't sure what, until we met today."

"I haven't shown the jug to you yet." I had returned it to Judith Wheeler before driving out to Maes Knoll.

"The wind is wrong. I felt it as soon as I came near Dundry. They've been playing, in their fashion, waiting for the moment. One of you will weaken, or be clumsy. You'll show the jug to a colleague, who—too curious—will open it before you can speak. You'll turn it on its side, and the wax will crack; Judith Wheeler will go to bury it once more, and trip, drop it. They'll be gathering to make that moment, now the jug can be felt. It's how They work."

We were back in the land of Capital Letters.

"I wish someone would tell me who 'They' are."

She didn't answer.

A bird sang; a tractor crawled past the car on the road below.

Few people would call me an impatient man, but at times, I grow tired of those who act as if they have mysteries hidden behind their ears. And I remembered a time, in Abbot's Elk, when I had used words I did not know, standing barefoot in the blush of a Spring dawn...

"I have caused the Greenway to be run; I know the mask which are not masks," I said, perhaps a little theatrically. I would have suited the stage, I think.

Which got those eyebrows working.

"I wasn't told you had the Cunning," she said, her voice softer.

"I haven't." I held up my hands—look, nothing up the sleeves. "But let's say I've blundered into this sort of thing before. Not quite *this*, obviously."

"Okay. I don't know exactly what we have here, but I can smell the Children of Angles and Corners on you. Do you know of Them?"

I shook my head.

"It's hard to explain, unless you've been taught, shown. 'They' are something dark, ancient, known from the first days that people ever strode these hills and valleys. They foster still-births and dying cattle; ruin lives and weaken bridges; They delight in our misery, suckle on our failures."

"Actual creatures? Monsters?" I didn't know quite how much of this to swallow.

"If you like, but trust me, definitions won't help you get your head around Them. How does a tuna describe a shark? They live—exist—askew from our lives, until They find a way through. Older than monsters, we say of them."

"So this isn't about tricksters like pixies, or brownies, those sort of folk?"

I watched her face twist between derision and sheer horror at my ignorance.

"No," she settled for, very clipped.

"And the jug, the witch-bottle?"

"The Children are vengeful, mercurial. They know the Old Ways, and they like the weak spots of the land, so places rich with myth suit them. Like this area. That's where Their name comes from—Their crooked pathways, Their ways into the World. So, what age would you say this jug is?"

"It's typical of the sixteen eighties, sixteen nineties. Severn Valley clay, I'd say. Probably made as a single item, not one of a batch. It may be unique. There's no record of another 'Woden' jug that I can find. A ceramics expert might—especially if the jug was chipped—be able to look at the material used, and give it a more exact place of origin."

Beth thought a moment.

"You want my best guess?"

"It would be better than mine."

"Then I'd say that someone, centuries ago, was troubled by Them, and had the jug made for a single purpose—to keep the Children far away," She gestured to the tump. "They chose to put it in a beacon place, an ancient place. Look at the view Maes Knoll commands. There must have been a lot of worrying things going on at the time, to try such a thing."

Her comment woke a few brain cells.

"War?"

She frowned. "They love any form of strife. It draws them. 'War brings the woe-mongers', as we say. Why?"

"Well, look—there was the Monmouth Rebellion ravaging Somerset in 1685. The jug could easily have been fired around that time." I knew my history, at least. "Chaos and uprising, ending in bloody battle at Sedgemoor—and a fair number of hangings." I warmed to my theme. "And then, when it was exposed, another war. 1941."

"Buried in one war; unearthed in another. That would suit Them. And the charm must be so much weaker than once it was. Did a bomb fall on Maes Knoll, exactly where the jug was hidden, just by accident? I wonder who might have brushed a harassed German bombardier's mind, over thirty years ago?"

I got to my feet.

"What does Judith Wheeler do, then? Break it apart, bury it once more? Or let me sent it to some dusty museum far away, and let it be forgotten?"

"That's a hard one. They have the scent of you now, and of the Wheeler woman. Who else has seen it, been near it?

"My friend Margaret. She's left for Ireland. Oh, and Judith's father. The chap who found and opened it."

"Their contact with him would be Their first touch in this part of the country for many years. Their first whisper of opportunity. I say that, but don't think of Them as people, with the same basic thoughts and motivations. The Children are as 'wrong' and unlike us as anything you will ever meet. They'll peel the fat from under babies' skins, drown family pets, and drive people to suicide—simply for idle amusement."

The cynic in me wondered at that. I'd known people who... well, never mind.

She might have heard my thoughts.

"It doesn't stop at single incidents, Mr Margrave. It doesn't stop until They're sated, if They come in numbers. You've heard of those deserted Medieval villages that the archaeologists find from time to time?"

"Emptied by the Plague and the Clearances, yes."

"Not all of them. Some were ruined and emptied by another evil."

Was that possible?

I was quiet the rest of the way down.

Somehow my new acquaintance had found a bus to get her near Maes Knoll—a magickal act in itself, given rural services—and so she had no transport. I said I'd drive her to Judith Wheeler's house, to see the Woden jug 'in the flesh'.

If I puzzle you, I should admit that I already had a rudimentary acquaintance with Beth Trethick's kind of knowledge. She and her ilk were said to be the people of small magicks and the old ways—the Cunning, basically, which only means 'knowing'. In storybooks, the wise ones, the hedge-wizards, and counsellors. The ones you went to when you really believed that a witch was out to get you, or that some malign influence possessed your life.

Almost every village in these Isles would have had one once, though he or she may have been called a herbalist or a healer. Everything I knew suggested that they were the real version of people who sold crystals from over-priced shops at Glastonbury, and put on Marks and Spencer robes to cavort in the woods. And poor, harassed Justin, when he wasn't try to decipher a dusty wine label, or admiring a Hepworth in the galleries, believed in calling on whatever might be useful when times grew hard.

For I had picked up those 'rags', as per my conversation with Margaret earlier in the day, and I was no longer so sure about the state of things. I had even been in brief contact with a newspaper editor I knew. The reports were true. If you could lay misfortune like a blanket across a stretch of countryside... house fires in Winford, with no apparent cause; tuberculosis from nowhere around the Nortons, in cattle and men; a rush of tranquilliser prescriptions in Dundry, and a sudden spate of fights, illnesses, paediatric emergencies, in half a dozen other villages.

All reported since a woman near Dundry dug up the Woden jug.

Judith Wheeler was not well.

We found her pale, shaken, lying on the sofa in the parlour, with her arm in a sling. The front door had been open, a woman in a District Nurse's uniform nurse just leaving.

"I was lucky," said Judith. "Mrs Granger, the nurse, was cycling past. She heard me cry out."

Judith had been cleaning the Welsh dresser in the kitchen when she heard faint voices at the back of the house. As she turned on her steps, the dresser, well settled in its place, made a cracking noise, tipped forward and caught her shoulder. It almost fell right on top of her.

Beth gave me a Look.

"My best china's broken." Judith shifted uncomfortable, favouring her arm.

"Better than your neck," I said.

I went into the kitchen, and the dresser lay there, the upper portion almost split in two. Oak needed help to break like that. When I reported this to Beth, her cheek twitched, a tic below her left eye.

"Where is the jug?" Snapped out at Judith.

"The... the witch-bottle? Under the stairs. You can go and see if you—"

Beth dragged it out and set it down in the hallway, examining it out of Judith's sight. Which didn't take long.

"I don't think there's any doubt. Mr Margrave, I need to protect this place; you need to find out what happened that night in 1941."

"Is this about my dad?" asked the injured woman when we rejoined her. I felt a bit sorry for her, and tried to form a reassuring smile.

"I need a little more information, Judith, that's all. Do you have the address of the care home?"

She pointed to the cupboard, where I found an address book. D for Dad. The place was almost in Bristol, and on this side of the city.

"Is he, um..."

"He gets confused. But he has his good days. If you're going, tell him I'll be over on Friday, all being well—don't mention this silly fall."

"Ms Trethick will look after you." I hesitated. "You can rely on her."

Cars these days have too many gears, and the one I'd hired had less of them by the time I reached the Elmtree Nursing Home. It was as if the damn thing were fighting me all the way, and I wished I'd had time to hire a driver as well.

Elmtree was a large Victorian villa, converted into a facility which was hard to negotiate. Former servants' stairs and corridors confused my hurried brain, but a cleaner guided me to Jethro Wheeler's room. He looked a lot like his daughter.

"Mr Wheeler, hello. I'm Justin, one of Judith's friends."

He peered at me from his chair, watery eyes only half-focussed.

"Judith's not here."

"I know. She sent me to have a chat with you." Close enough to the truth. "About the war."

"You a reporter?"

"Yes," I descended into bald-faced lies. "We're doing a series..."

Jethro Wheeler had a bent frame—he must have been in his eighties—but a strong voice. I teased him into the open with a few remarks about the air-raids, and he was soon spouting easily. Like many of us as we age, past excursions were clearer than recent weeks, and he had no problem giving chapter and verse as to that night on Maes Knoll—up to a certain point.

"You opened the jug," I said. I said it twice, because he had gone silent.

"You ever had rats, Mr Margrave?" came the eventual response. He spoke with a Somerset burr, with 's' almost a 'z'.

"As pets?"

"In your house, under it, round it. That was the way of it. Like having rats in your head. And small, thin voices... Cork in one hand, jug in the other, and the smell of it, like all the piss and droppings ever made by all the rats there ever were..."

He jerked in his chair, as if surprised at what he'd been saying.

"You a reporter?"

"I'm Judith's friend, remember?"

"I still hears Them, smells Them... like rats, you know?"

I thought of folk songs, of deals made with shadows; the beat of the bodhrán and a warning refrain...

"Did They offer anything, ask you to do anything?"

"Can't say They did." He narrowed his eyes. "But I could feel them, prying, looking to find a way into me. I corked it damn fast, and buried it where They couldn't go—and I have ways."

He fumbled under his blanket, and brought out a large, crude iron nail, four or five inches long.

"I'll prick Them, if They come," he said, his loose dentures grinning.

And that was all I could get from him.

Back at the Royal, I showered and went down to the front desk to add a day or two on to my stay. There was a message for me, from Gareth, one of Margaret's Bristol friends:

Accident at Holyhead before the ferry left for Ireland. Margaret in Valley Hospital. No need to call—doctors say minor stroke, or seizure. Recovering well, sends her love.

Judith, and now Margaret. I did not think that Beth Trethick would call these accidents.

Insane though it might seem, I was beginning to believe in the Children of Angles and Corners.

The scrape and the scratch of it, claws on the door-step, eyes in the angles and paws in the dark; mutter and murmur, gape at the green-rings, push through the moss-banks where hate cuts the air. The oh-so-sweet honey of death-beds and fever cots, sharp from the sorrow-bound, weak and resentful. And the warding at large, torn from its high seat, borne from its safeness, back in the hands of the stupid and small...

Coming, coming...

"He buried in the air raid shelter," I said to the Cunning-woman. "And I've had a look at what's left of it, in the back garden. Corrugated iron. And there was scrap iron in the second hiding place."

Beth nodded. "Iron has power. Enough to bother Them. Then his daughter moved it, and They came back. They want to be here, amongst us."

"Why?"

"To foster anything that hurts, and worries, and divides. It's what They feed on. Misery and distress. Any other harm They cause it for pleasure. Your friend Margaret—what happened to her was for fun, simply because They had touched her, even briefly. If allowed, They'll be a scourge on all the lands around here, until They're sated." She gave me a sharp look. "And don't be fooled by small starts, Mr Margrave. There will be deaths."

I didn't have much choice but to believe her.

"Have you a plan?"

Judith was asleep in her bedroom upstairs, and we could speak freely. I'd reassured her that her father was fine, and safe. He was certainly a lot less worried than I was.

Beth paced the parlour, her boots leaving smears of soil on the carpet.

"I'm an accounts clerk for Woolworth's, Mr Margrave. I like puppies, and a few beers. The Cunning comes from family blood and history; some of the time, it makes me more scared than complete ignorance would. I'd rather this were someone else's problem. And it's eating into my sick-leave. My boyfriend's not too pleased, either."

"You sound almost human."

We grinned at each other, and she sat down. Her dark brows came together.

"But as for plans... Are you strong, Mr Margrave?" she asked.

"I wouldn't be the first person to turn to if you wanted furniture moving. That Welsh dresser–"

"No, no. I was thinking about will, and stubbornness. Such people deal better with the Children. The uncommitted and indecisive tend to fall by the wayside. Because I have an idea, but we would need someone strong at the heart of it."

That didn't sound promising. "Go on."

"The best we might do is to renew the ward, the single purpose of the jug—which means someone must be the bond-maker, the key. Better than starting from scratch. But Judith's too vulnerable and confused. Besides, Woden is a male figure. It pays to stick as closely to the original making as possible..."

"And dear old Justin is to hand."

"It's you or her father, really. Men who know of the jug."

It was tempting to volunteer the old chap from the care home, but the sad ghost of my conscience must have been hovering nearby.

I agreed to do it.

I always kept a travelling bag with me, and so I stayed at the house, along with Beth. There were fresh claw marks on the outside plaster,; a chicken had been gutted, messily, on the edge of the lawn, and the rest of the hens had fled, as had the cat. Hardly surprising.

When we weren't talking, we could hear Them—voices slightly too far away, nasty voices. Not words, more an insidious feeling of threat and malice which ran along your nerves and swirled inside the caverns of your brain.

Like radio waves from a foreign country, whispered in a foreign tongue.

"They're calling out from the Half-World. They would sound much louder, be more of a threat, if I hadn't raised my own wards around the house."

Beth was on the sofa; I was propped in an armchair, surround by cushions.

"Such as?" I was curious.

"Such as a Cunning-woman might know. I'll share trade secrets some other time, Mr Margrave." She paused. "Do you ever think about your name?"

"Justin?"

"Margrave. A walker on, a protector of, the borders. Lord of the Marches—Mark-graf. And here we are talking about touching the Half-World, a true borderland."

I sighed. "I'd rather not go there, to be frank. It interferes with my digestion. But speaking of names, why Woden—does that have some significance? Are the Cunning Folk pagans?"

"We're pretty much anything we want to be. Atheists, even—as long as we touch the land, and remember the Old Ways." She scratched her armpit, and thought a moment. "I imagine our predecessor, whoever he or she was, chose to have Woden on their jug because the Children would recognise the name, and its resonance. These were Anglo Saxon lands once. And with Woden's Dyke being here, yes, it must have seemed particularly appropriate."

"Reasonable enough." My back hurt. I wasn't built for sleeping in chairs. "So where do we do this? And when?"

"It will have to be on Maes Knoll. And as tomorrow is Wednesday..."

"Yes?"

"Wodensday, Mr Margrave. Might as well draw on what we can get." She was tired, as was I.

I had one last question, prompted by the sight of that eviscerated chicken. There might be dogs, or foxes, or some such animal around, but...

"How dangerous are these creatures, physically?"

By asking that question, I saw that I had fully and finally bought into Beth Trethick's interpretation of events. Oh dear, oh dear...

"The Children?" She pulled a blanket over her and stretched out. "Who knows? I've never faced Them. But I hope that Woolworths will miss me if it all goes wrong."

A reassuring note on which to go to sleep.

Wriggle and writhe, the Half-World is opening; hungry, so hungry...

We did not tell Judith Wheeler what we were going to do. In the morning I helped put the dresser back up, and as I cleared away broken dinner plates, I went on about the ways wood could warp in the heat and damp of a kitchen. And I said that, although I gave no credence to talk of it bringing misfortune, I would take the jug away that night. Just to settle her mind.

When she said she might walk up to the village, Beth and I encouraged her. Fresh air, a little exercise. In her absence, we made our preparations. Or Beth did, and I listened.

"No iron on you. We want Them to focus solely on you and the jug, whilst I do what I can to keep you standing. No crosses, religious symbols, anything which might bother Them. No talismans, amulets, or similar paraphernalia."

"Do I look like a man of paraphernalia? Unless They object to hand-made Italian shoes and a rather nice Art Deco silver tie-pin."

"Lose the tie-pin, Mr Margrave. Just in case."

I checked all my pockets, removing keys, loose change and one of the iron nails I'd purchased in Bristol.

"I am ritually naked," I announced.

She looked out of the parlour window.

"Dimpsey soon."

"I'm sorry?"

"Dimpsey. What we say in Somerset—that time when dusk is almost upon us."

Judith returned not long after, and the three of us had a light tea together. Gammon ham and fresh bread. I talked about some harmless art finds from my past, adding a few poor jokes, trying to keep Judith at her ease.

When she was up in her room for an early night—she was still a little shaken from her fall, I think—Beth and I took the jug out to the hire car.

"I would have liked to have the rooks with us," she murmured, "But this has to be done at night, which is not their time."

I could feel the jug now, like a leaden weight in my hands, and with 'dimpsey' came the voices once more. In some ways, it was more annoying that they were too low and distant to make out—you kept trying, straining, to catch something intelligible. Rat-scratches on the air.

The Children were under the floorboards of our world.

We had a fifteen, twenty minute drive to the east—not the crow's distance, but further because we had to curve round by the small village of Norton Malreward. The radio in the hired car crackled a lot.

"And in local news, a number of sheep have been found dead on pasture land near Dundry South Quarry. Police say that the bodies bear some signs of a dog attack, but are not ruling out human agency..."

"Not animals, nor human agency," said Beth, turning the radio off. "They are growing confident."

Near Norton Malreward we parked and walked west, up through the farmland to reach Maes Knoll. We both had decent flash-lights. What else Beth had in her backpack, I couldn't guess.

A full moon pierced the country darkness, showing the way but setting more shadows than felt comfortable.

"So, is the moon a friend of ours?" I picked my way across a boggy ditch; I'd never worn a pair of hiking boots in my life, but was beginning to consider their value more seriously.

"It's the moon," said Beth from ahead of me. "It can be used, for good or ill."

At last we were on solid grassland, the slope up the side of the knoll.

Maes Knoll looked larger, more important now. Were the wights of Iron Age warriors watching our approach, wondering why we dared their fort? Or was it rabbits? More comforting to think of rabbits crouching under the bushes, simply annoyed to have their suppers disturbed.

As we reached the main heights of the knoll, there was a chill wind, where there had been none before. Around us, Somerset slumbered, a patchwork of fields, woods and villages; to our North, Bristol was on fire with street-lights and motorway lights, shop neons and hotel displays. I thought of Jethro Wheeler standing where I stood, a war around him.

And I could hear Them clearly at last.

Out from the gore-grass, up from the mire; tumbling, laughing, with mouths agape. Flesh to tear, bellies to rend—out from the corners, through every angle; here for the blubber-man, his soft flesh waiting. We are coming, coming...

"Try to hold on until the right moment." called out Beth, her tangled black mane loose in the breeze.

The right moment. The Children had to be there, in our world, when I renewed the witch-bottle, for it to work, Beth said that I needed to know what I was binding, that this was no time for vague moves. As I stepped away from her, making myself alone and obvious, I felt Their presence on the other side of a wall of icy air—and They felt me, reaching out from the Half-World to enter my thoughts.

Where They found something They could use, and unlike Jethro, I couldn't just slam the cork straight back in, seal the Woden jar.

Waiting, waiting...

They tugged at my past, at the Margraves who had been, the ones who were weak and lonely. They brought back all the small hatreds I'd encountered, week after week, month after month, whilst growing up; the weaknesses in me and the blows I'd taken. Half-forgotten but never forgiven, from shameful gym sessions and showers after rugby; late nights in unlit alleys, the sound of those who scorned me. Fat Margrave—queer boy, shirt-lifter, loser...

'You touched him, I saw you, your hand on his arse.'
'A kicking will teach you.'
'Kiss her, you bum-boy. She wants you, she wants you.'

A callous stranger, a kindly desk sergeant...

'Get along home, son. And steer clear of them woods, there's some bad'uns up there.'

My parents, stiff, distant, always muttering in the other room, always sighing as they spoke of me to 'decent' people. The voices we collect, and cannot un-hear. And now these other Children, finding me ripe, undefended. I was weeping, shivering in the cold, half-propped against the side of the tump—but to my own surprise, I was also angry.

How dare They?

I think I snarled, or as good as did so, and I held the Woden jug up in my left hand—*left-hander, sinister, hello sweet-heart*. With my right hand, though my fingers didn't want to obey me, I twisted the cork, snapping the wax, and I pulled.

Ahhh, opening, opening...

They were there.

And They were beautiful. Beth Trethick had lied to me.

Out on the razor-edged winds, out of the Half-World, with the border no longer guarded. Tall, slim figures, wreathed in gossamer, princes of air and darkness—I could not count them, or turn from the light of their long, slender limbs and Their perfect faces.

The Children of Angles and Corners, with eyes of moonlight.

I knew I should shatter the jug forever, and let Them play here, on Maes Knoll and Dundry Hill, in the gentle meadows and broad fields; Their places, barred to Them by envious lesser souls. The Cunning was no more than sly obstruction and control, and the Cunning-woman, only a few paces away, was a small, mean creature...

In that moment, an accident of the breeze brought a stench to my nostrils, the rotting, rat-piss stench from the jug, and with that came another memory—Bainley, proud prefect and school golden boy, as he forced my head down over the urine-slick toilet bowl, as he fumbled all the while with my zip and trouser belt. Bainley, who was as beautiful as the Children—but only on the outside.

"Justin!"

But I didn't need Beth to spur me on. I thought of 'Bonny' Cheyvis, and the razor he took to his wrists after one of his failed affairs; my dear friend Helene, her sculptures unfinished, a shovel-load of barbiturates in her half-finished Bacardi and coke. Of those who had lost entire careers over one ill-chosen night of love, one newspaper photograph, and how I had survived, even prospered.

Of how difficult it was to be human—which these creatures were not.

"Look at Them, Justin." Beth was on her knees, Their pretty fingers tearing at her clothes, her hair, her skin. Blood ran from one corner of her mouth as she wove steel wire between her fingers, pattern after pattern, the iron-tinged glamours that were helping me stand firm. "LOOK AT THEM!"

All glamour fled; illusion fell.

When people talk of something being indescribable, they do not usually mean it. They mean that some basic verbal skill had temporarily failed them. I could describe the Children, but I choose not to.

You must settle for whatever terrible memories you yourselves have—malice and anger distorting a woman's face, a man's cheap, bullying rage; the warped pleasure of a damaged child as it hurts anything, anyone, it can grasp—and the slobbering greed of those who already have too much.

These things are only part of the Children of Angles and Corners, wrapped in stick-limbs and claws, outlined by harsh, triangular gashes in the night which might or might not be their cruel mouths.

Beth, of course, had not lied.

They bore down on me, trying to stay my right hand and claw the jug from me; They drove me back against the tump, but I had seen Them now. I had judged what They were.

I thrust out the jug, not trying to shield it.

The Woden jug, on Woden's Day.

"Third, High, and Just-as-High." A memory of eddas and verse I had read over the years. "He knew you, hung on a tree to be sure of what you were."

On the Bartmann jug, surely crafted for only a single purpose, the one-eyed face was alive in the moonlight—or it suited me to believe that.

The salt-glaze writhed; I bit down on the inside of my cheek until the blood came—a somewhat more difficult and painful act than I had anticipated. The Children shrieked and swirled, and a crooked claw lashed at my face, connected, but I was too busy to pay attention.

I spat blood into the open neck of the jug.

"Margrave!" I yelled into the storm of Them. "Border-Lord. So do fuck off, the lot of you!"

My right hand arced and drove the cork back into the jug with all my strength.

Time is malleable, ductile, whatever you want to call it. That moment twisted and lasted, one half-second stretched so long and thin...

A man and a woman, both bloodied, stood alone on Maes Knoll, on a warm August night. There was ice in Beth's hair.

"Are They...?" I said, putting the jug down on the grass.

"Yes." She had lacerations across her face and the backs of her hands. The steel wire formed some sort of cat's cradle between them. Its purpose, she'd said, was to give me purpose, stop me from being wholly dragged into Their illusion. It seemed to have worked.

"I feel like—"

Four figures coming up the slope, tall, dark.

"More trouble," I moaned.

"No." She managed a hoarse laugh. "The Cunning Folk of the Southwest, come to finish things. They were ready in case we failed."

"Only four of them?"

"That's about all we have between here and Salisbury. We're not what we were, Mr Margrave."

A woman who must surely have been in her nineties; a teenage girl, and two very ordinary looking men. Even the old woman would top Beth Trethick by eight or nine inches. They had spades over their shoulders.

"They'll bury the jug deep under the turf, and place Words in the soil of Maes Knoll, that no one digs here by accident or purpose. Magpie and mole will keep watch for us, so we're not caught unawares again."

Beth ushered me down the mound, back to the car.

"They know what to do—they don't need us."

"The accidents, the illnesses..."

"Will stop. And everyone will forget them, given a week or two."

"It isn't only here, though, is it?"

"Some other day, some other place, anywhere where the night is thin, They will try to enter again. But we've done what we can for today. Don't bring me down, Justin."

It seems I had been permanently promoted from being merely Mr Margrave.

At Judith Wheeler's house, we let ourselves in with the spare key, splashed our cuts with antiseptic, and fell asleep in our parlour-bedroom. The armchair was far more comfortable this time.

* * * * *

IDIDN'T TELL MARGARET the truth. Partly because she didn't need to know, and partly because she was a gossip—as am I—and giving her the full story, whether she believed it or not, would cement me into a role I didn't want.

'How was Dundry, then?' they would ask in the galleries and dining rooms, and smirk, or lean forward, eager. There were enough stories about me in circulation already.

We dined at *Le Bon Couteau* towards the end of August, and I listened, sipping a decent Bordeaux, as she told me that the doctors could find nothing wrong with her.

"Over-work," I said.

"What happened about that witch-bottle thing?"

"Oh, some people who knows their stuff better than I do took it off Judith's hands."

"But all them goings-on around Dundry—"

"Sometimes a fish is just a fish, Margaret. Maybe someone upset a black cat, or broke a mirror. Anyway, I gather it's quiet in those parts now."

She looked disappointed, and made up for it by ordering a huge plateful of profiteroles, dripping with a dark chocolate sauce. I would have joined her, but my waistline had suffered enough from another few days of West Country cuisine. The dessert waiter was a tall, rather striking man in his thirties, very attentive, and I might have given him my card, except for one thing—there was a tattoo just visible beneath his rolled-up shirt sleeve.

It depicted a broad, bearded face, with only one eye...

STILL SHE STARES

FOUR

"THE CHILDREN OF ANGLES AND CORNERS." Marcus shakes his head. "I don't... look, I'm sorry, but I find that one hard to believe."

"That must be a comfort, my dear." Margrave fingers the silver ankh at his neck. Today's cravat is bottle-green, loose above his usual linen jacket. "Disbelief has its place, but sometimes it's no more than a luxury, one which not all of us can afford."

Stefan pours more wine. "I don't have a problem with the weird stuff—my grandma came from Poland, and she blamed Baba Yaga for everything that went wrong, even her faulty toaster."

Margrave doesn't smile. "I try to avoid that sort of extreme, but the Children... too dark a thing to be mocked, too different. Wait a minute..." He reaches deep into a trouser pocket. "I don't care for silly amulets and trinkets, but this has never left my side in the last few years."

He holds up a long, thick iron nail, square-sided and old.

"A gift from those who know."

Losing the battle again, Marcus glances at Stefan. At thirty seven years old, his partner remains an eager puppy-dog, wanting more. And it's only nine in the evening.

"There's time for another... reminiscence," says Stefan.

Their guest—their friend?—doesn't respond immediately. For the first time in their presence, he appears uncomfortable.

"You're too tired, maybe, Mr Margrave?" Marcus tries not to sound hopeful. "I could ring for a cab."

"No, not tired, Marcus. Cautious. This next tale is not entirely mine to tell, nor can I give it my usual voice. I was involved as it unfolded, but I was not there at the conclusion. If it has a conclusion." He looks down at his wine, as if forgetting for a moment why he holds it. "Not everything ends, you see."

"Please go on, sir." Marcus has cornered himself. *Margrave—a walker on, a protector of, the borders.* That's what the Trethick woman said of the old man.

Marcus Evenche doesn't especially want to walk the borders.

He doesn't really want to know that there *are* such places.

"I believe," Margrave begins, "That I would like to get this one off my chest. I have never recounted the full story to anyone else, and perhaps now that I know you both a little better, this is the time..."

WHERE THE THIN MEN DIE

New York, 1975

H
E STUMBLES AS HE WALKS *across the stage, and some of the audience chuckle, believing it a signature of his act. The truth is he had a minor stroke eight months ago. With his ancient suit and the battered slouch hat which almost covers his eyes, he used to think he looked like a black Teddy Roosevelt, a Rough Rider of the boards. These days he feels more like Franklin R, headed for a wheelchair and death on the job.*

It could be worse. Archie Bowles, the Voice of the Funnies, died last year, and he was only fifty two; the Bronx Nightingale, Ellie Potsvitch, coughed up her innards alone on the L before she hit the big four-oh.

It's not a long warm-up. A few minutes of patter, to get the saliva flowing, and a joke or two—wife-and-mother-in-law, nosy neighbors, and hungry dogs.

And then comes the routine itself...

"Black Harry's dead," said Rosalee, folding up the paper. "Didn't you mention him, a while back?"

Tomás frowned. "You shouldn't call him that, these days. It was a stage name, and not one he ever asked for."

"Harold Freedman, then. He was black, and he's dead. You're hung up about that sort of thing."

Which was what a white girl from the Boston suburbs would say. Tomás had to accept gigs wherever he could, and test the mood every time. He'd started out explaining that his father came from a town in Argentina, not from some vague 'Spanish-speaking world'—and got nowhere. He ended up settling for Latino or Hispanic, whatever they wanted to call him on the day.

If it meant a mostly white crowd looking for novelty, or a black crowd just waiting for him to put a foot wrong, that was what it took to meet the bills. Rosalee typed, and not so well; her jobs rarely lasted longer than a few months.

"I saw him once," Tomás said, before he could stop himself.

"Where?"

The White Diamond, a mixed-crowd place which spoke of uneasy truces, a laying down of Puerto Rican knives and Bronx baseball bats. His father would have called it a black-and-tan saloon.

"Oh, around."

"Was he good?"

"I... I don't remember."

Rosalee pushed the paper aside, losing interest; Tomás looked through his scuffed briefcase, wondering where he'd put the notes he made last night. He found the crumpled sheets and flicked a glob of egg mayo off them. His sandwich was leaking out through its torn paper bag.

So this guy, this Polish guy, goes into a bar... something like that. He wasn't sure how many Poles drank in the Crazy Pine. It was 135th and 7th, so probably none. Safer not to make any Italian jokes, though.

He was trying not to think about Harold Freedman.

* * * * *

THE BUS TOOK HIM most of the way to 135ᵗʰ Street. Another Latino guy, buried deep inside in a shiny suit, made a sign Tomás didn't recognize; three black kids, fourteen or fifteen years old with serious Afros, snickered at him. He was no more at home here than he was at the polished walnut dining table of Rosalee's parents.

He didn't feel safe in Harlem, but then he didn't feel safe in New York. The city was a monster constantly on the edge of starvation; a monster which sharpened its claws on coke-high socialites and street heroin overdoses with the same indifference, which made its body of garbage and tenements, spiked through with shining towers.

The Crazy Pine was easily found, a new joint which had never seen a real tree of any kind. Unpainted dry wall inside, Formica and disinfectant. The stage, barely six feet across, was opposite the bar.

"Delgardo?" asked a bored voice from by the pumps.

Tomás nodded. "Yes."

He took in the thick-necked owner of the voice—maybe forty-five, fifty; stained T-shirt, jeans and a crew cut.

"Get up there, then. Gimme five minutes, no filler."

Tomás clambered up. The stage was sticky, and he could see the glitter of broken glass, tiny stars across a dark night of linoleum. He'd read through his act again on the bus.

"Hey, the Big Apple. Want to know why they really call it that? Ask Mayor Beame where he..."

It was polished, pertinent. Crew-cut pulled a sour face a few times; smiled twice.

"Okay, I'll give you an hour, week on Friday. Twenty dollars and a cut of the door."

"I'll be there."

"If you ain't, no loss to me," muttered the man, and pretended to polish a glass.

The audition was over.

The eyes under the slouch hat should be a deep, lively brown. They're not. One is watery and large-pupiled; the other is a discolored white, like some sort of cataract. Old folk in Harlem—the ones who cling to fragments of the past and still don't approve of TV dinners—remember a conjure-woman who walked their streets in the 1920s, a woman with one eye of milk and honey. He doesn't discourage such talk, in case it draws the curious.

He undoes his suit jacket, trying not to tug a button off altogether. He hates sewing—big, blunt-nailed fingers—and his left hand doesn't work as well as it used to.

There are seven or eight soldiers sprawled in the front row. Large, angry men; small, angry men. General Trần Văn Trà is on the Ho Chi Minh trail again, and South Vietnam won't be around much longer. A few of them want to be back there; most don't even know where they've been.

He ought to cancel, but he has no choice.

"I have a lot to tell you," says Harold Freedman.

As Tomás made his way back from the Crazy Pine, he saw that 'Black Harry' had briefly caught the imagination of the newspaper editors. Bored with reciting the city's failings or another litany of homicides, they'd pushed Freedman forward as human interest.

He bought a couple of different papers, sat down on a bench and read, taking occasional bites from his egg sandwich. They wrote briefly of Harry's upbringing—a family with no money, a boy with no father. Not one that anyone would name, anyway.

Everyone in the family called young Harry a funny guy. He did his time telling jokes and stories, picking the banjo, whatever got him a meal. It never paid much, but he grew to be a familiar face around the smaller clubs and bars in the forties and fifties.

One obituary mentioned how Richard Pryor pointed Harry out at the Village Gate. That would have been in the mid-sixties. Freedman stood alone, to one side of the audience; Pryor called him a black icon, but never mentioned him again. The press didn't bother to cover Harry when he was alive. You had to have TV or Vegas to get the real talk going.

Freedman had two routines. One was a stand-up act, although it was rare to see an aging black man in the role. The vogue was for young, cutting-edge performers. Freedman's act was tired—and safe, far too safe.

His other routine... that was known only on the edges of the New York club circuit, and he didn't do it often. The few people who had seen it would never say what he actually did.

Tomás knew why.

The next bus didn't come, so he walked to the subway. Four in the afternoon, which was OK—you didn't take the subway after six if you could help it. The walk took him past the 'Sinsational' Peeporama, which had replaced one of the local theaters.

8mm Art Films, the posters proclaimed. Porn was gripping the Big Apple with painted nails which covered deep, embedded dirt. The men behind it made money, and built empires; the girls it drained put powder over their injection sites, ice cubes on their nipples, and smiled—a rictus of small hopes never to be realized.

The subway was crowded. He lasted three stops and a hustle from a pock-marked white guy with missing teeth, who lisped out a few bad jokes. One of them was from Black Harry's act, and Tomás suddenly needed air. He got off a stop early.

Out on the street, he was in sight of the block where he lived. Ten minutes walk. He began to breathe properly, walking round burned-out Pontiacs and leaking hydrants like a native.

The joke hadn't been Freedman's. It was simply one of those tired gags that went the rounds, year after year. No need to get paranoid.

There were plenty of other things in New York to bring on that sort of feeling.

* * * * *

Tomás Delgardo was born in England. His father was an Argentinian-American working in London, his mother an artsy society girl from Chelsea. They'd married in the spring of 1949, in a flurry of raised eyebrows. Tomás, their only child, followed soon after. He'd expected to spend the rest of his life there, but when he was fourteen, his father announced they were moving to New York. No warning, no discussion.

His parents never did tell him why they uprooted—nor why they divorced eighteen months later, when he turned sixteen. His mother went home, and phoned at Christmas and on birthdays; Tomás remained with his father, an electronics engineer, but the teenager had no gift for any of the sciences. Instead, he wrote bad poetry, failed to complete a novel, and ended up working the clubs. Delgardo Senior joked about circuits and 'the circuit', but disappointment stained his smile.

In 1973, Tomás was commiserating with himself after a failed gig when he met Rosalee, pretty and smart. They moved in together, and were married a few months later. She wanted to do set design, but there were no openings—there was money in her family, but neither she nor Tomás wanted to beg.

They lived in a brownstone apartment where the rent was bearable, and the tenants paid the local cops to keep the stoop free of pushers and prostitutes. Rosalee had painted the entrance hall in muted greens and yellows, the comfortable side of psychedelia.

When he made it back from the audition, she was by the window, drinking coffee with Nicolette.

"Ay, goat head," said Nicolette, white teeth in a dark face. She and her flatmate Angie were Caribbean, maybe from Barbados. He wasn't sure about that odd accent. Models, presented as the exciting New York black look, which caused some tension with models actually from New York.

"Hi, Nico." He threw his briefcase onto the sofa. "I got the gig."

"Do ya ting, man. Got to split—shoot in Astoria tomorrow."

Rosalee noticed him watching Nicolette's hips as she left.

"Yeah, she's beautiful. Want me to go into modeling?"

He was tired, but he grinned.

"You'd crush them all."

"White and regular aren't in," she said. "You think the Crazy Pine might be a regular?"

He didn't know. His life was patchwork—a script for a local radio skit; two other gigs this week, and a birthday roast coming up for a man he hardly knew. It paid the rent. He'd been asked to play a bit-part Mexican in a play the week before, and had refused. Borrowed Argentinian pride. Rosalee didn't understand, but let it go.

"Mind if I go to Marky's?" he asked.

"No. Back for nine—I'll do a casserole."

"Thanks, chica."

Marky's was only a block away. It held the best and the worst in Tomás's line of work. Beat poets long past their sell-by date; stand-ups who phoned their acts in, thick with bourbon; a few genuine talents. Commiseration over failed gigs was tinged with secret glee, and triumphs received with brittle salutes. 'I should have got that slot,' was the real tune as the glasses clinked together.

"Black Harry's dead," said Mike, the bar man.

Tomás squinted at him. "I heard. Why are you telling me?"

"Okay, okay. I thought you knew him."

"Not really."

But he knew more about Freedman than anyone else in the bar. He'd been there, at the White Diamond...

September 1973. Tomás was weighing up the competition, and if he admitted it, looking for styles to imitate, material to 'borrow'. Things hadn't been going well. Booed off stage at the Mimosa Club; bottles thrown at him at a red-neck bar. He could put his own spin on anything, he told himself.

Black Harry completed his comedy routine to a scatter of applause; most of the patrons in the low-ceilinged room abandoned their tables for the bar. As the performer gulped down a beer, the door by the stage opened to reveal Martha, the wrinkled, bleach-blonde woman who ran the White Diamond. Tight red dress and plastic pearls.

She blinked in the spotlight, looking around at the remaining audience.

"Any of youse wanna see Harry throw more of a punch?

Tomás said yes, as did about a dozen others. Maybe there was a blue version of the act—edgier material altogether. It didn't seem to fit with Freedman's tired expression, but there was nothing worth taking from what had gone before.

The passage behind Martha led to the abandoned cinema club next door. The frontage was boarded up; the seating hadn't been touched. Horsehair stuck out of the seats where rats had been in search of bedding.

Black Harry hobbled in after them, and had trouble with the steps onto the stage. Tomás went forward and helped Freedman up.

"Thanks, son."

The old man's breath smelled of pear drops, his clothes of stale beer. Close to, his face might have come from a curled sepia photograph taken a hundred—or a thousand—years before. Tight-curled hair, stiff with gray, and a few days growth on his chin. The eyes confused you—you were torn between the depths of one gaping pupil and the cloudy white of the other.

Tomás had his hand under the other man's elbow. Beneath Black Harry's jacket, beneath dark skin and wasted muscle, deeper still, he felt something he didn't want to feel. Something demanding, though what it demanded, he had no idea.

He realized he was staring, and let go.

"You tread the boards, son," said Freedman. "You've the look of us."

"Learning the trade, sir."

"I wouldn't. Wouldn't stay for what's a-comin', neither."

Tomás laughed nervously and found a place in the front row of seats. The woman next to him asked what was going to happen; he admitted he didn't know.

Freedman took off his jacket, and rolled up frayed shirt sleeves. He had no microphone, just a stand to which he clung for support.

"I have a lot to tell you," he said.

A half hour later, Black Harry put his jacket back on and left the stage, guided off by the owner. Some of the audience were weeping. One man rushed out, screaming 'Myra' or 'Moira'; a couple of young men in cheap suits were struggling with each other at the back, swearing in Italian. One had blood across his mouth.

Tomás stayed in his seat, stunned. The woman to his right was clutching at a leather bag the angry red of a newborn child.

"The man next door—Al Parker—he's touching my kids," she said, and her shoulders convulsed.

Dazed, Tomás swallowed bile. "How do you know?"

"Al was here, next to me—between us. He smiled, and told me. He smiled, for God's sake. He said he puts his hand up their dresses, and promises them things... Jesus, they're eleven years old."

"He couldn't have been here."

She pushed him away. "Didn't you see him? He's a big man, red hair. You must have done!"

He wasn't sure what he'd seen—though he knew he hadn't seen Al Parker or anyone like him.

"You should go home."

She wiped her eyes, nodded. "I need to tell Ted. He'll sort that son of a bitch out."

"Maybe... maybe it wasn't real."

"HE SPOKE TO ME!"

Tomás let her go.

The room was almost empty now. One of the Italians was propped against the wall, mopping his bleeding face with a handkerchief; the other had gone.

Tomás had seen, and he had heard, but not Al Parker. His mother had been on his other side, where a ferret-faced guy in a check suit should have been. At times he thought he could see the man through her. She had bouffant hair and her fingers played with a silver necklace. His father gave it to her for her thirty fifth, and she'd loved it once, but she never wore it after they came to the States.

And she told Tomás things. The words went in, and his brain knew what they meant, but he couldn't process them.

After the White Diamond he drank himself into a stupor at Marky's, got dragged home by a friend, and in the morning it was alright. Black Harry's act had to be smoke and mirrors—hidden microphones, projectors, whatever. And a lot of research into his audience—but that sounded ridiculous. Maybe there'd been acid in the bar-nuts.

Nothing that happened at the White Diamond had really happened.

He proposed to Rosalee the next afternoon. It wasn't a bad decision, but it came from all the wrong places, and only he knew that.

Later that same week he stared into the bathroom mirror. He told himself that he would find Freedman and ask how it was done. One day. But he never did.

He never dared.

They always look impatient after the intro. They're eager for something vulgar or scurrilous, for mean-minded jokes about those they envy or fear. The sex lives of the stars; jokes that play with familiarity and contempt—the Polacks, the Canucks, even the blacks if this old man has it in him. Won't be the first time they've heard a black guy look for favor by sticking it to his own.

He doesn't have any of those, because he doesn't write this part. He only sets the scene.

It's time. He's getting thin now, thin like stained gauze on a cold night's breeze, bloodied bandages in the branches of a dead tree. Thin like black rice paper.

And as he fades, others come, eager to talk. Shadow people who settle in shadow seats, slivers of the world the audience left at home. Recognition and whispers. People start to look around, puzzled faces and a twitching of hands.

He clutches at the fake pillar on one side of the stage; his hands feel rough plaster, but only barely. He's stretched so thin he can hardly draw air into his failing lungs...

In the third row, a man starts to argue with no one, with a sliver of air and darkness.

"You gonna raise that again, huh? You gonna start?"

The audience pays no attention, because they all have their own shadows and slivers, born of misery, lies and the minutiae of never being what they wanted to be, never quite grasping the prize.

A squat Master Sergeant stares around him, his broken-veined nose matching flushed cheeks, and starts to rise to his feet. One of the other uniforms is muttering to him, hand on his arm, telling him it doesn't matter any more, that his crew understands.

Freedman gasps, seeing a bad one coming, and he feels so thin that a single spit might pass through him...

Un-noticed by the Master Sergeant and those around him, the wiry black soldier at the end stands up, tugs a handgun from the back of his belt.

"You. Will. Never. Give. It. A. Rest," he shrieks, and jams the muzzle of the pistol under his chin." If you love your brother so damn much, go and screw him instead of me!"

Only Freedman hears the shot. He's too thin—and too old—to react. He knows we have all failed someone.

The first few times he thought he'd worked out what was plaguing him, that it was something easy to grasp. He'd been brought up with stories of haints, with whispers from the grave, and could have handled that. Five-spots and mojo bags, they might have helped.

But then he worked it out, and it was much worse.

Black Harry was stretched thin so he could touch those who touched his audience. He summoned the living—and the living had far more to say than the dead.

* * * * *

ON THE TUESDAY, Tomás did the birthday roast. Lame jokes about Freddie Sumner, a balding accountant with a poor sense of humor. The money came from Freddie's office, and Tomás suspected that they'd set it up precisely because Freddie wouldn't get half of it. The accountant's wife acted amused, and spent too much time in the kitchen pressing Tomás to beers and sandwiches. She gave off a heat, a need, which was oppressive; he declined to stick around afterwards, uncomfortably aware that she wasn't wearing a bra.

Trudging back to the brownstone, he saw an elderly black guy sitting on the sidewalk, right in front of the tobacconists on the corner. The steel shutters were sprayed with gang signs and obscenities. The man's left leg was in some sort of caliper, strapped on over patched corduroy trousers. Tomás had taken good money for a bad night, and he reached into his pocket for a dollar bill.

The man looked up.

"Jes' restin'," he said. "Takin' in that cee-gar smoke, dreamin' o' Havana."

There was no smoke; the night air smelled of burning slums and dog shit. Tomás fingered the notes in his pocket, and asked what he considered to be the most stupid question of his life.

"Did you know Harold Freedman? Black... uh, Black Harry, some called him. Old-time comedian, used to work the clubs around here."

A frown, wrinkles like the corrugations in the shutters behind him.

"Ain't never met him. Colored feller, was he?"

"Yeah."

"Dead?"

"He had a stroke which did for him, last week."

"Most all o' us headin' that way, soon enough." Narrowed eyes checked out the younger man's best performance suit and the less-than-best shoes. "Want me to tell you 'bout it?"

Tomás stepped back. For a second he thought that one of the man's eyes had widened, and the other gone white as milk.

"No." He thrust a dollar into the man's hand, and ran, ran for home...

* * * * *

A N HOUR LATER, after a bottle of wine, he placed a call to London. The wine helped cushion the cost, though he knew Rosalee would be pissed with him.

A cultured English voice eventually answered from the moon, or so it sounded. Echoes and emptiness.

"Margrave."

"Justin—it's Tomás Delgardo."

"What on earth's the matter, dear boy? It's two in the morning here."

"You're up, Justin. You're always up. Look, please, I need the truth from someone. About my parents and the move—in '64."

In the lunar wasteland, the clearing of a man's throat.

"Put the telephone down, Tomás—you can't afford this call. I'll ring you back."

He made a strong cup of coffee, because he didn't trust himself; poured out another glass of red because he needed drink more than trust. When the phone rang, it sent ice through his belly.

"You've known my mother most of her life," Tomás started, before the other could speak. "And I know something happened, just before we came to New York."

Margrave was from another generation, a world of art, beauty and occasional self-destruction. He was also the nearest thing Tomás had to a god-father.

"It isn't pleasant," said Margrave. "But I imagine you know that, from the way you ask."

"I've already heard it. Some of it."

His mother had told him, that night at the White Diamond. Harold Freedman had let her tell him, but the words had been buried so deep inside him that, until now, he could pretend they weren't there. And there was always the chance that it was all a lie.

After thirty minutes on the phone, he knew that it wasn't.

"What... what happened in the end?" asked Tomás. He'd broken the wine glass against the wall, and was watching runnels of red find their way to the carpet.

"In the end?" Margrave sounded sad. "Stevie Slater was a prime bitch, dear boy—a listener-in, a steamer-open of letters. A venomous beast without the charms of his serpent kin. We hushed it up, naturally. I was seeing Leo at the time—Leo Chancel, you remember him, the kindest of fellows. He dealt with your father; I took care of your mother."

"And Slater?"

"The little sod recovered, but the marks couldn't be cover up. He went to try his hand—and his arse—in Prague. If there is any justice in this world, he went under a tank in sixty eight."

"Thank you." Flat, drained.

"It won't do any good, you know—mentioning it to your mother or father. She's happy enough now. I saw her at Sissy Metcalfe's gallery last month." The older man paused. "Who stirred this up again, Tomás?"

"Harold Freedman," he said, and put the receiver down.

* * * * *

WHEN ROSALEE AND NICOLETTE got back from a party downtown, he broke.

"My dad screwed another guy, during a bad patch in the marriage. And... shit happened."

It wasn't the best way to greet them as they giggled their way into the flat. Rosalee took in the wine stains on the wall, the glistening shards, and her husband's expression.

"You know where the glasses are, Nico," she said, calm.

And he told them the story—not only what he'd heard from Margrave, but everything that had come out two years before, when Black Harry raised shadows and ruined lives. When Tomás saw a woman who couldn't be there, her face tear-stained, her fingers playing with a silver necklace as she sat in her Chelsea flat, three thousand miles away...

Stephen Slater, an angular twenty two year old little better than a rent-boy, flattered and charmed the handsome Mateo Delgardo. Delgardo's marriage had become sedentary, sexless, and somehow he fell for bright talk of other pleasures. They met in anonymous hotel rooms across London, and did what men do—until Slater started doing what Slater did. Turning up on the edge of work events; 'chance' arrivals at Mrs Delgardo's arts happenings. Suggesting certain interpretations of business trips, letting his hand linger too long on Mr Delgardo's arm.

Slater had letters, and few would care if they were forged or genuine. Outside of the right 'scene', such letters could cripple a man.

"My mother dealt with it," said Tomás.

The two woman sat opposite him, sobered, fascinated. Rosalee's knuckles were white.

"How she do dat?" asked Nicolette.

"She had my father write to Slater, and arrange a meeting one evening. "

The black girl nodded. "She pay him off for licking his mout' too much."

Rosalee closed her eyes, letting her long blonde hair fall over her face; Tomás wet his lips.

"No. She met Slater in an underground car park, near Piccadilly."

Nicolette's eyes widened; Tomás slumped, committed to finishing the tale.

"There was no one else around. When he sidled over and asked for money, she said that she wouldn't pay a penny to scum like him. That any

more mention of her husband, ever, or the slightest word to the police...
well, she warned him. When he laughed, and suggested what he might
do next, she took a knife out—a craft knife from her workshop—to
prove how serious she was—"

"She cut him?" Rosalee's head stayed low.

"She caught him off balance, and when he fell, she drove her heel
into his crotch until he could only whimper. Then she cut him—in more
than one place—and left him there, sprawled in his own blood and piss,
to limp his way home or bleed to death. She didn't really care."

There was his mother in his memories, smiling as she took a cake
from the oven; laughing at the antics of a puppy at a friend's party. Pretty dresses, and a hug at the end of the school day. And there she was
in some urine-stained car park one night, a knife in her slim, artistic
hands...

"She... she fix dat boy-skank good." Nicolette no longer looked
comfortable. With a squeeze of Rosalee's hand, she left for her own flat.

Tomás got up, and began a half-hearted attempt to sweep up the
broken glass.

"That's why they came to the States," said Rosalee at last. "To get
away from what had happened."

"I guess so."

She held him in the night. It didn't help.

*He doesn't think he'll be able to do this much longer, however hard the need
drives him. It was never his choice anyway, but now his body is giving in. The
pain in his liver is worse, and the blood pounds in his veins, looking for a way
to corrupt the flesh beyond.*

*Better than having it sprayed across the back of an old cinema seat, may-
be—half the young black soldier's head is missing. A woman has called the cops,
but they probably won't even come. The city's going to shit.*

*Harry never knows what they're told, by their friends and neighbors, lov-
ers, mothers, husbands. He doesn't want to. He didn't ask for this, and he doesn't*

determine who turns up from the shadows. Someone else will carry on when he dies—tomorrow, next month, next year. Someone who's seen his routine, and never let go of what they heard. Never really left the performance.

It always lingered with one or two of them, like it lingered with Harry so long ago in a North Carolina roadhouse, his only attempt at touring. He helped an old man up onto a soapbox after a blues session, an old man who said he had something to tell folk. That was when he first heard those words, and saw what it meant to go thin...

Truth is a dreadful thing. Harold Freedman would like to feel sorry; he'd like to make people smile, nothing more than that.

It wasn't to be.

Tomás managed a short set at the Conga King, a bar packed with plastic palms and plastic people. They like his film references, his skit on Gerald Ford; they didn't like the older stuff, the early, warm-up part, and he realized that he'd used material he'd meant to drop. Material which went back to the sort of act Black Harry did, years ago. Why the hell had he done that?

Afterwards, he sank a large gin in one corner, shook hands with a couple from Illinois, and wondered where all this was going. He'd felt different during the gig, like there was something he needed to do—the truth about his parents' past was a worm under his skin, twisting and turning inside him, and he began to wonder about those who were watching him.

Lies and secrets...

He pushed the empty glass away and took up his briefcase. He would have to rework some of the material for the gig at the Crazy Pine. If he had that as a weekly slot, and could get spotted by an agent... it might cheer up Rosalee, who was finding him hard work at the moment.

He didn't blame her. She trusted him, but he didn't trust himself any more.

Black Harry was dead, and things had changed.

He looks out at the tables, waiting for the chatter to subside, wondering if it ever will. He's already done the introductory jokes, which didn't make much of an impression. A green spotlight shines in his eyes, but he'll have to live with it.

It's a small crowd tonight. Hard-faced Italian construction workers, unable to tell the difference between the rubble of their days and the rubble of their nights. Couples in love who live with their parents, surrounded by damp ironing and the smell of three day old bolognese sauce being boiled up again. They have nowhere else to go to be alone together. Uncomfortable wives, dragged out by husbands who use these evenings as an excuse to get tanked. They pray their men will pass out on the sofa later.

A cop, already a quarter way through a bottle of cheap whiskey. He shot a black kid two days ago, but all the kid had was in his hand was an Afro comb. The cop can't decide if he cares or not. The whiskey might give him the answer.

At the table nearest to the stage, a man and a woman. The woman is young, attractive, with soft blonde hair swept back, and she looks worried, distracted. The man is dark-skinned and must be forty years older than her—he limped in earlier, from streets which steam and groan, favoring a calipered leg. They don't seem to know each other.

He folds his jacket on the back of the wooden chair, the only feature on the cramped stage. He's beginning to feel... thin, stretched out around the people in front of him. He's here, and he's being pulled like taffy, drawn thin across the crowd. So stretched that now he can feel the people they know, and the people who know the people he know, a terrible web of interconnecting failures and deceits...

It'll come, because it has to, and it'll change the expressions on those faces, maybe change the rest of their lives.

Already there are strangers in the audience, sliding between the seats, setting shadows where shadows can't be, and other voices are ready to speak...

"I have a lot to tell you," says Tomás Delgardo, as he begins his first and last performance at the Crazy Pine.

STILL SHE STARES

FIVE

WHEN THE OLD MAN has fallen silent, Stefan shivers.

"That... that's dreadful. Forgive me, sir, but how can you know all that detail, if you weren't there?"

"Because I knew almost everyone involved. And..."

Marcus looks up, interested despite himself; Margrave's voice becomes more hollow, wistful.

"Because Tomás Delgado called me one last time before he disappeared, shortly after his night at the Crazy Pine. Poor child. He told me everything, as if he were in the confessional. It was a very, very long conversation—and I believed his every word. He told me things he couldn't possibly know, about people he'd never met.

"He was sobbing, distraught, at times; I said I would get a flight to New York the next day, and we could meet, look for some way to change things... 'There is nothing you can do, Justin,' he whispered. 'Nothing I can do. I'm so very, very sorry... for Rosalee. Please... don't come after me.'

"Neither I nor Rosalee heard from him after that call. The police were no use. I did pay for a Boston private investigator I knew to do some digging, but apart from a couple of reports concerning some disturbing performances in isolated Mid-West towns, nothing. If those were even connected to him."

"He had a lot to tell them," echoes Stefan. "Christ, what a bloody awful business."

"It doesn't make any sense." Marcus tops up their glasses. "Why Harry Freedman, why Tomás... why did any of it happen?"

"I have no idea," says Margrave. "But it did."

They finish their wine in silence. When the last bottle on the coffee table has been drained, Margrave looks directly at Marcus.

"So, my dear boy, we have reached a conclusion, of sorts. I need my sleep—today has been wearing—but next time, I should tell you why you thought you knew me. Or would you rather consign that to history, one of the rambling stories of a geriatric who is simply seeking attention in his dotage?"

Marcus winces. That's a little too close to what he said himself, in the early days of their acquaintance.

"I think... I think that you should come again, sir."

"Justin," murmurs the old man.

"I'm sorry?"

"I f I return, you must both promise to call me Justin. I tire of 'Sir' and 'Mr Margrave'. I don't need respect or recognition these days. If I ever did."

They agree to do their best.

* * * * *

EXACTLY A WEEK LATER, the three sit, companionable, in the court-yard once more. Margrave expresses his dislike of Hirst—'Better suited to supervising a biscuit factory,'—and his interest in a couple of up-and-coming Chinese ceramicists—'Form and concept fused to create an inner space'; Marcus shows him a few watercolour sketches by an artist who is getting noticed in the Antilles; the old man approves of her work, whilst admitting that watercolours are not his strong suit.

Stefan is the one to break the mood.

"So come on, you two—I've waited long enough. Who is this Auntie Vi?"

Marcus takes a deep breath. "She was a voodoo mama. Almost everyone around our way was scared of her."

"No, she was an obeah-woman," says Margrave. "A Trinidadian should know better."

"Same difference."

The old man clicks his tongue reprovingly. "Auntie Vi knew almost nothing of voodoo—no more than I did, certainly. She would have been terribly cross if she'd heard you say that. She practised obeah, the small magicks used in many parts of the Caribbean

Stefan is fascinated. "And you went to her because you needed help with something inexplicable, a cursed vase, an antique mirror which—"

Margrave laughs. "You are so very imaginative, dear boy! In fact, I met her because I had guests coming from Jamaica at the time. A sculptor and his wife. I was in Brixton Market, looking for salt-fish and plantains. I had rather hoped to provide a meal which made them feel welcome."

"Oh."

"In the end, my friends preferred to go out for a vindaloo, though they only told me that part later in the day. But anyway, there I was in the market, a delightful part of town—covered stalls on either side of the street, bustling with trade, overflowing with the sights and smells of produce from all over the world. Jackfruit next to King Edward potatoes, yams nestling up to early forced rhubarb from Yorkshire. It reflected the general liveliness of the community, Brixton at its best, with Black and white mingling, yelling, swearing, laughing.

"And whilst at the market, I crossed paths with a pinch-faced little Black woman, elderly. She was wrapped in more than one dark outdoor coat, and wore a battered black top-hat. Hard to miss. When she fingered fruit, the stall-holder gave it to her; when she complained about prices, the goods in question were immediately knocked down to mere pennies. She was obviously important in the neighbourhood, but I had no idea why."

"And you made enquiries about her."

"How very convoluted of you. No, I spoke to her, there and then, as we stood by a stall groaning with plantain and sugar cane. 'The people here seem to be somewhat in awe of you, madam.' I said. And she screwed up her face, staring at me with dark, narrow eyes.

"'Mi doan know yuh, bwoy,' she replied. Her voice had a peculiar high lilt to it.

"'Margrave. Justin Margrave. A pleasure to meet you.'

"As I came to learn later, you didn't address Auntie Vi without permission. Or you weren't supposed to, I should say. She took hold of my forearm, and I saw that her fingers were withered, claw-like. Only on her left side, though—her right hand was untouched by whatever had afflicted her. She had a tight grip, almost painful.

"'Margrave. That a name mi doan like. A prying', pokin' sort o' name.'

"'It has been said,' I agreed. 'But we all do what we must, even if we're not always terribly keen on it. Isn't that so?'

"And I met her gaze, which clearly threw her off. I suspected that it had been a long time since someone didn't wither like her hand when she stared at them. She let go of me, and spat twice, once on each side of her laced-up boots. I remember the stall-holder's sudden intake of breath— and the old woman walking away, muttering to herself.

"'That Auntie Vi, mister," he said. "She mebbe boiling a black cat for you tonight.'

"I raised my eyebrows. 'How very unfortunate for the poor cat. Why would she do such a thing?'

"When the old woman was well out of earshot, he told me that she was trouble. People who didn't pay Auntie Vi proper respect had accidents, misfortune. No one knew exactly which island she was from, or why she had come to Britain; no one knew exactly what she did all day in her cramped flat, full of herbs and murky glass jars. You went to her when something bad had happened to you, and the minister was no use;

you went to her when your husband was beating you, or your wife unfaithful. Or just when you took against a neighbour. Auntie Vi always had the remedy."

"That was what they said," Marcus agrees. "And she hated kids. Terry Brown broke a bottle of milk on the landing outside her flat—it was an accident—and the next day he was suspended from school for fighting. He'd not done a thing, but two other boys swore he'd been looking for trouble, and they had bruises to prove it. We all knew who had made them say that, and that they'd given each other those marks the night before, behind the kebab shop. She voodooed them."

"I'm not getting through here, am I?" Margrave sighs. "Voodoo is a religion, an entirely different matter—think of her more as one of the people who helped me with the Children, if you were listening."

"But those people were good," says Stefan.

"'Good' is an entirely different issue, my dear. They were what they were. But anyway, Auntie Vi and I crossed paths in seventy eight, seventy nine, and I though little of it at the time. Margaret Thatcher came to power only a few months later, and many of us were trepidatious, wondering what she would do."

"Clause 28" Stefan chips in. "'Thou shalt not promote homosexuality, nor support its promotion'."

"That came later, yes. It was an uncomfortable time, and a duplicitous one at that—as ever, many politicians nurtured their own various types of closets, well away from the public eye. Some were gay, some were less than choosy either way, and a number, as always, were simply unfaithful to whomsoever they had been saddled with by convention or ambition. More shockingly, as came out later, there were child molesters walking the most sacred corridors of power—you remember what I told you of Piccadilly? That period had a lot of dirt under its nails, the nastiest sort of dirt you can imagine.

"It is a politician—but a decent one, as it happens—who brings us back to Auntie Vi..."

AUNTIE VI

FIVE

Brixton, 1981

I WAS DINING WITH ARCHIE CRANE at a decent enough French restaurant in Kensington, one rainy February night, when an awkward subject arose. We had argued about Hepworth's legacy over an onion-based rustic soup, disagreed about the Arts Council whilst dipping into a bouillabaisse, and were about to dissect a Polish gallery owner when Archie's expression changed to one of annoyance.

"Margrave, I almost forgot to mention. I have a friend who may need help."

"Then you should help him."

He toyed with his spoon. "It's not... well, it's more up your alley, so to speak."

Oh dear. I knew what that meant.

"Go on."

And he outlined the general situation as our bouillabaisse bowls were cleared away. This friend was a leading London councillor and campaigner, not a bad sort. I shall call him Mr Smith. His public life was earnest and well intentioned; his private life was squeaky clean (Archie said this part as if slightly disappointed), but complicated, for he had formed a liaison with a young Black woman from Brixton, by the name of Glory. Archie knew Smith well, and for all Archie's many, many faults, he was of a 'liberal' political tendency, and no racist. There was, it seemed, a genuine and mutual attraction between boy and girl—but there were problems.

Glory herself was apparently extremely pretty, and intelligent—she worked for a housing charity—and a number of the young Black men in her neighbourhood considered Smith's actions to be poaching, taking what was rightfully theirs. In a way, I can see their point—the sweet-talking colonialist arrives on their shores to seize their assets.

Her parents and uncles, aunts, meanwhile, were strict, Windrush-generation Jamaicans. Folk who, whilst they did not want a fancy white son-in-law, did not approve of their young people's blunter remedies in such a case, such as having Smith threatened, or beaten up in a back-street, to make the point.

"So, as I understand it," said Archie, "When the usual range of parental lectures and stern commands didn't achieve the results they wanted, the family went to a peculiar old woman called Auntie Vi. Some sort of local witch, Smith says—a nasty piece of work."

I kept my lips sealed, nodding for him to continue. Tapping his spoon on the table in an idle rhythm, he smiled.

"Well, you know? Margrave, old boy, everyone says you're the chap for that sort of thing—the unusual stuff, I mean..."

The evening ended, as you might expect, with my agreement—without great enthusiasm—to act as a go-between and speak to Auntie Vi. There was no point in me going directly to the family, who were strongly opposed to people of my 'nature'.

The tale of Glory and Mr Smith is not important in itself, by the way. A mean thing to say, I suppose. It was important to them, of course, but for me, it served only as my proper introduction to the woman known as Auntie Vi.

I chatted to Smith over the telephone, cross-questioned him as to his intentions, like a prospective father-in-law, and got an impression of a decent sort; I managed to meet with Glory in a discreet cafe, and I was impressed.

"I love him, Mr Margrave. He's a good man."

Female beauty is a somewhat abstract issue in my case, but I was taken by her large brown eyes, and by her forthright manner.

"Mum isn't sure; dad... he still lives in the fifties. He won't have me marrying an outsider, and a white one at that. He thinks I should be with some enterprising Black guy, raising a 'proper' family. Sod that. I want a career, to be known for myself, not for whose ring I wear, or how flash my car is, y'know?"

I knew. "So... Auntie Vi."

Some of the spark went from Glory's big eyes. "She terrifies me, always has—'Shi ave duppy behind har back' is what they say around our way."

"Sorry?" That last part, delivered in a strong West Indian accent, had lost me.

"Auntie Vi has ghosts, spirits, following her, that's what they mean. That you're screwed if you cross her, basically. It sounds stupid, but..."

Who was I to argue, after all I'd been through?

I reassured the young woman, airily, that I knew a bit about such matters—which puzzled her, I think—and that I would see what I could do. I was ready, or so I thought.

I had always found Brixton and its surrounds to be a vibrant, interesting area, but only weeks before there had been the tragedy of the New Cross fire, a house party where thirteen Black youngsters had died in a sudden conflagration. Despite it being the view of the police and fire services that the whole thing was just a terrible accident, some locals considered it arson, possibly with racist intent, and it had happened against a background of increasing tension.

Unsurprisingly, the streets there were not... comfortable. I could sense the mood, although curiously, my age and style of dress have always worked in my favour there; enough people had seen me around before, and I clearly wasn't involved with the authorities. Apart from the occasional sneer, or cry of 'Batty-man!', which ought to have offended me, I was unmolested—I believe most of the locals were merely amused by the large middle-aged fellow in the linen suit, with his cravat flowing in the breeze. Perhaps they hoped I was an eccentric music producer or a television agent?

A local painter, Anton, met me in a coffee bar, and after we had discussed his latest works—Caribbean Art Deco, you might call his general style—he offered to take me to the dilapidated block of flats where Auntie Vi lived. Anton didn't believe in duppy or deity, he just thought that the old woman was the sort of crazy it was best to avoid.

The block had been up no more than ten years, yet its poorly-cast concrete facade was already crumbling away. The lift was out of order, and we went up three flights of stairs, until he pointed to a scratched, battered door with a bunch of dried leaves pinned to it.

"I wait outside," said Anton. "Got some canvas to show you later, mon."

The door was partly open—I knocked, received no reply, and gently pushed it a little further ajar. An entrance hall, cluttered with empty bottles and Tupperware boxes of all sizes, the contents of the latter unclear; the odour of stale beer and bitter herbs. Given the disorder, the flat might have been burgled a few minutes ago.

"Hello? Are you home, madam?"

"Mi here." Auntie Vi emerged from what I guessed was the kitchen, her good hand dripping an oily yellow liquid. "Why yuh trubbel mi, Missah Margrave?"

"You remember me?"

"Oh, mi memba yuh, Missuh. Yuh like de plantain."

"Ah, yes. I am sorry to bother you, but it's about a young woman—Glory." I used her full name, but do not wish to repeat it here. "Mr Smith is anxious, hearing that you have been retained, asked to discourage any further... association."

"So 'im fears mi." She reached behind her, and wiped her hands with a threadbare Coronation tea-towel.

"Fears you, madam? I don't think he has the faintest idea of what's going on. He is in love; that affliction is returned. I am not, in general, in favour of interference with such affairs. They will break other's hearts, ruin each other, or whatever, soon enough without you or I having to poke a stick into it all."

She took this without comment, motioning that I should come with her into the cramped kitchen.

"Di tea ready. Come."

I couldn't guess what was bubbling on the discoloured stove top, but opposite it stood a clean formica table, taking up most of the free space. There were two straight chairs, two china cups, and a teapot.

"I'm sorry—were you expecting company, or waiting for a client?"

"Mi see yuh comin'," she said. "Yuh tink Auntie Vi no knowin' who come to taak? Sit, tell mi bout dis Smith."

There followed one of the stranger conversations I have had, petitioning an old Black woman as to the virtues of a man I barely knew whilst sipping some sort of pale herbal tea. The chair could barely carry my weight and creaked alarmingly; the acrid, oily smell of her kitchen was oppressive, and most of the time, her only response was a widening or narrowing of her small, dark eyes. When she did speak, it was in that blend of English and—as I had learned from my vindaloo-loving visitors—a version of Jamaican patois.

When I finished, she nodded her head once.

"Mi tink yuh right."

"You do?" Not what I'd expected.

"Mi said. Dis Glory, she no go far wit' dem bwoys 'round heah. She need mooah. Mi tell puppa, mumma, mi see dis—di gyal do good wit' dis Smith."

"But he's white, and that brings its own difficulties—for both of them."

"Dem buy mule, dem mus' feed 'im."

By which I guessed she meant that what happened after they got together was their problem, not hers.

I was somewhat taken aback by our conversation, having expected imprecations, curses, warnings—or a refusal to listen to me at all. All I could do was ask if I might have another cup of her brew, which despite its initial sharpness, had surprisingly subtle undertones. We drank, and talked... I risked ridicule, and spoke of two or three 'less usual' encounters of mine, finding her an informed, receptive listener to those. She could be irritable, sharp, but she was not the woman I had been led to believe.

When I realised that almost an hour had passed, I remembered that I had someone waiting for me, and with reluctance, took my leave; she assured me that she would deal with Glory's family. Her parting words were: 'Mi see you 'gain.'

I couldn't tell if that was an invitation, or a foretelling.

Outside, in light drizzle, I took a few deep breaths. Anton was smoking a fat roll-up on the corner, and two policemen were closing in on him. I didn't like their determined tread, or the cold look on their faces.

"Are you waiting for someone, son?" said the older one, a tall man with 'BULLY' stamped on his forehead. Or it should have been. It was a sneering challenge.

"I wait for him," said the artist, nodding towards my approaching figure.

That amused the bully, but confuse his colleague. The police were becoming notorious for their use of the 'sus' law—stopping and searching people 'under suspicion' of intending to engage in criminal activity. This was being disproportionately aimed at young Black men, engendering a lot of heat in the community. I could see where the current encounter was headed.

"Is there a problem, officers?" I spoke in my clearest BBC voice, looking the tall one directly in the eyes. The other constable said something to his colleague—I think he used the word 'ponce'—and they turned away to plod down the road.

Anton's hand was not steady as he took a last drag of his joint. It wasn't fear, though.

It was anger.

We both knew what was going on, and said nothing more about it.

* * * * *

I VISITED BRIXTON a number of times in the next few weeks, and always called in on Auntie Vi. She was certainly a woman of her own making. Concerning her time before coming to Britain, or even when she came over, she never spoke. I suspect that it had been traumatic, troubled. She may even have been abused at some time in her life.

"Mi neva love nuh mon," she said to me, and in such a way that you knew there was pain behind it.

But she was quite a psychologist. The 'witch' image, the ominous muttering of an obeah-woman, had earned her respect, and I believe that once on that path, she saw no way of leaving it. She had chosen her face for the world, and if some feared her, that had its value at times. Elders in the community nodded to her or avoided her; young people laughed, occasionally, but not too loud and not too near her. She went to church once a week and sat apart others, singing along in that cracked, sing-song voice of hers.

Despite her reputation, most of her work centred around healing. Her herbal mixtures, salves and potions followed obeah practice, and she sold her services at a reasonable price, when she had diagnosed what she thought was wrong with a petitioner. Sometimes, she said to me, she told them that they were idiots and needed to go to hospital immediately. 'Dead folk doan pay nutten.'

I grew to like her, although any display of such an affection was met with suspicion.

"Tell me, do you have a problem with the fact that I'm gay?" I asked her, when she was being particularly cold. "Or the fact that I'm white?"

"Mi got nuh problem wit yuh, bwoy. But yuh want fi like people— mi nuh like anyone. It safa."

It was safer.

I saw that as sad, but had to respect her choice.

* * * * *

I DO NOT KNOW if April is always the cruellest month, but this particular April was certainly not a kind one for Brixton. The police were undertaking yet another crack-down, an operation to tackle street crime, which was once again leading to Black people, especially young men, being challenged, threatened or arrested, whether or not they'd done anything criminal. Some had, no doubt, but these blunt, indiscriminate actions were fuelling local anger. I wasn't surprise—I had seen blatant racism in action more than once here, and did not like it one bit.

Although I didn't want to be in the area around that time, I'd promised Auntie Vi that I'd take her a piece of African art I'd come across—a horned wooden carving of a seated figure, about eight inches tall. I'd been told that it was an *ikenga*, a sacred thing from Nigeria, and she'd expressed considerable interest.

The cab driver who dropped me off by her block of flats gave me an odd look as I passed him his money.

"You maybe want I should wait, mister?"

It was late afternoon, and Auntie Vi could be slow getting to the point; a number of our meetings involved me trying to polite and wait for her to finish a story or a recitation of wrongs.

"No, thank you. I'll be a while."

He looked unhappy, but drove away.

What the old woman and I discussed that day is unimportant—I did decide, however, that she was would be a better companion for the *ikenga* that I would, and made it a gift to her. We talked at the kitchen table; she cooked us spiced chicken, with ackees and spinach, washed down with her herb tea.

"It's getting late," I said at last, looking out of the window. A twisting column of smoke marked the dusk sky not so far away. "Looks like there's a fire somewhere around Railton Road."

"Be plenty burnin' dis night," she muttered. "Yuh be careful, mon."

I wasn't sure what she meant, but reassured her that I always was—possibly an untruth—and said that I'd walk over to the tube station, where I could take the Victoria Line. A ten, fifteen minute stroll on a dry spring night.

It is a measure of my foolishness, or my lack of any 'psychic' gift, that in making my choice that night, I walked directly into the Brixton Riots.

Much has been said elsewhere of that time, by people better informed than I was. Almost every street corner held a group of excited youths, both Black and white, with runners seeming to dash from group to group. Occasionally a clutch of police officers stood at vantage points, not overly excited, but wary.

"Is there trouble, officer?" I asked a sergeant holding an empty polystyrene cup in one hand, a radio in the other.

"Go home, sir." Brusque, disinterested.

"That was my intention," I replied, but he was no longer listening.

I had to see. My weakness, as you know. Instead of the most sensible, logical move, I headed towards the smoke—and as I did so, additional flames lit the horizon in more than one spot. If this had been anywhere else in London, I might have suspected an IRA bombing; here, I thought that I had a better idea of what was going on. The young people of Brixton had decided to fight back.

As I came closer to Railton Road, often known colloquially as the Front Line, the signs became unmistakable. A white teenager in a parka ran past me, away from the smoke, clutching a portable television and three or four cassette players; two men in cheap suits trotted in the same direction as I was heading, one of them with what looked like a television camera on his shoulder.

"It's a bloody riot, mate. A proper riot at last!" yelled the nearest when I called out to them. He was excited, in a manner which I thought somewhat unhealthy.

The closer I got to Railton Road, the worse the situation was. Black men holding snooker cues and bricks, a couple of the men with head wounds, un-bandaged; a jewellers' shop with the plate glass shattered, and a burning car on its side in the middle of the street. More fires appeared in the distance every minute, and some of those running past me or milling around on the street had more than empty milk bottles ready to throw. They had petrol bombs.

Courage and idiocy both lead us into disasters. I have always tried to avoid an excess of either. It was, I decided, time to back away, but when I found what I thought would be a promising alley, it was choked with smouldering rubbish; when an obvious gap opened in the protestors, it closed before I could reach it.

I began to lose any notion of which direction to take, and when I thought I had worked it out, my route was blocked by a fire engine—which was reversing away from the nearest blaze. It soon became obvious why—people were throwing bricks and pieces of paving stone at it. The wind-shield was already shattered.

Somewhere inside my mind, an icy wind was growing, and there came to my ears—above the fury and clamour of the riot—a sound I had never thought to hear again.

That sick, hungry whisper from beneath the floorboards of the world.

'They love any form of strife. It draws them,' a woman had once told me. 'War brings the woe-mongers.'

Well, there was more than enough woe in Brixton that night. Not that I thought for a moment that They had started this—tonight was a purely human disaster—but They had surely sensed the cracks that the riots had created, and wormed their way through, or close enough. I had somehow thought of Them as rural things, echoes of old woods and hill-tops, isolated villages—but what was London, except a fractured mosaic of villages and petty towns, pressed tight, too tight, together?

The Children of Angles and Corners were feeding, and as I could feel They were there, so They could sense me. I had no doubt that They wanted me to be aware of who had returned, after what I had done on Maes Knoll.

They wanted me to see hurt, and—I imagined—to be hurt. That would be Their hope, anyway.

Dazed, I turned yet again, and came out onto one of the larger thor-oughfares, just off Railton Road. Here was a more brutal kind of insan-ity—vehicles and waste-bins on fire along the road, car and shop alarms shrieking their own painful song; protestors and rioters intermingled, sometimes arguing amongst themselves, sometimes flowing and reform-ing, shouting out slogans, rallying cries. A building further up was on fire and beginning to collapse...

Eyes in the angles, claws in the corners, and so close, the thin-ways opening; sweet on rasping tongue is the kin-strife, the mewling of men and their fears, the failed-lives and follies...

"They not from round here!" said an anxious, elderly Black man, pressed into a doorway.

I thought for a second that he could feel the Children, see Them, but he was pointing to a group of white youths with scarves across their lower faces as they smashed a shop window, laughing. Many others were local, though. I recognised a few. The flames reflected off anger, confu-sion, excitement—the potential for change and justice woven with that unmanageable chaos that can grow within any mob.

A lone constable, helmet-less, blood running from his forehead, screamed at me, waving his baton as if beating off a cloud of flies. I stumbled out of his way, and saw lines of police forming up further along Railton Road itself. They were fumbling with truncheons and plastic riot shields—nervous under-studies who had been given props and pushed on stage. Many of the police had no protective gear apart from the shields, and one was holding up a dustbin lid to fend off burning missiles, but for those who ran through the streets—their streets—every uniform held an enemy.

At the same time, the crowds jeered, and a boom box—I believe that is the word—was blasting out Mr Bob Marley's 'Get Up, Stand Up'. A fine song, but with an alarming aspect in such an atmosphere.

The Children would be lapping up the hatred.

Not far from me, two teenagers were trying to lift a very large, dark-skinned woman who must have been jostled off her feet—she was dressed as if on her way to church. And a squad of officers with protective helmets and better equipment were heading our way, which was hardly comforting. The situation had descended below any rational level, and if you were not in uniform, well, having a Radio 4 accent was of limited value now; bystanders were being assaulted just for being there, being in the way. Innocence was not a word which interested either side that night.

In that moment, I saw the boy.

He was seven, eight years old, standing in the middle of the street. A dirty white T-shirt against brown skin, and torn jeans, too large for him, hanging low. Only his head moved, turning one way then another, a clockwork thing with no comprehension of what was happening.

I could understand that—to his left was a crowd of yelling men with improvised weapons; to his right, a dozen or more grim-faced policemen, clearly ready for a fight. None of them were seeing the boy.

The untutored psychologist inside me saw dissociation in his face, and I could imagine him being trampled any moment, whilst an echo of the Cunning told me how much the Children were delighting in such a delicacy. Were they, on the edge of our senses, clustering around him? I went from stumble to purposeful stride, meaning to pull him into shelter.

The car appeared without warning, shooting from an adjoining street, clearly out of control. There was a screech of failing brakes, the smell of burning rubber, the panicked expression on the driver's face as the yellow Cortina skidded across the road, too close to the child. It might miss, but...

I leapt—possibly for the only time in my life—and managed to grab hold of his T-shirt, tugging him back; the car crashed into a lamp-post, showering us with broken glass and fragments of the concrete support. I was on the ground, bruised and somewhat shocked, the boy cushioned by my generous frame.

The police surged forward regardless, with the clatter of truncheons against riot-shields; rioters and protestors would still clash where we lay. I held him more tightly, hunched over him, and that whispering filled my head, until...

"Mi tink yuh go now. Dis nah yuh place."

A high voice, audible above the terrible night; a small, heavily-swathed figure in black, outlined by torches, headlights and burning vehicles. She stood by the wrecked car, unflinching, apparently unbothered, with her bent top hat pulled low, her face in shadow. The nearby flames danced in a cold, fell breeze, but she raised her withered hand.

"Dis nah yuh place," Auntie Vi repeated, and then: "Mi tell all yuh dis, fah sure—who doh hear, do feel!"

Her sharp words penetrated everything. I started calling out that something else was here with us, something wrong, but she silenced me with a gesture of her other hand.

"Mi nah fear Dem!" she snapped. It was impossible to know whom she was addressing, or which Them she meant.

Maybe that didn't matter when you were Auntie Vi.

The people around me looked suddenly awkward, as if they'd forgotten what they were about to do; the police advance, so determined a moment ago, faltered. Someone was yelling out orders behind them, but none of the officers appeared to understand. It was as if no one was sure any more why they were there.

You can say that this was a reflection of the general chaos. You can say, believe, anything. But it was as I tried to rise that I saw the choking smoke itself swirl away from where Auntie Vi stood, saw the air shimmer around her withered fingers...

I would swear that she was closing the Half-World, ignoring the whine of unhearable voices, their appetites thwarted.

The police officers backed into Railton Road, milling and losing formation; the crowd began to break up and move off in other directions, seeking their wits. We were alone—as much as you could be that night in Brixton.

"Mi know 'im," she said, standing over me. Her old-fashioned button-up boots were inches from my head as the damaged lamp-post sparked and sputtered nearby. The driver of the car had disappeared. " 'Im mamma dead."

"He lives around here?"

"Na far."

"I don't think he's very well." I saw a child in shock. He was clammy, eyes wide open and unfocussed; his dark skin was tinged with grey, and his scalp was bleeding.

The old woman looked down, nodded. "Yuh bring 'im, mi set tings rite."

I carried the boy, through knots of strangers, some angry, some scared, until we made it back to her flat. I was reaching the end of my own resources by the time I laid him down on her bed. His pulse fluttered; his eyes stared, blank, unseeing.

Auntie Vi told me his name, and I spoke it to him, repeating it, trying to draw him back from whatever limbo he had entered. There was no response.

"We should get him to Accident and Emergency."

"Dis night, wit all dat happen?" She scowled. "Hush yuh mout'. Like mi say, mi set tings rite."

So I sat on the end of the bed, holding the child's hand, and I watched as an obeah-woman worked. I could tell you what she did, and the words she used, but I will not. I have no right to do so. Suffice it to say that there were certain people, spread out across our lands, who would have understood. In Somerset towns, in Sussex villages, deep in York-shire dales—they would have nodded, maybe added their own touches, but they would have agreed. The boy had brushed the Half-World, I suspected, and had to return.

Which he did. By dawn, he slept, curled up on her bed, his breathing steady and his colour good.

"You knew what else was there, didn't you?" I said, exhausted, ach-ing. "The others—the Children.—"

"Mi know nuttin," she snapped. "An' tell nuttin. Betta dis way, Bor-der-mon."

I stared at her. "What did you call me?"

She drew her lips back in a sort of smile. I think.

"Border-mon. Yuh tink mi not know, Mistuh Margrave? How yuh always ends up where tings 'appen. Sum'dy mus' watch di borders, bwoy. Betta yuh dan most."

Lost for an answer, beyond any reasonable reply, I dozed on the end of the bed for the next few hours, next to the child. It was around ten in the morning when I woke, with no sign of Auntie Vi or our patient. I had to assume that she had taken him back to his father.

I needed to go home.

Along Railton Road, fires still smoked, and small groups of people, mostly male, clustered at the corners of roads. Some were wary, others appeared almost... triumphant. They had achieved a sort of victory, I suppose. They had faced the power of Babylon, and survived.

A visibly-damaged police car drove slowly along the road; two constables, looking like sacrificial virgins awaiting their fate, stood by a charred telephone box. To me, the morning air smelled like pain—pain and distrust.

I did not go back to that part of London for a while after that. Not out of fear, nor from disapproval, but because Brixton had to forge its own future.

I hoped that such a future would now include a boy called Marcus...

STILL SHE STARES

SIX

MARCUS REACHES FOR THE BOTTLE, pours until the glass will hold no more, and drinks. The other two men sit quiet—Stefan digesting what he has heard; Margrave placid, eyes half closed.

"You were there," Marcus says, when his wine has gone. "That's why I thought that I must somehow know you. It was from that night in Brixton. You were bloody there, Justin!"

"I was," said Margrave.

"And Auntie Vi..."

"She probably saved your life. I won't ever be sure. You may have recovered in your own time, I suppose. Shock is odd in that way—and young minds can be remarkably resilient."

Marcus has to put the glass down, before he snapped its stem. He feels tense, angry, but doesn't know where his anger should be directed. At the old man?

"But you've been coming here, telling your stories, for what, two, three months? And you never thought to start with this? You never thought to tell me the truth about my own life, about Auntie Vi, about... oh God, wait—'Who doh hear'. *She* said that, in 1981?"

"She did. But as you say, it's a common enough expression in the Caribbean."

"But—"

Stefan squeezes his arm. "Hey, it's all right, it's done, over."

Marcus pulls away.

"How long *have* you been watching me, Justin? Was the whole Perot thing just an excuse to see how I was doing."

The old man sighs. "Yes, dear boy, absolutely. You are hugely significant, Marcus Evenche, and I have had nothing better to do for over three long decades than to keep an eye on you, to help your every step in this terrible world."

Marcus recognises sarcasm. He flushes.

"I... look, I'm trying to take all this in."

"I know. Dear boy, when I heard about the Perot being here in London, I felt I really should do something about it, given that I knew the truth. And so I asked around, wondering how my appearance at *The Hummingbird* might be received. It was then that I learned who the owner was. As you can imagine, that interested me. The note on my card—I wondered if it was time for you to know about that episode in your past. I may have been wrong in waiting, I admit."

"No, you weren't." Marcus lowers his head, his chin close to his chest, and takes in long, slow breaths. "You weren't. I wasn't ready when you first came. If I hadn't heard about the rest, I might not have believed the full story about Auntie Vi or the... you know. Them."

"And now you do?" asks Margrave, almost teasing.

"I believe... enough. Stefan is a terror on the Internet—so much of what you've told us, it's like the history beneath history. The worrying part that you don't tell the kids."

"Or most of the adults."

Marcus nods.

"You must remember," says the old man, "That Auntie Vi is the one who did what was needed. I was simply there, and feeling lost. If you draw anything from my tales, you must see that for much of my life, I have been merely a witness. Oh, I have acted from time to time, not always wisely, but most of all, I have chosen to notice such things, rather than turn away.

"And so if I differ from others, it is because I have been a willing witness. Could I have done more? Of course—but once you start to believe that you can change everything, that you have importance, then you court vanity, pomposity, and eventually a kind of madness. Besides, sometimes we are helpless anyway."

"That isn't very re-assuring," says Marcus, but he can feel his tension dissipating.

"I didn't intend it to be."

"Brixton, though. My dad never mentioned any of this."

"Auntie Vi told him not to. 'Mi wud luk bad,' she said to me—there was her reputation to keep up, remember? She had helped without petition or pay, which wasn't her *modus operandi*, and she had no intention of explaining herself."

"Probably wouldn't have changed anything," Marcus admitted. "Dad was a disaster, mum died when I was small, and the family took a long time to forgive him. They thought he'd worked her to death, given the mess he made of every job he took—and he wouldn't go to church either, another strike against him. It was... hard, back then."

This time Stefan stands and put his arms around the other man, protection from a storm of memories.

"It's all right, love."

Margrave clears his throat theatrically.

"She never even explained to me why she was on that particular street at that very moment, by the way. She did, however, watch over you. That was what I also needed to tell you. She was the reason why your family came together again."

Stefan looks over Marcus's shoulder.

"She told them how things were? Smoothed things over?"

"No." Margrave is smiling again. "She told them that the spirits had spoken to her, and that misfortune waited in the branches of their trees, in the corners of their houses. That their beer would sour, and their sweet potatoes rot. They must make things right, or suffer the consequences. If they hadn't listened, she might have 'helped' matters along. That wouldn't have surprised me."

Marcus thinks of Auntie Vi—and of Peter Carew, and so many sad lives.

"Were you around when she... passed on?"

"Around? I sang along at her funeral, and we partied; we all laughed, and saluted the pinch-faced little woman who had cursed every one of us at one time or another. Violet Mercy Hall. That was her full name, though I gather that no one ever found a birth certificate, or any indication of her origins. Talking to Anton over some remarkable jerk pork that day, we both wondered if even her accent, her patois, was assumed, part of the image she had chosen."

"Still, I'm glad you were there, Justin—at the funeral. Very glad. And... thank you."

They sit subdued, each lost in his own thoughts.

"You never said what happened to Glory and Mr 'Smith'." Stefan's sudden, over-cheerful, interjection is artless, but effective.

"A happy ending, my dear. They left Brixton, moved to the outskirts of Birmingham, where Glory had distant relatives, and had three healthy children together. To the best of my knowledge, they're doing well. He gave up politics eventually, to open a food bank; she runs a local housing association."

"Cool."

"And if you think that otherwise I have brought you only doubt and worry, consider this—people stand guard below Maes Knoll; the masks are safe in Kemberdale, and..." He loosens his cravat. Around his neck, almost lost under a fold of skin, is a necklace of tarnished silver beads, clearly many years old. "The Berber women still play their *rebabs* and grind pigments in the Souk al-Dkhaan. We take such small comforts as we can."

He stands, leaning on his cane. "But now I really must be off, I'm afraid—though I have a gift for *The Hummingbird* in the hire-car outside."

"You've never driven here before, Justin."

"Ah, but I'm not returning home after this. I'm going away, you see, and a late flight awaits me at Heathrow. You recall Cesare Gallo, my Italian friend? He's retired now, and has his own vineyard a few miles from Brindisi."

"In Puglia!" says Stefan.

"Quite. Where else should I go but there, to heat up my ancient bones and sip the finest wines on Earth."

Marcus doesn't understand what he is feeling as he takes in that news.

It can't be loss.

"You'll be back, though? One day."

Margrave looks at their awkward expressions. His smile is fond, tinged with amusement.

"We shall see, dear boys. We shall see." He take a set of car keys out of his jacket. "Stefan, if you would be so kind as to bring in the package from the back seat?"

When the deed is done, a large, flat parcel propped by the doorway, Margrave shakes each of them by the hand, a long, warm moment. Marcus feels a damp prickling at the corners of his eyes. Irritated with himself, he smiles too hard, laughs too loud, as they say their farewells.

"You'll have a wonderful time over there, I'm sure."

"Oh, I imagine so." Margrave's expression is playful. "Cesare has the most marvellous carved Venetian bed, once stolen from the chamber of a seventeenth century Doge, so they say, and re-assembled by dissident monarchists in Bonaparte's time. Imagine, boys, rutting where a Doge once said his prayers."

Marcus tries not to imagine two eighty-year old men 'rutting', in the Venetian or any other style. "You... you should write to us."

Stefan's look is scathing. "Or Marcus could learn how to use email properly."

"Or that," Marcus concedes.

"I do have one final word for you, my dears, and for once it has nothing to do with Half-worlds, sculptures, or masks. It is more to do with the future I wish for both of you. Speaking of poor Peter Carew reminded me of this, the other week, and I meant to say it earlier.

"In the nineteen seventies, even bold Margrave could be arrested for being found in a hotel bed with another man. The art and theatre scenes had a tendency to cover for their own, but that did not help those outside it. Do you know what was said of us, fifty years ago? 'Those who suffer from this disability carry a great weight of loneliness, guilt, and shame all their lives.'"

Margrave regards them from the doorway, and somehow he seems taller, younger, in that moment. The broad grey-felt hat goes on his head; the onyx-headed cane taps the tiled floor. And he straightens his extravagant cravat, an Imperial purple blossom at his throat.

"The politician in question meant it kindly, with compassion—but he was also wrong. This life, this identity which informs our existence—it is not a disability. I have never felt guilt or shame over being what I am, and never will. So stand firm, dear boys, with each other, with your identities, and..." He winked at Stefan, "Let those who hate go fuck themselves!"

The door closes behind him, and they stand there, uncertain.

Something has passed by them, through them, and what it was, neither can be sure. Not yet.

"We should see what he's left us," says Marcus. To talk of Margrave himself feels lame, inadequate.

"There's an envelope with it."

"Let's find out what we have, first. I can't imagine him giving us anything that doesn't have some meaning."

"A Bernini sketch? A Tisanetti?"

"We should be so lucky."

The thick brown paper is so heavily reinforced with tape that they have to cut it or tear it in places, but they only need a brief glimpse underneath to know what they have.

It is 'Who Doh Hear'. The painting has been re-framed without ostentation, set in dark timber which is polished to a lustrous sheen.

"Wamara." Marcus strokes the satin-smooth grain. "Guyanese rosewood."

"Rosewood—super—but I don't get it. Why would he give it back? He bought it from us, after all."

"How would I know? I'll put it where it gets some decent light, so I can check it over."

Marcus lifts the painting up against the far wall, and eases it onto the rail, where it hangs once more in place, exactly where it was the night Justin Margrave first visited them. They'd never decided on what to put there instead.

"Poor Celine." Stefan folds up pieces of torn wrapping paper. "I don't really want to look at her again, after what Margrave told us."

"I think... I think you should."

Stefan mutters something under his breath, and joins Marcus, who is folding up his spectacles. Three spotlights, aping soft, natural daylight, fall across the painting.

It's a long time before the younger man speaks.

"He must... surely Margrave's had it re-touched."

"No." Marcus's voice is matter-of-fact. "No, you can see the original brushstrokes, the same pigments—and if you get nearer, the old varnish is intact. No one's worked on this picture since Aristide Perot painted it."

"You're sure?"

"I'm absolutely certain, Stef, love."

The same lush Guyanese foliage surrounds the reclining figure; light, shadows, all hold their places as before. Celine Granger lies upon her couch, but now her limbs are supple, graceful, with no trace of their former stiffness. Her fingers no longer clutch; they caress the air, and her eyes do not stare—they are no longer cold pinpoints, but instead are bright... alive.

Marcus opens the envelope left with the picture, to find a simple note, written in an unmistakable copperplate hand.

I sat with her in the marcher lands, by the shifting borders where unkind shadows gather, and I have done my duty. The rest, the future, I pass to you. M.

Side by side in the open doorway to *The Hummingbird*, drawing in London—its restless, over-lit night, the smells and sounds of far too many people trying, failing, seeking—there doesn't seem much more to say.

Except...

"'Duty', he wrote. Marcus, are we supposed to... do something, after hearing all that. Are we meant to try and be what he was, or do we just watch our backs and hope for the best?"

"I don't really understand what we heard, 'dear boy'." Marcus shrugs. "I think... that he just wanted someone to be aware of what he has been, has done. To remember him."

He lets go of Stefan's hand, and turns his back on the night. There is a single bottle of the Salice Salento left in the kitchen wine rack, and he needs to find where he put the corkscrew down.

For one last taste of Margrave.

ACKNOWLEDGMENTS

SINCERE THANKS TO EVERYONE who has been so supportive of this project, including my incredibly generous partner Sarah, Steve Berman at Lethe Press, author James Bennett, a staunch spokesman on the need for queer narratives, and the many readers (you know your own names) who—often to my surprise—asked for this to happen. I was there in the nineteen seventies, a time of too much pain and prejudice to be silent. Thanks also to our current dog, Biscuit, whose ravenous appetite and tendency to eat shoes have made me need to try and sell more books.

ABOUT THE AUTHOR

JOHN LINWOOD GRANT is a born-and-bred Yorkshireman, raised on the bleak North Sea coast—presumably by some sort of parents—and eventually dragged inland (but not out of Yorkshire) to train as a zoologist, the least practical option available. He honoured his academic excellence by working as a bartender, running a bookshop, and then entering the health sector as some sort of training officer and social researcher. Somewhat plain speaking, he annoyed senior staff in the Department of Health and voluntary sectors for some years before becoming terribly anxious about everything and catching agoraphobia.

As it was clear that something practical had to be done, he abandoned his past life and, at the age of fifty-eight, decided to enter that most lucrative and celebrity-spattered of fields, writing strange and peculiar fiction for small and independent presses. This went surprisingly well, except in terms of income or celebrity status, and combined nicely with his habit of taking in rescue dogs, especially lurchers. He now writes and edits enormous amounts of dark prose from his ramshackle kennel in West Yorkshire, his agoraphobia exacerbated by the fact that dogs have eaten all his shoes. Tall, 'large-boned', and with his own beard, he describes his personal trudge through life and his sexuality as colourful, because he dislikes labels. His main ambitions are to be less poor, have more dogs, and finish his project, completing all the remaining fragments of unpublished M R James stories.

ABOUT THE TYPEFACES

This book is typeset in IM Fell Double Pica, a modern revival font based on The Fell Types which take their name from John Fell, a Bishop of Oxford in the seventeenth-century. The original typecase was cut by Peter de Walpergen in 1684 then digitally reproduced by Igino Marini, an Italian civil engineer.

The titles and drop caps are typeset in Special Argument, a handwritten font designed for Youdiful Creations by Judith Westermann in Münster, Nordrhein-Westfalen, Germany.

Milton Keynes UK
Ingram Content Group UK Ltd.
UKHW010752010724
444982UK00004B/330